BRAD BUJNOWSKI

To Martin, With Love

HARLEY
HOUSE
PRESS

First published by Harley House Press 2021

Copyright © 2021 by Brad Bujnowski

Portions of this book are works of fiction. Certain names, characters, places and events are products of the author's imagination, and any resemblances to actual events or places or persons, living or dead, is entirely coincidental.

Portions of this book are works of nonfiction. Certain names, places, events and identifying characteristics have been changed.

First edition

ISBN: 978-0-578-95841-5

Editing by Jocelyn Carbonara
Cover art by Philip Studdard

This book was professionally typeset on Reedsy.
Find out more at reedsy.com

To the memory of my dad, our Papa.

And to the memories of my mom and brother who both left us too soon.

Contents

Foreword

I consider myself lucky to work on a lot of books. In the past year alone, I've helped around fifty authors in some capacity—writing, editing, or coaching. *To Martin, With Love* secretly became one of my few favorites.

The themes are universally appealing—of a complex relationship between father and son, made even more layered by non-linear events and characters. Brad Bujnowski relates to us in matters of loss, connection, and yearning to understand someone or something that eludes us. We all were born with a father, or have loved or lost someone—and we undoubtedly have cherished memories, regrets, and unanswered questions. Right?

Brad deviates from the norm through his absolutely skilled mosaic of this father-son story—turning concepts like time into playthings, and matters like race relations into understated drivers for his characters. This memoir (with a twist of fiction) becomes four-dimensional, moving on multiple levels at once, with comedic timing and irony no doubt honed by Brad's own experience as a comic. It made me laugh, cry, and pause in awe—often within a single page.

The book's imagery is like a moving slideshow—vividly casting us into scenes. We see the complex relationship between childhood, end-of-life, and everything in between—while freezing frames long enough to elicit wonder. Whether through an innocent day after a snowstorm as a young boy, or a tense moment in the ICU as a physician attempts to normalize the abnormal, Brad gives us the lens to witness his devotion, joy, pain, and crystal-clear perspective.

I believe the story will make you think of your own life, as you witness Brad's interactions with his father. Through flashbacks and thoughts of the future—woven into seventeen hours of their present—you'll consider how you intersect with your loved ones. It's an important story which probes effortlessly at our own perceptions and interactions, without demanding anything of us other than a willingness to read.

When I least expected it—since I thought this was simply a memoir about life, relationships, and mortality—a secret is uncovered that kept me turning pages until the very end. Expect to be surprised, maybe even a smidge shocked.

To Martin, With Love is a gift for its prose and perspective. Come for the memoir, stay for the mystery!

—Jocelyn Carbonara

Editor, Ghostwriter, and President of Spiritus Communications

"The distinction between the past, present, and future is only a stubbornly persistent illusion."

                                 &

"I never think of the future—it comes soon enough."

—*Albert Einstein*

"Time dilation, in the theory of special relativity, the 'slowing down' of a clock as determined by an observer who is in relative motion with respect to that clock."

— *"Time dilation," Encyclopedia Britannica*

Prologue

How did we get here?

Me, sitting in the front row with all the questions. Dad, lying there under Old Glory with all the answers. Mom, waiting for him, out in the cold near the interstate, plot 251. My brother, floating just south of us.

I hate the front row. Always have. This one's the worst.

Don't get me wrong though. I'd rather be in this heated mausoleum chapel than outside in the frigid winter slush, icy rain pellets attacking my face and muddy snow pies ruining my dress shoes. But I'd really rather not be anywhere near here. I suspect others around me feel the same.

The three soldiers seem unperturbed by the shitty weather. Duty calls.

Lingering ice shards trapped in my hair keep melting onto my scalp. The chilly droplets ruin the mood of the place when they land and steal my attention.

It's been a long morning. Dad's been patient.

I miss him.

They're right. It waits for no one.

HOUR 1: The DRIVE

A waiting its next feeding of daylight and disorder, and blissfully ignorant of the drama it would produce, the new year slept.

Until the cordless rang.

Slowly, as it woke to the shrill trill, the day-old decade uncoiled itself while leaving me submerged in a dream. One of those where the ringing seemed to be part of the dream itself, and vivid enough to remember and retell.

But it was never remembered nor retold. That possibility ended when my wife dazedly picked up the phone on the nearby antique nightstand and snapped at the caller, waking me as well in the dense darkness.

"Hello? Who is this? Who?!"

She was much more defensive of her sleep than I was, and a random call in the middle of the night was not going to receive her usual silky-smooth response. God save whoever was on the other end of the call if it went much longer.

She fired back tersely, "He's sleeping. Can I take a message? Hold on."

I loved her for trying to protect me. And I could tell by her short but groggy replies she was tired and not fully awake either, and probably hadn't fully encoded who was calling and ruining her sleep. I had yet to open my eyes and wanted to get back to that dream.

"It's the hospital. It's about your dad," she said as she rolled to her right to hand me the phone. My arm stretched to find her, the dream evaporating as I grabbed the phone.

"Hello?" I offered in a sleepy drawl, my head still on the pillow.

It wasn't the first time we'd been awakened in the middle of the night regarding my dad, but we had just seen him the week prior, and he was in great shape, all things considered. I was confused. And still waking up.

"This is Callie at Havenshore Hospital. Dr. Clayton would like to speak with you. One second please."

The drowsy haze began to subside as I quickly tried to recall a Dr. Clayton in the roster of doctors on my dad's healthcare team. Primary doc? Cardiologist? Primary's backup? No luck. And Dr. Clayton didn't give me much time to make a connection.

"Hello, this is Dr. Clayton, I'm the emergency room physician at Havenshore. Your father was brought in a little while ago. He was in a lot of pain. His vitals are okay now, but we've done a CT and his stent is leaking."

His voice was friendly, clear, professional, and had a sense of urgency but not panic. Very effective in getting my attention.

My eyes were still closed as I fully exited my dream and absorbed his introduction.

"Hi. How is he? Can he talk? Is he, uh, uh, coherent?" I asked, a little tongue-tied but wanting to know if Dad was lucid, if he was still mentally capable and engaged. Ever since I could remember, he was always mentally capable and engaged.

"Yes, he's talking. We're helping him with the pain and watching his blood pressure," the doctor answered confidently.

I felt somewhat relieved knowing my dad could communicate, and if he could communicate, then he could make decisions.

"Do you think I need to come down immediately, or can I wait till morning?" I asked, wondering how focused I needed to be and how quickly I needed to act.

My dad had made other trips to the ER over the past few years, and my responses had always been thoughtful and measured based on the diagnoses. It was one of the things I had learned from him; thoughtful and measured were good, panic and chaos were not.

Dr. Clayton was direct in his response.

"I can't tell you what you should do, but if the stent ruptures, he could go quickly at his age. Within minutes. It's pretty serious."

I got the point.

He continued.

"Also, his DNR instructions on file here indicate he does *not* want to have surgery to repair the stent if it ruptures, correct?"

With that question, I became very focused and alert.

"Correct, he wants to be treated with medication and CPR if needed, but no surgery and no long-term machines. He's not a full DNR, but one step away. If he's able to talk there, please ask him. Ask him to confirm."

I held Dad's healthcare power of attorney, and we had talked through his DNR previously, during a less critical incident at the hospital. Actually, it was the last time he was in the ER, for a fever and chills. At first, I thought he had a comfort-only, "don't touch me" DNR, but he wanted what I called "DNR Lite." If needed, he *wanted* to be saved with reasonable but not extraordinary effort. No rib-spreading, no cutting, no six-to-twelve-month recovery, no constant pain or machine attachment—nothing like that.

We had talked about it during that ER visit, about the possibilities. He wanted some basic assistance to keep living, to keep cracking jokes and see his grandkids—but he didn't want to rely on others or suffer without purpose indefinitely. I respected every word of his decision and wanted the same for myself when the time came.

"Okay, thanks," the doctor replied. Then he added, "Your father is nodding and agreeing here, too."

Yes, he was always capable and engaged, I thought to myself.

"Thanks doctor, I'll be there in about an hour and a half."

That goddamn stent! Every time my dad went to his primary doc or to his cardiologist for a checkup, they parroted the same basic message: *You're doing great for your age. Watch your blood sugar. Keep as active as possible. Here are your prescriptions. Come see me again in six months. And, yeah, that stent could kill you if it fails. Think about what you want to do if it does.*

The doctors were clear and direct with my dad, which he liked. So did I. They told him that if they went back in to repair or replace the stent, even in the least invasive way, the risk of him succumbing to the procedure or experiencing a long, painful convalescence was, at his age, very high. My dad didn't want any of that and his "DNR Lite" reflected it.

I clicked the OFF button and handed the cordless back to my wife. She had listened silently to the conversation.

"Is he okay?" she asked quietly, knowing his medical history as much as I did, including his aortic aneurysm and the eight-year-old stent, and how resilient he always seemed to be.

"No, I gotta go now. He's in the ER. His stent's leaking. Sounds serious."

I rolled over to get out of bed. The dim teal digits of the alarm clock showed 1:04 a.m.

I grabbed my glasses and cell off the nightstand next to me and shuffled in the dark to the bathroom, turning the knob and softly closing the door, trying to let my wife go back to sleep a few feet away. The tile floor was chilly, as was the entire upstairs. It always was before the thermostat kicked on, later in the morning around 7:00. I stepped on the throw rug, put my glasses on the counter, and glanced at my phone to double-check the time.

I was mildly startled to see the message, "Havenshore, 3 missed calls." I unlocked it and noticed a red dot with the number three on the phone app and was puzzled. It wasn't on silent. I checked the recent calls—yep, three from the hospital at 12:50 a.m. I missed all three. Hadn't heard any of them, affirming the deep sleep I was in. My wife slept through them as well. I put the phone down and looked at myself in the mirror above the sink, anticipating a long day ahead and grateful I slept hard for at least a couple hours.

The next ten minutes were a blur as I pulled myself together—hair, face, teeth, deodorant, decent clothes, wallet. I could charge my phone with the cable in the car. *Ready to go.* Hospital ready, at least.

As I walked out of the bedroom, my wife wished me luck.

"I'll work from home today," she said, "Keep me posted. Drive safe. Love you."

I stopped, walked to her side of the bed, and kissed her forehead.

"Thanks, love you, too."

I headed out again, running through the checklist in my head. *Phone. Wallet. POA—shit, forgot that.* I circled back to my dresser in our closet and found the four documents that normally accompanied me to the hospital—Dad's will, powers of attorney for his healthcare and finances, and the receipt for his burial plot, next to where my mom was buried. A large black clamp held them all together, making it easy for me to grab-and-go when one or all might be needed. I went downstairs, snatched the car keys and my heavy leather jacket, and exited the house quietly into the even-quieter darkness. It was the second day of the infant year, 2020, and it was cold, but not too cold. Thankfully, there was no new snow, and the streets were clear. I assured myself I'd get some coffee at the hospital.

I climbed into our Sportage, tossed the documents in the passenger seat, plugged in my phone, put my wallet in a center cup holder, pushed START, turned on the heated seats, and clicked the cruise control button. Each motion was executed out of habit, done repeatedly during the past year when visiting him at his house. I had a routine.

Dad lived directly south of us, about an hour and fifteen minutes on weekdays, between rush hours. A little faster on weekends. His house, our house since I was in fifth grade, was about ten minutes from Havenshore. I was hoping at that time of the morning I'd make it directly to the hospital in about an hour. Typically, the drive to see him was uneventful and always the same route: west on the Eisenhower to 294, south to I-57, exit at 298, then head to his house. I avoided the alternative that routed me to downtown Chicago, preferring to pay the corruption-laden tolls on 294 than to deal with the free logjam and mental cruelty of 24/7 construction traffic and the Dan Ryan Expressway. I'd say I was too old to deal with that, but honestly anyone of driving age was too old to deal with that mess heading east. Better to pay the tolls and retain my sanity, than to feel homicidal for a solid ninety minutes each way.

I scanned the gas gauge: *three-quarters full, easily enough for a trip there and back.* As I backed out of the driveway, I had a feeling this trip would be different.

I turned on the radio as I pulled away. It was 1:22 a.m. Then it hit me—*how the hell did he get to the hospital?* I really hadn't thought of it until then, having been stunned by Dr. Clayton's evaluation, then racing through an abbreviated hygiene routine and collecting essentials for the day. None of the calls I had missed were from my dad. He must have been well enough to call 911 in the middle of the night. He'd done that before, after a fall that bruised his elbow, triggering us to put a lockbox on his front door with a key for first responders. He'd also done it when he felt weakened by the flu, the most recent fever-and-chills ER incident. Knowing it would take me a while to get to him, he was confident the local EMTs would arrive quickly and take care of him. And they did.

Over the years and after a few health-threatening events, he became acquainted with the teams that responded in the "inhalator"—not many people still used that term instead of ambulance, but he did, as did I. And he gained confidence in their responsiveness and abilities. Dad was wired with pride and didn't accept help easily, but he liked the folks who arrived from the fire department. They were reliable and friendly and made him feel at ease.

And like my vehicle routine when I visited him, he had his routine when I took him for doctor visits or when he was a guest of the inhalator crew. He'd put on his Cubs hat, pocket his front door key, grab his thin, leather bi-fold wallet from the top drawer of his dining room buffet, and turn off the light in the kitchen. I assumed the EMTs came to his rescue again that night, but I continued to cycle through the possibilities in my head as I merged onto the Eisenhower and headed west.

A few minutes later, it seemed as if the car were navigating itself as it accelerated onto the nearly-empty tollway, then underneath the iPass truss of lights, transponders, and cameras—ringing up another seventy-five cents for the bad guys. I had maneuvered the route so many times before that the combination of instinct and familiarity—and the bareness of the highway itself—generated a safe, surreal confidence as I buzzed forward well above the speed limit. I needed that ghostly autopilot of self-assurance as I concentrated on other practical matters at seventy miles an hour, versus dodging potholes and semi-trucks or slow idiots in the fast lane.

A few miles later, I slowed and exited in the direction of Memphis, passing under the final toll bandit and fattening another politician in Springfield. I picked up speed again and began going through a variety of "what if" scenarios as I prepared for the worst but hoped for the best upon my arrival at the hospital. I turned down the volume of the radio and took advantage of the alone time. The cruise-controlled Kia careened along in Tesla-like fashion.

What if Dad pulled through the day, and the stent and its deadly leak stabilized? I tried to stay positive. *Would he want to have surgery to repair it, contrary to his DNR? Would he still be in a "resuscitative" condition, or would that become elective surgery? Would it matter? Would he be coherent and capable of deciding on what treatment he wanted?*

I hoped in that scenario, if surgery were an option, he would be as mentally present and as pain-free as possible to help decide how he wanted to move forward with the leaking stent. I suspected the doctors would tell him—*us*—that the leak was not sustainable and he—*we*—would need to decide what to do next. I hoped it would be *we*, not me, deciding that.

What if, worst case, I was too late getting to the hospital, and he was already gone? What would I do next? Call my wife? Yes, she was always a pillar of emotional calm and decisioning for me. *Should I call the kids?* No, not until morning when I could devise a plan. They were all back to their post-holiday, young adult lives, thrilled to have spent time with my dad while they were here, and he as well with them. Bad news would surely hit them hard.

What if I had heard the first three calls on my cell? Too late to change that. *How do I get a death certificate? Who do I call for funeral arrangements to bury him?* I'd figure that out later, I reasoned in the car, pushing it out of my mind.

None of that post-mortem trivia had concerned me previously, especially in the prior few months while I had worked with my dad to accumulate the required information to apply for his admission to a veterans' home that was fortunately just a few miles from his house and a few minutes closer to ours. He had objected for years to moving out of his home and living elsewhere, but started warming up to the idea the previous summer. He didn't demand it or have a logic for it, but I suspected he wanted to be around more people as he began to slow down and fade.

I didn't take it personally. I knew he appreciated my regular visits to help with the basics—groceries, home-cooked meals from my wife, doctor visits, hair cutting—but he started talking about other options. The veterans' home was one option due to his military service, and it was a good option because of the cost and location. As we started the application process in early October, it also became a vehicle to talk more about things such as his time in the Navy, his assets, my grandparents, and the location of critical records—not including the four documents patiently riding shotgun that he gave me at the time of my brother's untimely death. The application also required him to get a full physical and labs, which he did in early December, allowing me to hand-submit his final application that same day.

But we never discussed his final arrangements, the final-final ones, beyond the burial plots he had purchased when my mom passed away. I never looked into funeral homes, funeral costs, burial process, headstones—anything like that. It was probably because *I* wasn't ready for that discussion more than *he* wasn't ready for it. And I truly thought, confirmed by his physical exam, that he was in fine shape for ninety-five and funeral details could be investigated "later." *We had time,* I thought.

My eyes strained in the rural darkness from lack of sleep and paved monotony as I took back control of the car and veered onto exit 298, taking the ramp toward Charbonnay and the last leg of my trip. I figured I'd pass Dad's house to make sure the door was shut, then go to the hospital. My regular route to his place was typically void of hassle and took me straight past the public high school, my high school. Much had happened since I roamed the halls and locker rooms of CHS. But not in my mind. Mentally, I was stuck in the seventies—behind home plate, snoozing in study hall, at a devious party—whenever I hit exit 298, no matter how much had changed the past forty-plus years. That thought came to me as I moved unnoticed through the sleeping town, stealthily winding my way in the direction of the high school before turning down my street. *His street. Our street.*

As I approached Dad's house on the right, I saw his porch light was on, likely his doing to welcome the inhalator team. I pulled to the curb and parked to rest and reset my tired eyes—and check his front door. In the orange-yellow light that burned through the darkness, I could see from the car that his door was closed. The kitchen light was off, along with every light inside—dark like the rest of the neighborhood, porch glow excluded. All seemed well.

Part of me said to get out and verify the door was locked. The other part said to stay in the warm, leather cockpit and get to the hospital. Warm won, so I put the car in gear for the last ten minutes of the empty, dark drive and headed down the street. I was in the home stretch. Bruno Mars crooned from the Harman Kardons at mid-volume.

I hadn't gotten far from his house when my cell rang out, the loud surprise courtesy of Carplay. It was the hospital. Havenshore's number was in my contacts from visits past, and mine in theirs. I perked up quickly as I sat at the red light near the KFC where my brother once bucketed crispy legs, wings, and thighs. The light really had no purpose at that moment, as I was perfectly capable of managing my self-imposed traffic at the deserted intersection.

I took a deep breath and reached over, touching the green button on the display to accept the call. I didn't know what to expect.

HOUR 2: The ROOM

"Hello?" I said hesitantly, alternating nervous glances between the traffic light above me and the call seconds ticking by on the display.

"Hello, this is Dr. Bhatta at Havenshore hospital. Is this Mr. Grojnecki's son?"

"Yes," I gulped, as the light changed to green.

"I've taken over your father's case from Dr. Clayton. Your father is stable, but his stent is leaking as I believe you know. If it ruptures completely, it will be fatal. Very quickly. I just wanted to make sure you are aware of how serious his condition is," he said, confirming what I already knew.

"Thank you. Dr. Clayton told me the same," I responded. "I'm actually about ten minutes from the hospital."

With the doctor still on the line, I accelerated down Roosevelt Drive, relieved my dad hadn't worsened in the past hour—relieved the stent hadn't ripped, rotted, or unraveled completely.

"Okay, good. I just wanted to keep you informed. Goodbye."

Dr. Bhatta's voice trailed off as the call ended and the car went silent. Although I didn't learn anything new from the conversation, I was grateful that Dad had two seemingly competent, communicative doctors on his side, especially in the wee hours of the morning. I felt lucky and anxious at the same time.

11

Shortly after hanging up, I turned right and headed west on Jury Street, crossed the bridge over the Mennawa River, then turned and approached the hospital entrance from the south. The road was quiet, and I was envious of how the medical campus slept as I passed under two more traffic lights that gave me their full attention. I was familiar with the visitors' parking garage sandwiched between the east side of the hospital and the river, so I turned and circled around to park there.

Security lights lit up the side hospital entrance and parking decks. There were no enter/exit gates or ticket booth; parking was easy and free. I pulled into the garage and parked in the first space that wasn't painted blue or reserved. They were all available. The whole garage was available—empty, but for the Kia and me.

I let the car run and stayed warm as I pulled my tired self together. I texted my wife, not expecting a reply, to let her know I'd arrived safely, then unplugged my phone and stuck it in my pocket. It was at 100 percent, hopefully enough juice to get me through the day, but I wound up the lightning cable and put it in my coat, just in case. I slid my wallet in my back pocket and reached over to the clamped envelopes in the passenger seat. I shoved the four documents under my seat and made a positive mental note of where I was putting them, hoping to keep their whereabouts from evaporating in my sluggish head—*like the dream.*

As I opened the car door to get out, I checked the time on my Fitbit. It was 2:25 a.m. And eerily quiet. The emptiness reeked of the kind of temporary strangeness you feel when it shouldn't be that way, because it never is. Like when you walk into a room expecting to see a dozen people chattering away in pre-meeting small talk, but no one's there. Because you missed the email that postponed the meeting, and now you're there an hour early. By yourself, with a bunch of empty chairs and a white board with someone's fading scribbles and lines. Not horrible, just different. Weird and disconcerting until you realize why you're there and where everyone else is.

I was there in the garage because of that goddamn stent. Everyone else, for the most part, was home asleep and not praying for a tiny arterial sleeve to keep its shit together a little longer.

I pulled on the side door of the hospital, across from the garage, hoping to slink into to the labyrinth that had become Havenshore. It was the door I always used with my dad, but at that time of the morning it was locked—as I hoped it wouldn't be. Luckily, the cold air was still, and the temperature wasn't extreme, as I began to circle the building counterclockwise to get to the ER bay I had passed on the way to the garage. I walked briskly, fully zipped to my chin, but with no gloves. And no hat, no scarf.

I continued close along the edge of the hospital, eyeing the tree line across the drive, then turned toward a doorway a few yards away. I was hoping that would be my warm way in.

And it was time to find a bathroom. The cold air made that imperative.

I noticed "Hospital Personnel Only" stenciled on the door as I got closer and challenged its authority. Locked. I held my composure, and my bladder, and kept walking, finally making it to the ER entrance, brightly exposed in vivid lights and lots of red paint. The automatic doors parted as I walked in and looked for a friendly face to guide me to the goddamn stent. And to my dad.

A nurse perked up when she noticed me approaching her desk.

"Hi, good morning," I started in a friendly voice, though her blank expression indicated I either didn't look friendly or had perplexed her by arriving in the emergency room without an emergency. "My father was brought in a couple hours ago with a leaking stent. Martin Grojnecki. Can you please tell me where I can find him?" I was really trying to start off my morning there on a positive note. Flies with honey, as they say.

"They just took him up to the ICU. You'll have to sign in with security over there first," she replied stonily, having missed the memo on the honey. She pointed behind me.

I turned around to see the security guard, tucked away in a small cove behind a desk and sliding glass window near the front door. I hadn't noticed him when I breezed in, and he hadn't called me out when I walked by. He was a young, husky guy with dark hair, done up in full security guard garb, and was putzing around on his phone as I walked up to him.

He put down the phone when he saw me and gave me a clipboard with a sign-in sheet, when I told him why I was there. I provided my info and handed it back to him, asking for directions to the ICU.

"Go right, take the hallway all the way down to the elevators, then up to the third floor and follow the signs."

He pointed vaguely and replied with the scripted response before picking up his phone to restart the diversion I'd interrupted.

As I stood there soaking up his directions, I hoped the route would be as easy and quick as he asserted, but I knew from a life of hospitals, airports, and universities—ever-morphing concrete masses in confined footprints—that simple directions in a maze are still directions in a maze.

"Hallway, elevator, third floor, signs," I repeated out loud like in *The Wizard of Oz*, trying to encapsulate the directions into something catchy I could anchor in my foggy brain—and to allow him to correct my restatement of his directions if needed.

No reply.

"Thanks."

I tossed him my gratitude in a friendly tone, as he continued head-down with his YouTube or InstaSnapFace or whatever. Then, trusting his guidance, I headed down the long hallway, my eyes trained high, looking for signs of an elevator. Or a bathroom. Whichever came first, I was stepping into it.

It was a long, solitary walk from the ER. I tried to recognize anything along the way that reminded me of the time my brother and I had our tonsils removed at Havenshore when we were living on the farm, aka the ranch. We were roommates for the dual procedures. I remembered I had the bed by the window. I remembered orange sherbet after the surgery. Very cold, soothing orange sherbet. Both of us enjoyed it. One of the few things we agreed upon as kids.

It was a smaller hospital back then, and a roughly rectangular building as I recalled, with less signage required. And less artwork, too. In previous hospital trips with my dad, or to visit him there, I hadn't taken the time to reflect on that glandular event from my childhood, as I was usually occupied with keeping pace with him and his walker, discussing an itinerary for a doctor's visit, or bantering with him regarding his gripe-of-the-hour: *Parking is too far away. Appointment is too early. Admissions takes too long. Elevators are too slow.* The standard stuff.

As I neared a closed coffee stand and the hospital's darkened gift shop, elevator A appeared. I hoped it wouldn't come too slowly as I mashed my finger onto the button to summon it. Within seconds, the elevator landed, its doors immediately inviting me up to the third floor. After a quick hoist, they re-opened and, as if by providence, a unisex bathroom appeared directly in front of me. Fortunately, it was unlocked and ready for its first visitor of the day.

I did my business, then took a minute in front of the mirror to reassess my "hospital ready" appearance. *It was not my best effort,* I thought, vain like my dad, *but it'll have to carry me through the day.*

I took off my glasses and put them on the sink ledge, turned on the water, and took a deep breath. Leaning down, I rinsed my eyes to wash out the long drive and wake them for the day in front of me. I stared at the water plummeting down the drain as I cupped my hands to grab a drink.

God, please help me to know what to do and give me the courage to do it. The phrase had helped me get through the crappiest days at the office, so I figured it most certainly couldn't hurt to prime me for the hours ahead. The drain stared back and wished me luck.

I put the glasses on, my eyes still damp and untowelled, and inhaled deeply again. I let it out slowly, along with a whispered, "Let's do this," as I left the bathroom and looked for signs to the Intensive Care Unit.

I picked up my pace as I headed in the posted direction of the ICU. The hallway lights were slightly dimmed, and the night provided no additional brightness via the windows. After a solemn walk east, assuming my body's GPS was correct, past a small seating area and through a couple sets of self-closing double doors, the hospital lighting became more intense. I paused to check the signage as I entered the ICU. I wanted to make sure I was in the right place. Though I was sure I was, somehow it seemed like if I glanced at the sign one more time, maybe I could make fate change its mind about what the day held.

It was well lit, sterile, uncluttered, and quiet. A large visitors' lounge greeted me on the right, minus any visitors. I walked further to find doctors and nurses who could help me or direct me to my dad. The unit wasn't blatantly busy and lacked the hyperactivity and faux drama seen in *Chicago Med* or *Grey's Anatomy*. It was more like the controlled medical facility you'd want to see your dying parent being treated in.

I called out to someone sitting in a pod away from the main walkway, "Hello. I'm looking for my father, Martin Grojnecki."

I couldn't tell if she was a doctor or nurse, but she wore baggy blue scrubs and typed on a computer. The short brunette made her way over to me. She seemed tired but ready to help as I repeated myself.

"I'm Martin Grojnecki's son. The ER said he was moved up here. Can I see him?"

She knew who I was talking about and didn't need to find him in her database.

"Yes, we just put him in room 10 a little while ago. Come with me." I assumed she was his nurse.

She led me toward the corner of the floor, past other staff who chatted calmly and poked at computers. A few steps later and directly in front of us was a set of large sliding glass doors, with full-length curtains pulled closed on the opposite side. She grabbed the handle on the door and pushed, exerting just enough energy to slide it a body's width from the wall. Yes, she was tired, too.

"You can come in," she said, motioning me to follow her as she pushed the curtains away. I eased through the narrow gap and followed her inside.

"Hey, who let the big shot in?" my dad called out as he saw me enter the room.

It was an awkward, snotty tone I really hadn't heard out of him too often, but I could see he was smiling, so I let it go. He was propped up in the bed directly across from the sliding doors.

"This is Bryant, your father's nurse," the first nurse said, introducing me to a medium-build young man with thinning brown hair. Hell, everyone in that hospital looked *young* compared to my dad and me.

Bryant manipulated the tubes and machinery next to my dad as the other nurse left the room.

"Thank you," I called out as she walked away.

"Nice to meet you. I'm just getting him set up with his monitor and checking his IV. We want to make him comfortable here," Bryant explained, then shifted his attention back to my dad with a little extra volume. "How are you feeling, Martin? How's the pain?"

"My back hurts a lot; it's really bad," Dad complained.

"I'm sorry. I'll see if the doctor can step-up the painkiller for you," Bryant offered as he continued working dials and tubes.

17

I wandered over, away from Bryant, to the other side of the bed. Dad's ashen, scruffy face and bloodshot eyes looked tired beneath his partially-matted, partially-tossed white hair.

"Hey big guy, how are you doing? What the hell happened?" I asked as I leaned down to hug him, clutching him awkwardly around his weakened shoulders, careful not to jostle the tubes in his arm and nose, but firm enough to let him know I was there for him. *As long as he needed me.*

"I got up to go to the bathroom, and when I was in there, I got this really bad pain in my back."

He was clear but hoarse, his lips quivering, his cadence halting.

"I never felt that bad before. I could barely move, so I called 911."

Thankfully, he knew his limits and trusted the inhalator team—and was able to get to his kitchen phone to make the call.

That call for help landed him in an ICU room that surprised me in its size. It was more of a one-bed corner suite, with floor-to-ceiling windows that permitted a tranquil view of the river below, at night reflecting the walkway and streetlights running parallel to its banks. A dull mint-green couch extended across the base of the windows, not far from the big screen TV articulating from the wall. Room 10 was considerably larger than the other ICU rooms I passed while looking for him minutes earlier. I didn't know if it was because of the treatment he required or might require, or if it was an omen of the comfort they thought he needed—or deserved. In any case, I was glad he wasn't cramped and slighted. Neither of us were cramped and slighted there.

I kept holding Dad's hand while I turned to look for a chair. Lack of sleep, a long dark drive, and an anvil of emotions suddenly took their toll on me. I needed to sit.

As I stretched for a cushioned chair by the sink, Bryant secured the IV taped to Dad's forearm.

"I'll be back soon, Martin," he confirmed as he removed his gloves and left the room.

I pulled the sturdy armchair next to the bed and turned it 90 degrees. I held onto Dad's hand as I sat down facing him, my back to the sliding doors and to the large, round analog wall clock that stared down on us, its red second hand in constant motion, not stopping as I wished it would to preserve whatever time we had left. Dad gripped me back. His reciprocating thumb strokes told me he was happy to see me as I got settled. I was warm in my leather jacket and chose to stay that way.

His eyes closed, Dad looked content despite the tubes, the machines, and the pain coursing through him. It could have been because it was the first time he'd been in a bed in months, and he was enjoying whatever feeling bubbled up from the mattress under him. In the past year or so, he had stopped climbing the stairs to his bedroom at home and slept on the couch in his living room, a few feet from his recliner and TV. He kept an Echo Dot on the soft, oversized arm of the couch, near his pillow. Alexa woke him up in the morning, and she put him to sleep at night with Bing Crosby, Frank Sinatra, or one of his favorite swing bands. He had gotten used to that arrangement, but I suspected a bed, even a hospital bed, felt good to him again.

"Dad, the doctor told me your stent is leaking. Is the pain pretty bad?"

I was starting a conversation with a detail we both already knew.

"Oh, gosh, my back is killing me," he answered, "and my lips are dry. Everything else is fine, just a lot of pain."

Dad was someone who repelled pain, so I knew he must really be hurting.

"I'll see if your nurse can get you more painkiller when he comes back. Are you warm? Do you need another blanket? Is your pillow okay?"

19

I was trying to help with something I could actually control.

"I'm okay, it's just the pain," he replied.

He never asked for much, other than chocolate Dilly Bars and homemade applesauce. The Dilly Bars—bloated pucks of vanilla ice cream dipped in milk chocolate and frozen on the end of a tongue depressor—started many moons ago, when my brother and I were kids, and my dad would take us into town to his friend's dry cleaners to "shoot the shit" with him. The square, cinder block building was floor-to-ceiling-full of plastic-wrapped garments hanging from a rolling jungle of hooks, rails, and motors, serenaded by rhythmic blasts of hot steam and chemicals. The acrid smell of cleaning solution welcomed you at the front desk.

Across the street from the cleaners was a Dairy Queen, and our chilled go-to was a Dilly Bar or chocolate shake. Either was a tasty reward after inhaling the noxious fumes of pressed suits and starched shirts.

The applesauce, however, was a more recent phenomenon. Or addiction. His taste buds were obsessed with the homemade cinnamon concoction my wife cooked and I delivered to him every week or two. He couldn't get enough of it and was religious in using it as a fruity dip for his toasted Kroger waffles each morning. Like Minute Maid for some, a day without applesauce "was like a day without sunshine" for him.

"Hi Martin, the doctor's going to up your dose of painkiller," Bryant said as he returned smiling and spouting the good news.

"Thank you," my dad and I sighed happily together.

Bryant put on sterile gloves and walked to the computer station next to Dad's bed. He typed his access code and pulled up Dad's record, then with a small wand, scanned a bar-coded vial he'd brought into the room. Above the computer station was the monitor tracking Dad's vitals. Heart rate, blood pressure, oxygen, etc. Digitally and graphically. In various colors.

If that device were in my kitchen, I'd spend hours examining and deciphering it. Or I could just pull out my phone and find its user guide online in a few taps. But in that big room, on that day, I had little to no interest in the mechanics or biology of what I was looking at. I simply hoped not to hear loud alarms or see flashing lights. Or flat lines.

"Hopefully this will make you feel better, Martin," Bryant said as he withdrew the fluid from the vial with a syringe, then injected it in a tube attached to Dad.

"The doctor says it's okay to give you this every hour."

I turned my gaze to the big white clock with black numbers, and the second hand that disobeyed me. It was 2:58 a.m.

"Are you comfortable? Can I get you anything?"

I looked up. Bryant was talking to *me*.

"No. Thank you. Thanks, I'm fine," I replied, a little surprised he wanted to care for me, too.

"Okay, I'll let him get some rest now. I'll be back later to check on him." Bryant logged off the computer and pulled the curtain closed behind him as he left.

Dad's eyes drooped and blinked slowly as I started talking to him.

"Dad, is the pain any better?"

I didn't know how quickly the drugs were supposed to act.

"You know, I've had a good life," Dad confirmed to me, and to himself.

In the past few years, he'd recited that phrase more frequently. Not every time I visited. Some visits were more business-like or abbreviated than others, due to my schedule or his mood, and focused on the must-dos—unbag the groceries, inventory the home-cooked meals, fill up his seven-day pill tray, put his Ensure in the fridge, plug in his electric shaver, take out the garbage, test his blood sugar, take home the empty Tupperware.

But on most occasions, when we took the time to talk—recounting the week's news or sports stories or reminiscing about our past—or when the kids visited him while in town, many of those visits ended with his melancholy pronouncement, "I've had a good life. I wouldn't change anything." It was also his tagline after he'd have Alexa entertain me with one of his favorite tunes.

His wincing and effort to get settled in the bed answered my initial question.

"I know, Dad. I love you."

I needed him to know that before he drifted off.

But any drifting would have to wait.

"Hello, I'm Dr. Bhatta. We spoke on the phone."

The black-haired, bearded doctor entered the room, addressing me as he headed toward the bed with an easy but direct gait. He reached across Dad's covered legs to shake my hand as he leaned closer to query him.

"Hi Martin, how are you feeling?"

His voice was friendly and slightly raised to capture my dad's attention. "How is the pain?"

"It's bad, doctor," Dad grimaced.

"The new dosage of painkiller should help you. Let's see how that goes," Dr. Bhatta replied, then looked at me.

"We'll try to keep him comfortable with the painkiller. His vitals are good. He has a slight AFib, but it's manageable. I've called his cardiologist, Dr. Mahanti, and we discussed the stent leaking. There's not much we can do if your father doesn't want it repaired, but Dr. Mahanti will be in to see your father first thing in the morning," he explained to me, in a softer tone.

I assumed he meant first thing in the regular morning, which also assumed my dad would make it until then. I was aware of Dad's irregular heartbeat, the AFib, and I liked the cardiologist since meeting him at the time of the stent installation. My dad liked his doctors, too, and wasn't afraid of them—typically using them, and their nurses, as foils for his bad jokes and dry humor, or just to amuse himself with friendly conversation.

"Do you have any questions? I'll be around here for the next few hours if you need anything," he concluded.

"No, thank you. Hopefully his pain gets better."

I reached over to shake the doctor's hand again.

I appreciated his update, but there wasn't much for me to ask or do. We'd gotten to the point the doctors had been speculating about for a while. That goddamn stent was in control.

"Thank you, doctor," Dad offered in a raspy effort as the doctor walked away. I could tell his gratitude was sincere, as long as the painkiller worked.

Dad turned his head slowly and looked at me, the oxygen tubes in his nose swiveling in tandem.

"You must be tired," he said.

"I'm fine, Dad. Try to get some rest."

I coaxed him to relax, thinking that might enable the painkiller to be more effective. It made sense at the time.

But he was right; I was tired.

HOUR 3: The SNOW

It was 3:23 a.m. and pitch-black outside, but my mind was elsewhere. About fifteen miles and a lifetime away, to be precise. On another January day.

The day was white. So white. So very, very white.

I closed my eyes to see it again. That day, the whole day.

Even with my eyes shut, and that memory fading after fifty-three winters, the glare of that day was still blinding. Still painful to look at directly, even in my head. As if the sun exploded and landed evenly on a sea of new snow—not yet disturbed, not yet trampled, the calm white waves interrupted occasionally by a barn, a fence, a row of trees. Everywhere I looked was a thick, brilliant whiteness, painted violently for two days over nearly six acres of what was our ranch.

But that day, the third day, under a cold blanket of empty, blue sky, the whiteness was still. As if it were finally allowed to rest. I couldn't forget it, faded or not. I closed my eyes harder to try and remember more.

#

I remembered with a grin the mass of what the blizzard left behind. Not just the pure whiteness, the snow-covered sameness of the fields, the yards, the orchard, the pool area, or the total disappearance of everything below two feet, but the absolute mass of it all.

The long branches of the evergreens, pines, and arborvitae surrounding our small farmhouse sagged helplessly under the blizzard's remains; immobilized by oversized cloaks of settled snow. As kids, those dependable trees formed the foundation of our favorite forts and hiding places. They were our "bat cave" when it was warm—albeit full of mosquitoes and crickets, and whose sharp inner branches snagged and slowed us, unwittingly teaching us tenacity. The cramped, dark space between them and the house, a couple feet in some places and a few inches in others, had been ours and only ours. Just us kids, no grown-ups.

When clear skies called, especially in the summertime, those trees and the spaces within were our Xbox. Our Netflix. Our Call of Duty. Our sanctuary where we could lose ourselves in a game of hide-and-seek, cowboys-and-Indians, or army. Those trees—full and flourishing on the surface, dry and brittle, creepy and unforgiving on the interior—breathed endless fun and imagination into our days.

But on that day, everything exposed to the storm was smothered by snow. Not just covered, but suffocated by it. Nothing breathed below that spectacular white surface. And the mass of what fell continuously over the previous two days ensured that nothing moved below it either.

I remembered it was Saturday! And that I ached to get outside, beyond the trees ringing the house, to carelessly dive into that ocean of snow. As I looked east out the living room picture window with my little brother, cartoons played on the Zenith television behind us. *Rocky and Bullwinkle, Tom and Jerry, Bugs Bunny*—the Saturday staples broadcast from Chicago—were the likely distractions that morning. And maybe *The Jetsons*.

Unlike other Saturday mornings fixated on the TV and whatever animation showed up, we were focused on what had appeared outside: that expanse of gleaming snow that appeared out of nowhere. And as we stared at what would be our playground for the coming week, mesmerized by the awesomeness of what had happened so quickly and relentlessly, we waited. And waited. Waited for Mom and Dad to wake up and let our day begin. It seemed like forever.

How deep is it? Will it start snowing again? Will it be too cold to play in? Can we even get out of the house? Are the horses okay? Why were Mom and Dad arguing last night? When are they coming down? We asked those questions to each other, or to ourselves, as we waited.

After all this time, whenever that winter came up, I asked myself questions—about that day, that storm, that era of our lives. I didn't obsess over it—too many things had happened since then. Life happened. Death happened. Kids, cancer, love happened. But I was curious, selectively curious. When I got to the age to make sense of it though, it was almost too late. The childish, impressionable details of *what* happened on that snowy day stuck with me like the packed snow, but the details of *why* they happened, and the emotions and events surrounding them, kept melting away—or had never fallen my way to begin with. Time wasn't stopping, and the melting continued.

I tried to remember more about that Saturday morning inside the house. And if Star, our German shepherd, was with us yet, or was it the short-haired brown boxer? No luck. Probably because the inside that morning was in every way unspectacular compared to what was outside. Yes, the outside was memorable, to say the least.

I remembered we both wore the same style navy blue snow boots, likely from Sears. Or Montgomery Wards or K-Mart. And matching light blue stocking hats, knitted with the name, in white letters on a gold band, of the high school football team my dad coached in Mennawa—the Jayhawks. I remembered the stocking hats especially; I was proud to wear my dad's gear.

I remembered exiting the house with my brother, hand-in-hand, to explore and experience what the storm had left us, and what it had hidden. Our nervous anticipation quickly shifted to full-on thrill as we pushed hard on the metal screen door and opened it just enough to allow our short legs to plow into and over the heavy snow. It looked like Dad, or Mom, had shoveled a small clearing outside the door so they could get in or out of the house Friday night, but the overnight drifting voided much of what was accomplished.

The air was calm that day. The "real feel" temperature was what it really was, not less, maybe even warmer because of the sunshine pouring over us. There was no polar vortex, no extreme temperature to match the extreme snowfall. On the contrary, the cool, crisp air, warmed by the sun but cooling our busy bodies, added to the experience—allowing us to enjoy the wintery dump for hours without breaking to calm ourselves or to warm up inside. It was ideal weather to enjoy the aftermath of a debilitating storm.

As each of us squeezed around the door and took our first steps into the snow, we moved deliberately away from the house, our faces bleached by the southern sun and fighting the ubiquitous glare. After struggling a few strides, we stopped to survey what was everywhere around us, and in some places, above us. The depth of the snow was daunting; hard to forget when you're a five-year-old and waist-deep in your first real winter. I was thrilled for every inch of it that day.

The first spectacle was the near disappearance of the overhead garage door. Our attached garage had been partially swallowed by the snow and its drifts. In reality, it was a small garage and barely large enough to hold our whale of a Buick, if it ever did. But the overhead door, which doubled as a summer entryway to the house, had become a barely-visible shield holding back the blizzard. And in our eyes—in our pre-K perspective—the near covering of a door that size signaled how strong and severe the storm had been. But only enough to elicit a faint "Wow!" before twisting to look at the next display of nature's wrath.

Behind us was the Buick. At least the top of it. Parked on the south arc of the gravel circle drive, the car was buried by the storm.

Though we were both awed by the sight of the garage door being mostly covered and unusable, the sight of the monster Buick entombed by the snow was paralyzing. I squinted to make sure what I was seeing was what I thought I was seeing. The glare off the snow and top of the car made it difficult to focus, but yes, it was our car.

I turned around and just looked at my brother. His eyes were still locked on to the vehicle, his anxious breath fogging faintly in the cold air. Excitement returned to nervousness. I let out a louder "Wow!" and urged him to keep going.

Over the years, I always urged him to keep going.

Until he couldn't.

Moving a few feet further, we saw beyond the Buick the outlines of bare trees and fence posts poking out of the snow within and around the south field. The field was the smallest and least interesting of our property's fenced-in spaces, full of weak, skinny trees that grew randomly near the road, then gradually thinned out and ultimately became rough plots of low grass and craggy brush as the field tapered toward the stable. Its southern edge, which separated us from our unknown neighbor's property, was a row of larger, unmanicured trees and bushes, with rusty barbed wire fencing woven as straight as possible between it all.

It was the field where our horses roamed and grazed most of the time. But on that day, there was no roaming, no grazing. There were no horses. There really was no field. It was just more of what we saw everywhere else we looked that day, a mass of lazy, gluttonous snow doing its best to jacket anything upright it hadn't already consumed.

A few steps further into the snow and still battling the glare, we saw our two pale yellow barns standing stoically in the sea of white. They both protruded out of the snow like massive buoys, though firmly planted and going nowhere. The drifts crept high up the sides of each barn, covering the asbestos siding in their ascent.

The two-story barn furthest from us was the stable and hay loft for our horses, Nick and Apache. Mom loved the horses; Dad maintained them. The other barn, midway between us and the stable, was only one level but larger and used in many ways: part tool shed, part auto shop, part junk storage, part kennel for dogs, cats, rabbits, and goats. Just west of the circle drive, it was big enough to house tractors and farm implements, which was probably its primary purpose. But it really excelled, along with the other barn, to provide the most epic hide-and-seek playground and "war" theater imaginable from spring to fall. On that day however, after the big storm, both barns stood silent in the background behind the main attraction: the snow pile!

The snow pile rose up on the northwest edge of the circle drive, between our house and the one-story multipurpose barn. It was a huge pyramid-shaped mound of snow that towered over my dad's weary Ford pickup truck, parked and pointed at the base of the pile. In our eyes, the pile was a mountain. Practically, it was probably ten to twelve feet high at its peak, and at its base it was the width of two, maybe three, cars side-by-side.

Without prompting, we both headed toward the pile, no longer holding hands or anxious about what we'd seen outside. As I trudged first, sometimes losing my balance in the depth, my brother followed. The path I carved bluntly for him with my knees and boots was just big enough for him to navigate without holding on to me. In our heads, we raced toward the pile; for our legs, it was more of a plodding trek.

The creation of the pile was a mystery. It was just there, waiting for us, a few yards away. And when we got to it, we were like puppies with a rabbit, exhausted and ecstatic but totally clueless as to what to do with it next. First though, we emptied our boots to relieve the icy chill we had accumulated. I struggled to help my brother get his little rubbery boots off and then back on, as we sat and fidgeted with excitement in the snow, wiping away snot with the backs of our hands, our fingers turning a cold pink until they were rescued by our gloves. It was the only part of that day that seemed real and intentional, interrupting the excitement and make-believe of everything else we did.

Once re-booted, we headed to the side of the pile opposite the truck and gazed up at that mammoth, menacing heap of bright white snow begging to be attacked. We looked at each other, both perplexed by its existence and its size. Then we did what brothers always do—we scooped up snow and attacked each other instead. Not so much with snowballs, but with whatever our little, uncoordinated gloved hands could grasp.

We both laughed as we dodged and flailed, our faces becoming rosy and numb from direct hits. The snow was lush, and the direct hits were brutal on our fresh, young skin. But it was a snow day like no other, so a face full of snow just came with the territory.

My brother, however, thought otherwise.

That became very clear after a snow-laced flurry that initially had us laughing wildly at the chaos of hurling chilly semi-projectiles at each other. Our almost two-year age difference gave me a hefty advantage in the battle, and I took full benefit of it, as I always did. But my brother was determined. Even at that age, he wasn't going to let me win without fighting back.

And he did.

He countered my heavier, better-targeted tosses with a rapid series of windmill-like arm sweeps and snow kicks, gradually devolving into crying and yelling as he rushed into my oncoming pitches and felt those cold direct hits on his face. As I laughed at his effort, and at the spontaneous thrill of being carelessly deep in the snow around us, he screamed with frustration as I taunted him to keep coming.

And he did.

As did his tears. And his screams.

And I laughed. And I taunted.

We were brothers. But I was the bully that day.

And every day.

Worn out and defeated, my brother retreated a few feet but continued to cry and scream at me, kicking snow and telling me to "Stop!" I laughed at him but stopped pummeling him with snow. There was so much more to do that day—more to be explored and experienced—it wasn't worth jeopardizing it on another argument with him or another fight I would win.

I yelled, "Shut up and stop crying! Dad will hear you!"

I always yelled that at him.

His crying turned to slower sobs as he, too, realized what was at stake that day if he continued. But he was still mad, evident by the wet scowl and red face under his capped blonde hair. I'd seen that look before, and would see it dozens or hundreds of times in the future—a look of frustration and determination, but mostly of contempt.

We turned our attention back to the pile and wiped the snow off our faces as best we could. Though he continued to mope, his face made slushier by his runny nose and the leftover sobs, my brother stopped the wailing that dulled our fun seconds earlier. But as we pushed through new snow around the base of the pile looking for adventure, we heard a shout.

"Hey, are you guys fighting?"

The sound of my dad's voice surprised and rattled both of us.

"If I have to come out there, you're coming back in the house for the rest of the day! Hey, do you hear me? Answer me!"

He had heard my brother crying and poked his head out the front door to yell his disapproval. There was no calm in his voice. He was definitely pissed.

My dad never issued an idle threat. And many times there was no warning prior to being on the receiving end of his ire. Basically, if we

31

couldn't discipline ourselves, he'd do it for us. And we knew that well. No questions, no negotiating, no debating. No excuses. We weren't really scared of *him*—most of the time he was fun and engaging, and liked being with us and having us around him. A guy's guy, and we saw that. We were afraid of the other moments, when he decided we needed his full, forceful attention, usually accompanying a fight between my brother and me. That's when we were petrified.

We both shouted back to him, "Yeah, okay!"

Then my brother yelled, begged, in his tear-stained voice, "Dad, come out and play with us! Pleeease!"

We didn't hear a response. But for me, it was good news that my brother's request went the route of "Let's have some fun!" rather than "He's hurting me!" else my dad would've been out that door, in the snow, grabbing our jackets and dragging us into the house in no time flat.

That's how the discipline worked. Quick, direct, and with force. Sometimes painful, always demoralizing.

So we went on our way, circling the base of the pile, playing tag, and diving into the untouched snow. It tasted cold and clean whenever it made it to our mouths; we sampled and ate it without fear or permission. How could you not? We laughed in the sun as we made peace with each other and were carefree kids on a sparkling, blizzard-induced day.

Having both fallen after a solid tag, we sat in the ivory trench to catch our breaths and get the snow out of our boots again.

"You think he'll come out?" my brother asked.

"I don't know," I replied as I emptied my boots and put them back on, not really caring if Dad came outside with us.

"What should we do now?" my brother probed, as he shook out his boots mightily with his numb little hands, shaking most of the snow onto his lap.

"I don't know. Let's go by the car."

I was curious about the Buick a few yards away, hidden under the snow drifts, like a toy in a sandbox. But as I started towards it, with my brother trailing close by, I got another idea.

"Let's build a snowman!" I announced, turning around quickly to see if he agreed.

His smile confirmed he was on board.

Without hesitation or discussion, we both started to gather snow around us, pack it in our hands as best we could, and drop it on a single pile to build the base of the snowman. I couldn't recall if that was our first-ever snowman, but our process indicated it was. My brother had no useful history constructing one at three-and-half years old, and my lame effort was shaped more by recent Christmas TV shows than legitimate hands-on experience. But we tried.

We exerted every ounce of energy we had to scoop up snow, carry it a few feet, and groom the growing mound into something resembling Frosty's perfectly round base, like we'd seen on TV. We worked with passion and teamwork. There was no bickering or judging. I accepted that my brother dropped at least half of what he picked up, as he packed and brought it to the mound. I, too, was a less than perfect craftsman, but I tried to mitigate my clumsiness by moving more snow, more quickly than he could. Net-net, we were inexperienced, inept, and inefficient. But we were focused and working together, like ants on their hill. And laughing the whole time.

As the mound grew, definitely looking more like a mound than a spherical Frosty, we heard Dad's voice behind us, heading our way.

"*What* are you guys *doing?*" he asked.

We both stopped and immediately turned around. He'd startled us, our attention devoted to Frosty's construction. We quickly tried to interpret his question—*was he still pissed and focused on the "doing," or was he curious and wanting to know more about the "what"?*

33

I answered him somewhat hesitantly as he approached us via the misshapen path we had carved from the house.

"We're, we're, building a snowman."

I was significantly more excited about what we were doing than my reply revealed, but also unsure if he was in favor of our plan. My brother stood frozen, his cheeks red and chest heaving from scooping and piling snow, as we waited for Dad's response.

My dad kept walking towards us, taking advantage of what we'd cleared away but still laboring through the deep, uneven snow. He was a strong, stocky man, healthy as a horse, with a full face and fuller jowls. Just under six feet, just over two hundred pounds, he wore no hat that day, his graying crew cut exposed directly to the sun and cool air.

#

He carried much of that presence with him during his next fifty-plus years, toggling between crew cut and shaggy. And when the muscles and joints ultimately weakened, and his vascular plumbing clogged, he kept his mind strong and his spirit healthy.

But that spirit was slipping away as I looked at his pale, inert face.

I closed my eyes again to hold on to what was left.

#

HOUR 4: The BEST

A s he advanced towards us in the snow, Dad was wearing his old, cuffed work gloves along with his faded, brown jacket and blue mechanic's pants—his standard winter uniform for feeding the horses and cleaning the stable. I assumed that's where he was headed.

"Can I help?" he asked.

With those three words, he immediately melted the anxiety that had frozen us as we waited for him to make a demand or chase us inside. In either case, we had feared the worst. This, however, was the best.

My brother happily screamed, "Sure! Are we doing good?"

Dad lumbered closer to us and our mound of snow, which looked nothing like the smooth, bulbous base we envisioned—as we'd seen on Christmas cards and wrapping paper a month earlier. I sensed he wasn't happy with our ugly creation, as he took a few seconds to inspect our hand-molded mess and prepare his critique.

Dad smiled and offered, "Yeah, it's a good start. Let me show you a faster way to build."

With that reply, we became a team of three. Like when we did jigsaw puzzles, or made model airplanes, or rolled up coins on Sundays. We were a solid team, and each of us had our role—my father was the mentor, the journeyman, the instructor and demonstrator. As a schoolteacher and coach, he excelled at that. And as a machinist mate in the Navy, he was also an accomplished mechanic and overall do-it-yourselfer. Nothing that was mechanical gave him pause. He could assemble, diagnose, and repair everything in the house, around the house, on the ranch, or in the driveway. And he had the tools to do it. Before moving to the ranch, he had built his own house, our house, from scratch with his father. So he was a capable leader of our threesome.

My role on the team was more of apprentice, learner, main helper. My brother was the laborer—get this, watch that, throw this away. He didn't hover over the car engine or pool pump with my dad like I did. Partly because of his age and attention span, mostly because I was intrigued and curious, and my dad was happy to answer and guide me.

"Here, pack a good ball of snow in your hands like this," my dad demonstrated to us. "Then take it and start rolling it toward where you want your snowman to stand."

He started with a baseball-sized snowball, plopped it in the middle of new snow, and slowly rolled it to the size of a softball, then a basketball. The snow was packing well that day.

"Take this one, keep rolling it over by the snow pile there. You'll have to roll it sideways sometimes to make it round."

My brother watched, then followed me as I took over the rolling from Dad. It was difficult to keep the ball rolling while also pushing our way through the deep snow. But we were determined.

As the diameter increased in the forward direction only, so not really a ball anymore, Dad yelled more instructions.

"Now get on the side of it, and push it sideways toward the pile."

Almost miraculously, as we pushed from the side, it started taking the shape of the Frosty we'd seen on TV, getting larger and larger as my brother helped me push the heavy base along. As we pushed, we intuitively started packing the surface with our gloved hands to smooth it out and fill the uneven spots. My dad helped push it the final distance to its resting place, about midpoint between the multipurpose barn and base of the snow pile.

"Nice job, boys!" Dad proclaimed, as the three of us stood happily in awe of the imperfect globe we created.

Thankfully, it looked nothing like the lame mound my brother and I started initially. Our end-product reflected the mass of what was all around us—a heavy base, taller in height than my brother, and not moving any further.

For the next half hour or so that afternoon, while Dad tended to the horses, my brother and I used our new skills to roll the remaining two sections of the body together, positioning them close to the base. When my dad returned, he took over and rolled the larger midsection around a little more, adding to its girth, then lift-rolled it up the side of the base, centering it on top as best as possible.

The last section, the head, was somewhat easier for my dad to lift and position, though he struggled slightly trying to raise it to near his own height. Neither of us kids were of any help to him for that—I had to look up to barely touch the head, my brother had to look up further just to see it. But we were done!

Or were we?

"Okay, now get some snow and start packing it in the spaces where the sections touch," Dad directed, "like cement, to keep them from falling off. You do the bottom; I'll do the head."

Dad could have let us stop without doing the "cementing," but that wasn't him. We could have moved right on to the next step of humanizing our new Frosty, but not under his watch. "If you're going to take the time to do something, then do it right!" was what he always said. So we did. We scooped up more snow and shoved it in the crack between the base and the torso, pushing it in, patting it down, and smoothing it out as we circled clockwise. My dad maneuvered around both of us to finish off the neck, then came down to help us pack in and secure the waist.

When we finished, we all stood on different sides of our creation, admiring the result of our teamwork, mainly its size—nearly as tall and wide as Dad—and its stability. Its weight and the cement had it firmly positioned. And it was soldier-straight, no lean. Its only enemy of destruction was the sun and impending warm-up, but there was nothing we could do to stop that eventual villain. We stood quietly for a few seconds, looking Frosty up and down for defects, thinking about what to do next. Besides empty our boots again.

"Are you guys hungry?" Dad asked.

We had no concept of time that day, nor any interest in it, though it was long past cartoons and cereal but not yet getting dark. The sky was still bright as the sun sagged toward the horizon behind the stable, shadows in the snow getting longer by the minute. We still had time for snow-filled adventures, and the clock was not our concern. But our stomachs were.

"Yes!" we fired back in unison.

"Okay, I'll be right back. Come in and warm up if you want. Who's gotta pee?" he asked as he headed along the trampled path back towards the house.

"Not me," I said.

"Not me," chimed my brother.

My dad entered the house alone, as we sat down near Frosty to empty our boots.

"Can we put a face on the snowman?" my brother asked, as I helped him wiggle out of his boots again. "And a hat?"

"I don't know. We have to ask Dad."

As I looked at my brother—distracted by my own runny nose, icy fingers, and cold feet—my gaze shifted to what was behind him: the snow pile!

Until then, it had just sat there asleep—and without purpose, casually jutting out of the ground, like a fat big brother to our muscular snowman nearby. But my thoughts of what we could do with the pile were quickly replaced with curious thoughts of what Dad would bring us to eat.

That curiosity came to an end quickly, as my dad emerged from the house holding a brown paper grocery bag under his arm.

"Here you go!"

We scurried to get our boots and gloves back on as he headed towards us, our empty stomachs full of anticipation.

"Who wants a Slim Jim?" he bellowed with a grin, as he reached into the bag and kept walking.

Slim Jims! SLIM JIMS! My brother and I loved Slim Jims! Those greasy, foot-long, spicy meat sticks were our favorite snack, which we frequently shoved stick-after-stick into our mouths at the bowling alley, sitting at the bar with Dad and Mom.

We rushed towards my dad, eyes focused on the bag as we tried to stay upright in the snow. He pulled out three straw-sized sticks wrapped in bright red and orange plastic, and thankfully started tearing them open with his bare hands. Normally it was near impossible for my brother or me to open a Slim Jim by hand—ultimately resorting to teeth, scissors, or a combination thereof. With snow, gloves, and overall numbness that day, it would have been a no-win effort to try ourselves. He gave the first ready-to-eat treat to me, which I grabbed and quickly devoured—and the second to my brother, which he attacked as well. Dad ate the third one, then reached in for three more. Heaven had seconds for us that day.

"Thanks, Dad," I said after finishing my second stick.

I was immediately mimicked by my brother, "Thanks, Dad."

Our stomachs were happy. Dad put the slimy empty wrappers in the paper bag, cleaned his hands off with snow, then dried them on his pants before crinkling the top of the paper bag to close it.

"Let's finish the snowman," Dad directed as we spun around and headed back to our faceless creation a few yards away.

When we got there, Dad started calling out the contents of the bag as he reached in and handed us what he had found in the house.

"Here's a carrot for his nose, and a scarf for his neck."

My brother snatched the dirty carrot, and I took the dull-colored woolen scarf. Only Mom wore scarves.

"Here's a hat for him."

Dad pulled out his coaching hat, a billed cap of light blue cloth with the same "Jayhawks" lettering we were wearing. He slipped the hat over his crew cut and kept going through the inventory.

"We can use Oreos for his eyes," he explained, as he reached deeper into the bag and pulled out two wafers of our other favorite snack. He handed them to my brother.

"Don't drop them, or eat them!"

He smiled at my brother who frantically juggled the carrot and cookies in his little hands, trapping them gently against the chest of his nylon parka. We both eyeballed those Oreos as if they'd eventually be ours to eat.

"Here's a cigarette for his mouth."

Dad put the Marlboro 100, wet and creased from his glove, into his own mouth, then looked at me.

"Get a couple branches for his arms," he nodded to me, glancing over toward the trees surrounding the house. "We'll start putting the face on him."

As he talked, the huge snow pile stood silent behind him—casting its shadow at the house—while the snowman and my teammates were already darkened by the shadow of the barn.

I turned and started trudging through unbroken snow, dragging the scarf behind me.

"Wrap the scarf around your neck," my dad yelled, "so you can use both hands."

That format and cadence of his instruction was commonplace in our house. I reeled in the scarf and wrapped it twice around my neck, doing exactly what he said.

I worked quickly so I could get back to the fashioning and face-building that was happening in parallel—and to minimize the numbness creeping its way around my wrists and up my parka sleeves. Luckily, the first arm-to-be cracked off the tree with limited exertion. The second, however, was not so compliant. When it finally broke loose, I leaned back from the tree, wiped the snot from my nose with my other hand, and exhaled, "I got 'em!"

As I returned to the day's construction zone, my brother stood in front of my dad, both facing the snowman. Its Oreo eyes stared past me. I smiled to see a persona beginning to form—and assumed Dad had been the one to surgically implant the cookies. Then, in a quick, casual hoist, my dad lifted up my brother to Oreo-eye-level and instructed him to plant the carrot he was holding with his small, gloved hands.

"Put the fat end into the hole I started. Don't touch the eyes; they'll break," Dad warned.

My brother gripped the carrot with one hand and balanced himself with the other on Frosty's cheek. He pushed hard two or three times to insert the orange nose and keep it in place, but it drooped and barely stayed put as he finally released his hand. I wanted to get up there and do it myself but knew that would only start a war and end the day.

"Good job," puffed Dad, as he lowered my brother into the snow, "I'll put some cement on it."

He picked up a handful of snow to cement it in place, then took a step back to assess his work.

My brother looked up at the carrot, then up at my dad.

"Good job, Dad."

My dad's pink face broke into a wide smile. "Thanks."

Dad took off his glove and used his fingers to etch a wide smile for Frosty underneath the carrot. When finished, he pulled out the cigarette—lodged above his ear—grabbed some snow, then proceeded to cement the cigarette in the corner of Frosty's freshly carved mouth. The nicotine stick hung intentionally from the snowy lip like a James Dean prop.

Dad smiled again, happy with himself.

"Okay, where's the scarf? And the arms?" he asked as he turned toward me, still smiling.

Holding a branch in each glove, I walked closer to the snowman with his new appendages.

"Can I do one?" pleaded my brother.

"No, you did the carrot!" I snapped back, "I'm doing the arms."

He moped quietly, "I wanna do one," as I ignored him and inserted the two branches, roughly at midpoint on each side of the torso. When done, I shuffled backwards into more untouched snow, bobbing left and right to view my attachments. Good on strength and length, poor on symmetry.

"They look fine. Put the scarf on him," prodded my dad.

I unwound the scarf from my neck and clumsily threaded it from behind to circle the neck, cautiously dodging the arms, the cigarette, and the carrot with Dad's help in front.

"Probably should have put the scarf on first," Dad lamented. "Next time."

With no other additions to make, my brother and I scurried around next to my dad to evaluate our design and execution. Dad straightened out the scarf and pushed the arms into the midsection a little. My brother and I scooped more snow to further cement the base, as we attempted an improvement at a height we could easily reach. The head was flawless.

"Great job guys! A-plus today," Dad noted, shaking each of our heads with his palms, while all three of us beamed at Frosty.

Our chilly trio worked well together, bringing life to the frozen flakes. It was the best snowman.

But my sights were set on something better. And bigger.

"Can we climb the snow pile now?" I blurted out, wasting no time to seize the moment and remaining sunlight.

The shadows were getting longer, the brilliance of the cloudless sky waning.

"I gotta pee!" my brother ached, grabbing himself and looking up at my dad.

Dad pointed toward the tree where I'd found Frosty's arms.

"Go over there," he told my brother, who began to bounce a little faster.

"Can you help?" asked my brother, still staring up at Dad.

Neither seemed to have heard my plea to scale the pile.

My dad looked down toward me. "Do you have to go, too? Can you help him?"

"Okay, then can we climb the pile?"

I was fixated on that snow pile and figured this was how to get to it—help brother, climb pile.

Plus, I had to go, too.

"Yeah, sure, I'll be back in a minute," my dad countered. He headed toward the house, while we headed toward the trees—both excited to return to that massive mound but physically distracted for the moment.

We ambled through the snow as quickly as possible to the trees, threw off our gloves, and both struggled with our jeans' zippers before relieving ourselves in bright yellow, curlicue patterns on the pristine canvas around us. We exhaled and giggled together.

"Where's Mom?" my brother asked, fascinated by the paisley outlines he doodled in the snow.

"In the house, I guess," I replied, completely focused on returning to the pile, and not at all on where Mom was—or with having to share Dad with her that day.

And in the back of my head, I knew if they'd fought the night before, they'd fight again. My response was selfish and uncaring. I didn't want to have to think about how she was doing—or where she was. To me—right then—it didn't matter.

I doodled along with him.

When we finished our business, we zipped up and re-gloved—laughing and pointing at our spontaneous artwork—then headed back to the snow pile. Dad hadn't come out of the house yet, but we heard our dog barking—yes, it was the brown boxer, not the German shepherd.

As we got to the pile to begin our ascent, the metal screen door opened, and out bounded the boxer into the snow—barking excitedly to see us and to be in that strange mix of frigid, deep powder. Behind him came Dad, carrying the square, steel coal shovel he normally used to clean the manure from the stable and the boxer's crap from the garage in the winter. He also used it to shovel snow, which he started doing as the door closed behind him.

"I'll be there in a minute," he hollered to us as the dog jumped back and forth between my brother and me, thrilled to see us and wanting desperately to play.

As Dad shoveled toward us, we did our best to climb the pile, laughing and pulling at each other while the dog barked with approval. Skyward progress was slow, but we were thrilled to try. The pungent, comforting taste of the Slim Jims lingered in my mouth as I climbed and fell.

I started to climb again from the base and saw my dad out of the corner of my eye. He had shoveled his way to the passenger side of the pickup truck that was parked patiently at the base of the pile. He spiked the shovel into deep virgin snow to hold it upright as he opened the door to get inside.

"I'm backing up the truck," he yelled, as he entered the pickup and slid across the bench seat to the driver's side.

From my vantage point a few feet up the pile, I saw a dull, rutted path behind the truck, extending all the way straight down our lane to the main road, snow shoved to the sides like a heavy white gutter. Again, the overnight drifts had covered much of what looked to have been cleared, but it was obvious something had furrowed a path behind the pickup.

The dog barked and jumped on my brother as they played near Frosty. The boxer was winning. Both were happy.

The Ford's engine rumbled cautiously as my dad started it up. I watched as he stopped, started, and rocked the truck back and forth to nudge it in reverse. His face was calm and confident, not unlike his methodical progress backwards, away from the pile.

After backing up about twenty feet, he stopped and exited the driver's side, then hurdled over the snow a few strides to get to the space he'd just vacated at the pile's base. Sunlight dimmed as the day turned to shadows and the calm air cooled.

He grabbed the coal shovel again and pulled it out of the snow.

"Let's make some steps."

Circling the pile, to its side furthest from the truck and closest to Frosty, he petted the exhausted boxer and motioned my brother to move away. During the next hour, as the sun set and we continued to dive and laugh and flail in the snow, my dad carved, shaped, and constructed a staircase in the pile. It was a one-man job to form the treads and risers, but I watched closely when I wasn't distracted by dog or brother.

As we played around Frosty and the pile, eating snow and hurling it at each other and the dog, Dad repeated the process to build a dozen steps into the pile, not including the duplicates eliminated by collapse.

I could see him sweat the whole time, his face damp and nose running constantly. Dusk arrived as he finished the top step.

He slid the shovel down the side of the pile and lumbered down himself, taking care to avoid the stairs and any further collapses. My dad was a healthy, agile man—a two-sport athlete in high school, a football player in college, and a regular weekend golfer. The snow pile posed little challenge to his physical abilities. On the other hand, my brother and I looked up at the stairs in continued awe of the day, and of him. We were dying to head up but didn't dare touch those stairs until *he* said it was okay. Our interest in Frosty dropped quickly to zero.

"Can we try it?" I asked excitedly, as Dad stood back and again assessed his work.

The boxer had calmed and wandered over next to him, looking for a new play pal. Dad lazily patted the dog by habit, then took off his gloves, unzipped his jacket, and reached in and pulled out a soft pack of cigarettes. He stuck one in his mouth and lit it with the silver lighter from his pants pocket. The still air was friendly to the flame.

He took a long drag on the Marlboro, wiping his forehead with his sleeve, then exhaled and released us in a single breath.

"One at a time. Don't fight!"

He was drained. I could tell a beer was in his future—it would definitely be an Old Style night.

Hearing his admonishment, we both jostled toward the first step, where I pushed my brother to the side as I headed up. He started to whimper, of course.

"Hey! Fight, and nobody goes up! Hear me?!"

It was an exhausted yell from my dad. He wanted no part of our quarrel. And we wanted no part of his belt. Darkness had arrived with the evening, and we needed to cooperate to enjoy the pile.

My brother knew that as well, as I carefully restarted my ascent at the first stair. My dad and my brother, and the boxer, watched intently. Thankfully, it seemed that Dad had done a thorough job packing and cementing before my initial climb. I proceeded upward.

Each step felt sturdy and functional as I approached the top of the pile without hesitation. At the very top, Dad had flattened out a small, squarish platform with the shovel, just large enough to transfer our balance from our feet to our butts without tumbling off. He'd thought of everything.

He always did.

"Just sit on your butt, lean back, and slide down. Lean back!" my dad encouraged me.

He seemed as excited as I was, as he and my brother circled 180 degrees around the pile, from the staircase toward the side I was preparing to head down. The dog followed. They looked up at me as I sat and smiled, ready to descend from the platform. I took a deep breath and glanced forward at the dark headlights of the truck, convincing myself Dad had parked it far enough away to avoid me being a victim of its front bumper.

I leaned back, closed my eyes, and pulled hard with hands and heels.

It was a cold, bumpy ride down the pile. Snow flew up the back of my parka and up the calves of my jeans. My head bounced softly a couple times as the pile captured my stocking hat—but it was great! *Better than great!*

"That was SO FUN!" I screamed breathlessly, as my brother scurried around to head up the stairs.

My dad smiled as he grabbed the shovel and extended it up the slope to reclaim my hat, then tossed it to me as darkness fell. I was ready for my next slide.

"I need help!" cried my brother, as my dad and I headed back to the stairs and found him a couple steps up.

"Can you follow him to the top and make sure he doesn't fall?" my dad asked.

Normally, I was opposed to providing any assistance to my brother, but on that day, that night, I was ready to help.

"Sure," I replied, then coaxed my brother to keep going.

"Let's go!"

The crying immediately stopped, and we both headed up slowly, one step at a time, my dad following with the shovel performing repairs as we went. When my brother reached the platform at the top, I could tell he was nervous. His slow movements got slower as he crouched close to the platform.

"Just sit there, and I'll help push you down," I offered, not thinking of how that probably sounded to him.

"Don't push me! I can do it myself!" my brother yelled confidently as he swung his legs around and sat on the platform.

"Okay, just go then. It's fun. Make sure you lean back," I instructed.

He settled himself and scooted his butt close to the curved edge of the snow-packed platform. I crept up slowly behind to motivate and encourage him. I wanted him to go so I could get another turn.

"I'm stuck, just push me a little, okay? Just a little."

Music to my ears!

I grabbed him by the shoulders and pulled him back, then gave a solid shove to send him on his way. I watched as he slid down in the dark, ending in more of a hapless roll. He cried again as my dad helped him up. And I laughed.

"Stop laughing! You pushed too hard!" he screamed up at me, his tear-soaked face full of snow to match his jeans and his parka, again blaming me for his discomfort.

His stocking hat was snagged by the slope, similar to mine.

"Look out, here I come!" I screamed back as I pulled my hat down tight over my ears, scooted forward on the platform, and headed down feet first. It was another fun ride!

As soon as I reached the bottom, before I could stand up, my brother attacked me—throwing his gloves, arms swinging, and boots kicking. My dad still had him by the sleeve as he cried and flailed. The boxer barked wildly, thinking it was playtime again.

"That's it! Get in the house now, both of you!"

Dad was pissed, again.

"It's too dark anyway. Get inside!"

He'd had enough.

"I spend all this time making this thing, and you two just argue. Get inside!"

He held onto my brother as they walked to the front door, then waved at me to go into the house. The dog followed the three of us.

Then, as quickly as he had screamed and sobbed at me, my brother shifted targets and started sobbing to my dad, "No. No. Please! I'm sorry. Pleeease! Can we stay outside?"

My brother's change in direction happened so quickly, I hadn't even had time to blame him for the chaos.

Surprisingly, my dad stopped as we got to the door. He opened it and sent the dog inside, then reached around the frame and turned on the outside light overhead. The bare bulb glowed a dull yellow. He turned around and looked down at the two of us, both depressed and yearning to stay outside. I could see the frustration in my brother's face and the anger in my dad's. He looked at my brother first, then switched his focus to me.

"You get one chance. Anymore fighting, and it's over. No dinner and straight to bed. You hear me? I've had enough!"

He stared at my brother, looking for confirmation.

My brother stopped crying and nodded. His nose ran like a faucet. I looked at my dad and saw the tension gripping his face, his jaw locked and eyes glued to us. I nodded in silence as well.

The silence didn't last long.

49

"Dad, can you slide down with us?"

My brother innocently thawed the moment. I was relieved.

"I might be too big. You two go. I'll be out in a minute," Dad said as he disappeared back in the house again. We turned and raced back to the pile.

We got about two-thirds of the way up the snowy stairs when Dad came out of the house. Helped by the overhead light, we could see he was dragging a small wooden sled with red steel runners; a short rope tied to the front was his handle. He headed toward the truck. We stopped climbing as we both watched him drop the sled and climb over the snow into the truck. He cranked the engine in the quiet night.

On came the headlights! Focused on the downward slope of the hill, the beams fanned out and gave us a perfect view of our playground. Dad exited the truck while it ran and grabbed the sled again. We remained motionless on the incline, waiting for him to come around, not sure what he had in mind. He looked at me and raised the sled with the rope in my direction.

"Here, take this. It's heavy. Try it first before your brother goes down."

I reached down and grabbed the rope from him. The sled was heavy, but my adrenaline countered the weight, as Dad pushed it up from the bottom. My brother eased to the side and allowed me to pass him with the sled. He was on his best behavior; we both were.

When I got to the platform, I sat down and pulled up the sled, nearly dropping it—and nearly falling myself. I squeezed it in next to me on the two-by-two-foot pad and took a deep breath before continuing. My brother was quiet, but in the beam of the headlights, I caught him crack a smile under his snotty nose. He was happy again; we both were.

"I'll run a long rope up there tomorrow to make it easier."

My dad was always looking for improvements to his work, and to ours.

"Okay, now stand up, put the sled between your legs, sit on it, and slide down."

Easier said than done, Dad, I thought.

I carefully stood up on the platform as my brother, on the top step behind me, held the sled in place as best he could. I still had the rope clenched in my gloved hand as I worked to center the sled and straddle it on the platform.

I turned my head around and looked in my brother's eyes.

"Hold it, and don't push until I say so."

He knew what I meant as I turned back and slowly lowered my butt onto the sled. I felt more confident and started to grin.

The grin disappeared quickly as I stared hard at the Ford and its headlights below, wondering if I was going to slide into or underneath it.

"Dad, what about the truck?" I yelled.

"You'll be fine. I'll stop you!" Dad confirmed through a smile illuminated by the headlights.

Dad was happy again. A brief calm passed over me as he moved to the front of the truck and became my barricade. Then, from behind, my brother whispered assuredly, "It won't hurt that much."

My chest pumped quickly again.

I raised my boots and rested the heels on the sled, grabbing the rope with both hands. I breathed deep.

"Okay, push!" I commanded my brother as I leaned my head over my knees until it snapped back upon descent.

I skidded to the bottom, leaning to the right as I slowly approached my dad and the headlights. As I fell to the side, he grabbed the sled with one hand and my arm with the other.

I remembered his hand was strong, his grip was tight.

And comforting.

"Nice job. Was it fun?" Dad asked as he helped me to my feet.

"It was SO fun! I was going really fast, wasn't I?"

I was sure I was traveling at warp speed down the pile. I was ecstatic and ready for the next run, and heard my brother screaming at the top of the pile, "My turn!"

"Yeah, that was pretty fast," Dad confirmed, "just like the Olympics."

I wasn't sure what he meant, but he said it was fast, that's all that mattered.

"Go up and help your brother. I'll hand you the sled." I raced around the perimeter of the pile and headed up the dark, snowy steps. More cement was needed, but not that night. We were having too much fun to stop for repairs! My brother was perched eagerly at the top step as I scaled the stairs to reach him. Dad waited as I got settled.

As I turned to reach for the sled Dad had extended up the pile, he offered another improvement in addition to the long rope.

"When we're done, I'm going to pour some cold water on it to ice it down overnight. It will be faster tomorrow."

The three of us smiled together, as my brother repeated, "My turn, my turn, my turn!"

I laughed. My dad laughed. My brother laughed.

I remembered what made that day the best. It wasn't the snow, or Frosty, or the pile with the carefully chiseled stairs. It was *the laughter*. After the quiet and stillness of the morning, the day had turned into joyful chaos. Interrupted by flashes of yelling and crying, I laughed hard with my brother and dad that day.

It was the best.

As I grabbed the sled, still supported by my dad, I looked up and glimpsed Mom in the kitchen window, above the front door. The fluorescent light above the sink surprised me, as it stamped a bright square on the front of the house, unlike the dull radiance delivered outside by the Ford and the light above the front door. It also illuminated my mom's red hair as she stared out at our playground, a Marlboro 100 in one hand, a drink in the other—likely an iced highball of Seagram's and Canada Dry ginger ale, the recipe she had taught me to craft for her.

I hoped she would come out and play with us, but I was more focused on grabbing the sled and getting my brother down the pile so that I could slide again.

It was the best day. The very, very best day.

#

Little did I know at the time, the blizzard of 1967 was the beginning of the end for her, and for my parents. Mom was twenty-five. Dad was forty-two.

I slowly opened my tired eyes and squeezed Dad's soft, still hand a little tighter. It was 4:54 a.m.—time for *my* grip to comfort *him*.

HOUR 5: The YEAR

The drifting felt good. Unlike the cold, still-dark morning beyond the windows, my jacket had become a warm, leathery cocoon, trapping my body heat while I sat peacefully in the armchair. I held Dad's hand, and he returned the favor as I slid seamlessly in and out of reality. The random beeping of his monitor and regular compressing of its blood pressure device, along with Bryant's intermittent visits, ensured I wasn't truly sleeping. But it was infinitely better than sitting awake, bug-eyed, and relatively helpless.

As I scooched back in the chair and squared my shoulders with a flicker of new energy, I felt the toll taken by my seated contortion. My longing for sleep had outweighed my need for physical comfort, and I was paying the price the more I unwound my aging frame. Ergonomic, the armchair wasn't. But the brief pain of my twisted oldness was nothing compared to what Dad was fighting off in that ICU bed, or to what he'd experienced the last five or ten years.

Forever it seemed, Dad maintained his strength, mobility, and desire to stay fit. Golf was always his exercise of choice, more so as his hair whitened and his days emptied. A cold beer on the nineteenth hole and a need to compete were his motivations. And when the evil onset of macular degeneration in his late seventies forced him to forever put away his clubs, along with the dimpled white Titleist balls whose trajectory he could no longer follow, he kept himself occupied with dumbbell curls and stair climbs in the house.

He enjoyed being an athlete—and coaching. He thrived on the physical challenges and mental dynamics athletics required. Getting out of the sand trap, catching a pass in the pouring rain, calling the right play on third and long. It was more about that—the trying, the practicing, the sweating, the overcoming, the giving 110 percent, the enjoying your sacrifice, the high-fiving—than it was about winning. Or maybe it really was about winning; winning the matchups against roadblocks, self-doubt, and untried potential. Not the shiny trophies and exaggerated headlines from superficial tournaments and Friday night games.

He was still exercising his creaky anatomy as he crept up on the century mark and the aches and pains became more frequent and acute. When I picked him up for his doctor's visit in early December, he felt the need to show me he was still doing bicep curls, using the short bar only, no weights. He was proud of the strength he had left in him. I was proud of it, too. And again when he showed me later that morning how he was able to go up and down six or seven stairs in his foyer—as if he were practicing for his upcoming physical and wanted me to evaluate his performance before his exam. It was innocent, almost childlike.

I was impressed by his abilities, but more so by his faith in me to assess them—made possible by the pride he began to swallow a few years back as he headed into the final lap in his race against time.

And against that goddamn stent.

But in the hospital that morning, he wasn't curling or climbing anything. Pain, and not the good kind, had finally won.

As I rustled about in the chair, I let go of his hand to steady and reposition myself. On cue, his eyes opened slightly, staring forward, as he felt me vacating his persistent grip.

"Hey Dad, did you get some sleep? How are you feeling?"

I hoped there was positive progress. There wasn't.

"My back really hurts," he replied softly, his voice cracking, "and my throat hurts. Is there water?"

"I'll check."

I started the slow process to stand up and find Bryant, when he came into the room, pushing the curtain aside. Another nurse followed him.

"Hi Martin, how do you feel? Are you in pain?" Bryant repeated my similar ask.

Dad responded similarly as well, "The pain is really bad."

"And his throat is dry. Can he get some water?" I added.

"Sure thing," Bryant replied.

Then in a louder, slower tone, he announced to my dad his main reason for his visit.

"Martin, I'll get you some more painkiller and something to drink, but wanted you to meet Katie. She'll be taking over for me. She'll be your nurse today."

I reached over my dad to shake Katie's hand as Bryant finished his introduction. I greeted her in my half-awake state.

"Nice to meet you, I'm his son." Her grip was firm.

"Hi. We work twelve-hour shifts in the ICU, so I'll be here all day if you need anything," Katie offered to me directly.

Like Bryant, she had a confident, personable manner. And like Bryant, she was clad in blue scrubs and roughly his age and height but blonder, with more hair. And much more alert than the three of us around her.

"Hi Martin, I'm Katie. I'll be your nurse today," she confirmed with extra volume and a start-of-shift pep in her voice. "If you need anything, just let me know, okay?"

"Okay," my dad squeaked.

Bryant logged in to the computer and reviewed my dad's status with Katie as I reclaimed Dad's hand and tried to distract him from his discomforts.

"Dad, how do you think the Cubs will do this season?"

I really didn't care how they would do or have much to offer him in related commentary, but if anything would distract him or trigger a reaction, it would be the mention of the Cubs or the Bears. He was a die-hard fan of both, but more of a glass-half-empty die-hard. In his heart, he would always root for them at game time, but he set his expectations so low—which was historically appropriate—that when they did lose, he could say he *knew* that would be the result and feel righteous in his post-game critiques.

Between the two usually lackluster teams, the Bears were the biggest target of his venom. With Dad's football experience as a player and coach, he was exceptionally qualified, in his mind, to be an irreproachable armchair quarterback. No one in Bears' burnt orange and navy blue escaped his wrath, even after the macular degeneration began to flex itself.

Pick a player or a head coach in the last thirty years, and Dad had a salty opinion to share—usually including the terms "overpaid" and "lazy." And any outstanding performances or miraculous wins were secondary to the "lack of effort" or "sheer luck" he preferred to highlight. In his view, the more they played—or were paid—the worse they got.

And when I felt like getting him really cranked up, I'd mention Lovie Smith, the fired Bears' head honcho, four coaches back. He despised Lovie. I'd remind Dad that *our* taxes were funding Lovie's post-NFL, millionaire lifestyle as the highest paid employee of the state, the U of I football coach. Hold fuse, light match, watch fireworks. Every time.

The Cubs, on the other hand, played second fiddle to the Bears in terms of Dad's animosity, even though they shared many of his complaints: *overpaid, lazy, can't hold a lead, manager can't manage, no offense, no defense.* But the intensity of his Cubs disdain was less than that for the Bears. Probably because the baseball season was longer, and he needed to pace himself. Or because baseball wasn't his first love, and he didn't have any hands-on experience besides coaching Little Leaguers—including my brother and me—to inform his pessimism.

Or because he'd made a connection with the Cubs when we lived on the ranch, by driving frozen mini pizzas up to Wrigley—pizzas mass-produced by the Italian restaurant in our small town. Sometimes, when he drove that refrigerated truck in the summer, we'd pack the cab with all four of us, deliver the pizzas, then watch a game in the upper deck cheap seats before heading back south out of Chicago. Though there weren't many of them, those makeshift family outings to the ballpark—batting practice and foil-wrapped hot dogs included—made for memorable summer days and softened his lifetime scorn for the Cubbies, his Loveable Losers.

But his Losers became big winners in 2016 when the Cubs won the World Series, their first in his lifetime. In *our* lifetimes. Dad loved every minute of it, even as he kept complaining about the pitching and high-priced roster. The Cubs' 108-year championship drought had come to an exhilarating, game-seven end, and he was thrilled to see it, as much as his blurry eyesight allowed. He launched a championship smile when I brought him a blue "World Series Champs" cap a few days after the Northsiders took the crown, thanks to a solid inventory of over-priced gear at Kohl's. That recent winning season was another reason for him to cut the Cubs a little more slack than he did the Bears.

Dad was slow to respond to my leading question about his prediction for the Cubs' season ahead. I waited. Maybe it wasn't the right time to elevate his blood pressure. I hadn't thought of that before I opened my mouth. I was glad that at least I hadn't asked about Lovie.

Dad didn't disappoint.

"Pffft! They shoulda got rid of Maddon after they won the Series! Downhill since," he grumbled.

The Cubs had fired their relatively successful manager, Joe Maddon, towards the end of last season. A couple years too late, in Dad's opinion.

"I don't know. I liked Maddon. I think they blew it with their pitching. Now *that's* been downhill since," I countered, trying to keep him going—trying to squeeze out the vigor I knew he still had in him, like the last precious beads of toothpaste in a lifeless, wrinkled tube.

"Oh, jeez. Their pitching's horrible," he confirmed.

He was on a roll! I could have kept going position by position, player by player, and he'd have something to say about it. Negative, of course. But I was happy for any response. Lying quietly and half-conscious under a beige pile of sheets and blankets wasn't his style, and I was hoping to draw out whatever emotion or feeling he had left.

"Martin, I'm going to see if the doctor will increase the dose for your painkiller. I'll get you some water, too. We'll be back."

Bryant interrupted our bedside sports-talk banter, then left the room with Katie following him.

"What did he say?" Dad asked, not capturing Bryant's exit fully.

"He's going to ask the doctor about your pain medicine, and he'll get you some water."

"Good. My throat is so sore. Oh, my back!" Dad was uncomfortable, shifting himself in the bed.

It was obvious he needed a bigger blast of whatever narcotics they were already giving him. Like him, I shared a high tolerance for pain and seemed to need more than the normal dose of aspirin, Tylenol, or bourbon for relief. So I had a feeling he'd also need an extra jolt after the first couple hours in the hospital when he was still hurting. If the nurses came back to the room without a change in plan, I'd have to press for one.

I needed to distract him a little longer until they returned.

"Dad? Dad, the drive here was pretty easy today. Glad there wasn't any snow on the roads."

He wasn't much of a weather-phile, but I figured that might get him engaged in another topic we could both relate to. I was definitely a bigger critic of the unpredictable Midwestern weather than he was, likely because he was homebound and really didn't care much how warm, cold, rainy, or humid it was outside. Hell, he wore cutoff shorts around his house most of the year, making sure his thermostat knew who ran things.

"If it gets bad out, you can go home. You don't have to stay," he optioned unexpectedly.

He was always looking out for my well-being—respectful of my schedule, my health, my wife and kids. He never wanted to overstay *his* welcome when *I* visited *him*. And I had visited him a lot in the past year, since I retired and his health further degraded. They were mutually exclusive events but a timely coincidence.

I had left my job after thirty-four-plus years, choosing to take my chances without that biweekly direct deposit, versus continue the fifty-five-hour work weeks shuffling projects and problems inside the middle-management hamster ball. Over the years, as one would expect, I'd become fairly adept at the concurrent juggling and spinning—meeting deadlines, resolving jeopardies, managing people, learning new technologies, aligning and realigning priorities. Surviving the day so I could do it all again tomorrow. Rinse, repeat, and always faster.

But like the song, the thrill was gone. And had been for a while. BB King knew it. I knew it. And my wife knew it. So we made the decision to give retirement a whirl—without a plan, a priority, or another job in mind.

Then, within a month after cutting my corporate umbilical and sleeping past 5:00 a.m. on the weekdays, Dad's bout of pneumonia and subsequent rehab gave me a new job and a new priority: him.

He didn't ask for it. He never would. But I knew he was happy and grateful for the time and attention I could give him as he recovered. And I knew he preferred to be in his own home—fending for himself—than to be at the mercy of someone else, and more so, their decisions and schedule.

Havenshore took good care of Dad during his weeklong encounter with pneumonia, and again during his subsequent three-week stay at their rehab facility across the street from the hospital. Rehab was required, because even though his hospital stay was relatively short, the illness had sapped his strength, and being bedridden had taken a toll on his mobility, whatever he had left. His ankles and feet were swollen from water retention, and his knees and hip were chronically tender and sore long before being admitted. The doctors and specialists deemed it necessary to get him some focused help to walk and move around again, especially because he lived alone. Their rehab prescription was new to me, but I was glad they recommended it for him. And, surprisingly, he was, too. That's when Dad met walker, and vice versa.

His stay at the rehab facility was extremely useful and necessary for him, and me, in a number of ways. Primarily, and as intended, it helped him get into shape to move around his house and be independent again. As a coach, he loved to practice. More than the games, he loved the repetitions, the commitment, the gradual improvement. He loved the effort to become better. And during his time in rehab, he rekindled his love of practice.

When I called or visited him, I'd immediately get an enthusiastic update on his accomplishments in the therapy center. *This many steps taken. That many stairs climbed.* He was proud of his progress. And his commitment. More than once, I had to hang up with him because he was gung-ho to be on time for his therapy session. It was in those sessions where he was introduced to using a walker, and accepted it

61

without hesitation. As proud as he was, he realized he needed that walker to be himself again at home, and with a sense of security. He embraced its use, comforted by its stability. It was like a tool for him. And Dad loved his tools.

It wasn't his first brush with a walker, however. My mom needed one when her legs started to fail, eventually needing a wheelchair when they stopped completely. My dad was there to help her with both devices—and to carry her up and down stairs, to the bathroom, and to the car for doctor visits. His strength—physical and emotional—was taxed repeatedly during those tough spells, carrying her eighty-pounds in his arms and their world on his shoulders. Much of that started when I was in college and worsened after our wedding, well over thirty years ago, when he was about the age that I was in room 10. He still kept Mom's walker upstairs in his house.

Besides the physical benefits of Dad's rehab, his time at the facility also gave him a taste of what it would be like to live in an assisted living environment. Generally speaking, he didn't enjoy the flavor of it. He didn't like having a 24/7 roommate; sharing a TV, and battling TVs, annoyed him, as did someone else's snoring and bodily noises. He liked his video choices at home and the ability to crank up the volume as loud as he needed it, at whatever time of day he wanted. A roommate six feet away tended to get in the way of that.

But as much as he would have preferred a private room, he was unhappy with the lack of socializing he sought from others when he was with them at meals or in common spaces. He often complained he was the only one to start a conversation, and when he did, he didn't get much of a response from anyone else. They were "old people," he'd say, and he wasn't ready to just fade away like they seemed to be doing. Part of me wondered how much of that was true, versus how much of it was their "ignore this guy" response to him instigating some kind of verbal skirmish just to get the blood moving. Like me asking about

Lovie.

In the end, going to rehab gave him, and me, a baseline to evaluate the types of places or characteristics that would be acceptable to him if or when he moved out of his house. He may not have cared for the experience, but it was a welcome opportunity for me to learn what he did and didn't like.

Another benefit of his stint in rehab was time. Time for me. I had just gotten off the stress-covered flywheel of full-time work and hadn't planned to be in the business of rehabbed-parent caregiver so soon. At some time in the future, maybe—but less than thirty days after pulling the paycheck plug, no. Just because I didn't have plans to golf, cruise, or both, didn't mean I was ready to shift gears and hit the ground running as Dad's plus-one.

Over the years, he'd had some live-in support, for which we were thankful, as was he. But no longer, and by no one's fault or negligence. His independence, his pride, and his almost half-century familiarity with his living space persevered in the absence of others' assistance. However, when he was discharged from rehab and left the food and the people he was glad to leave, he would need some help, my help, to get back on his feet—walker included—and keep going. Three weeks' of rehab time was my friend. Mentally, if for nothing else.

When he did leave rehab, stronger and more mobile than when he got there, he returned home anxious but smiling. He was ready to catch up on all the *Gunsmoke* reruns he had missed—and to indulge in a few Dilly Bars and Genuine Drafts. But he had slowed. As much as the rehab had kickstarted his basic movements and confidence, he was still in his nineties, and the pneumonia was not kind to his defenses.

It would take months for him to get back to where he'd been, if he got there at all: meandering around the house with daily chores, climbing the stairs to his second floor or down to his basement, sitting on his front porch as birds and squirrels challenged his hazy vision, or taking out his garbage and trading barbs with his alley neighbors over sports and politics. *Lovie and taxes.*

But he tried! And he accepted the help of the in-home therapists dispatched by Havenshore to get and keep him moving around the house. Dad was still all-in on the therapy he received, and having someone besides me he could talk to, and probably flirt with, was an added bonus for him. He reveled in their approval of his leg lifts and stair climbs, and enjoyed being recognized for his late-life abilities, especially if he could surprise them; like his sleight-of-hand coin tricks that amazed our kids when they were young. And me when I was young. Dad loved how they—we—thought he was a magician.

Or when, a month after his ninetieth birthday, as we loaded a college-bound U-Haul with second-hand furniture from his garage, he decided he was the older, shorter, whiter version of Usain Bolt. With a minor burst of energy, he eased out of the lawn chair where he was supervising my son and me, walked to the south end of the alley, and told us to start recording him. We pulled out our phones, stood in the driveway and looked at each other, perplexed and curious, as Dad got settled.

Then, with no stretching or warm up, Dad started jogging north down the alley in our direction. He was clad in a blue-and-white T-shirt and ancient, brown, polyester pants—accessorized with Velcroed gym shoes and Fitover sunglasses to shield his sensitive eyes. His arms and legs pumped in alternate unison, and his head pointed toward the finish line. As he picked up steam and passed us, I yelled to him to "be careful." I hoped he wouldn't stumble into a pothole and wreck himself, or need CPR when his legs finally gave up. We kept the phones recording as he raced himself to the other end of the alley.

We were dumbfounded by his performance, and hurried down to see if he was alright once he stopped.

"Dad, are you okay?!" I wondered loudly.

"Papa, that was amazing! How do you feel?" My son, eyes wide open, was legitimately concerned. And amazed.

"Pretty good for an old guy, huh? How fast was I?" Dad panted, while he rested his hands on his knees, hunching forward to catch his breath. And waiting for the praise to burnish his virile ego.

"Papa, that was crazy! Nice job! Let's go sit down," my son persuaded him, guiding him toward the garage.

"You tore up the alley, Dad!" That's really what he wanted to hear from us, so I obliged.

Dad was proud of his moment on that warm August morning, hustling his worn physique down the pock-marked pavement, legs bobbing like rusty pistons past the garbage cans that marked his progress. He wanted us to know he *still had it*.

And I had the proof. The video of that block-long sprint was resident on my phone, five years later, as he lay motionless in front of me, allowing me to leave him if the weather was too troubling. But like him, I was committed. And staying.

At least twenty minutes had passed by the time Bryant and Katie returned.

"Hi Martin. Good news. Instead of every hour, the doctor said we can give you the painkiller every half hour," Bryant informed my dad as he logged into the computer and scanned another vial.

"I've got some ice chips *and* some water for you, too," Katie added with a joyous tone.

I took the Styrofoam cup of ice chips from her. She bent a flexible green straw at a right angle in the other cup and moved it to Dad's lips for a slurp. He took a long draw of water, relaxed, then took another. And another. He was definitely thirsty. He turned his head towards me, away from the straw, when he was finished soothing himself.

"Here, I can take that," I offered her.

I had placed the ice chips on the wheeled bedtable behind me, and did the same with the cup of water.

Katie stayed engaged with my dad, while Bryant slipped on gloves behind her.

"How did that taste? Good?"

"Yes, thank you," Dad whispered back to her, quenched for the time being.

I could tell he was thankful for that cold, wet relief, plain as it was.

"There you go, Martin. Hopefully that helps with the pain," Bryant leaned closer to my dad as he talked. "Katie will be able to give you your medicine every half hour now. Is there anything else you need before I leave for the day?"

"Can you speed up the clock?" my dad quipped, getting a smile out of all of us.

"You be good, Martin. I hope you feel better soon. You're in good hands with Katie."

Bryant put his hand on Dad's shoulder as he said goodbye. They looked each other in the eyes.

"Thank you," my dad said sincerely, "for all your help."

He meant it.

I reached across Dad and shook Bryant's hand, thanking him as well. I meant it, too.

"Martin, try to get some rest. I'll be back in a little while to see how you're doing."

Katie took over quickly from Bryant to give my dad comfort.

The nurses turned and exited the room together, pulling the curtain and sliding the doors shut. I looked up at the clock as they left. It was 5:44 a.m. and still dark outside.

I reached over and picked up the cup of ice chips, shaking it slowly into my mouth and trying to get a few to pop loose while avoiding a full cascade onto my face. The drip of cold water from what had melted was refreshing, as were the few chips I was able to shake free.

I put the cup back on the table and sat down again next to my dad as I sucked slowly on the chips tickling my tongue.

The back of his hand was cool to the touch but came to life when I squeezed it to let him know I was there. He rubbed his thumb back and forth across my knuckles, his overgrown nail pressing lightly into my skin. I leaned forward and rubbed his shoulder with my other hand, hoping his pain would dissipate. He looked at me quietly with his swollen eyes. I knew he didn't want to be there, but he wasn't surprised he was. He continued making soft grooves with his thumbnail as his eyes closed. I let him.

"Dad, try to get some rest again, okay?" It was really his only option, but I coaxed him anyway as if he needed it, which he didn't. His eyes had closed with the heaviness of the unusual morning and accelerated narcotic. I closed mine and tried to join him for a while, hoping Katie would be stealthy when she returned to kill more pain.

HOUR 6: The RANCH

Still nestled in the warmth of my jacket and lacking the requisite caffeine to improve my sleepy mood, I again slipped back a few decades to our time on the farm, the ranch. It was a place of undeniable fun and endless activities, like the snow pile. And the horses. And the swimming pool. And the minibike. And the barns. It was where I learned to ice skate. And to first drive a car—a handsome, sporty gold Skylark—on my uncle's lap. It was where garter snakes were our friends, and apples and cherries were at our fingertips, assuming we didn't fall. It was where our imaginations ran wild, and every day was an opportunity to replace and forget the day before it.

But it was also a musty duffle bag of memories that Dad liked to unpack at random times over the years—preferring to pull out the clean, crisp, laundered ones to reminisce about while leaving the rumpled, smelly, and sometimes ugly episodes buried and untouched.

I never probed him on the negative or unresolved times on the ranch, even as I grew up and collected my own negative, unresolved moments in adulthood and middle age. I didn't bother to dig into or analyze his life, or our lives together, especially the times I didn't understand or was too young to fully comprehend.

Like him, I preferred the lively, sunny experiences from our time on the ranch and in Beaufort, a small village surrounded by other small villages like St. Clare, Reedston, and Delmont. The joyful memories were easy to recall and difficult to put away. There were plenty of them, and I, like him, was afraid to lose them completely or squander them by being too lazy to revive them. Or overshadow them by those that required a deeper inspection to unwrap, and the emotional balance to accept and discuss the not-so-sunny contents.

In his eyes, life on the ranch was happy. I knew better, but chose to let him have his way—his life, as he saw it. Then again, relatively speaking, he was right—our younger, carefree life on the ranch was happier than what came in the turbulent decade or so that followed.

As I sat dozing in the ICU, my time there metered by that goddamn stent, I began to shake the duffle bag and empty it in my head—dirty socks and all.

The ranch wasn't the first place where I could remember us living. The first place was the one-story house my dad and his father built themselves, about ten miles northwest of the ranch in another small town, at the entrance to a subdivision of similar houses, near the river. The same river that flowed calmly past his ICU suite. There wasn't much I remembered of our time in that first place, other than the four of us, the boxer, and a long, heavy, tail-finned turquoise Buick—and the honey-brown paneled basement where my dad had erected a miniature train set. A train set I never saw again after we left that house.

I remembered the time I ran and dove head-first into one of our twin beds, impersonating Superman but underestimating my pre-school superpowers. I was four or five when the rectangular headboard opened a large gash in my forehead after I caught air and flew, in *Man of Steel* fashion—past the pillow and into the dark birch veneer. A half-inch scar on my forehead, just beneath my grayed hairline, was a perpetual reminder of the blood, tears, and butterfly Band-Aids from that final flight.

But my primary recollection from that first place was the time when

I apparently tried to boil water on my own but instead, somehow, created a bonfire in the kitchen—one that required a visit from the local fire department to extinguish, and necessitated our evacuation for the day. I couldn't recall what I did to start the blaze or how extreme it was, or how long we were without a kitchen, but for some reason I knew the replacement stove was electric, not gas. It was a useless fact but one that followed me into adulthood, driving me to triple-check our knobs and burners with obsessive regularity.

And I remembered my dad and mom being calm and concerned, while I cried, and we all waited with the neighbor lady in the house behind us. Over the years, Dad would bring up my pyrotechnics from that day whenever he wanted to point out a flaw or error of mine around others. I could barely remember what happened or how it happened, but he felt compelled to ensure I wouldn't forget it—and that others were informed of my wayward actions at the ripe old age of maybe five, max.

But regardless of how irritated or bored I was by the repeated telling of the story, I was sincerely happy to have not been on the wrong end of his belt or backhand for doing it. His calm that day was appreciated, though unusual, given the temper we saw, and felt, later in life. And the fact that he'd constructed that kitchen with his own hands would have given him ample reason, even in my book, to exact some home-cooked discipline on my butt. I was glad he didn't.

I don't know what drove us from that first place and out to the sleepy, rural hamlet of Beaufort in the mid-1960s. My dad always said that it was Mom's love of horses that caused them—us—to leave the custom, brick, hand-built, self-built, big-lotted home—minus the torched, rebuilt kitchen—for the ranch. It always seemed odd to have exchanged that newer first house for an old, work-infested, asbestos farmhouse and six acres of land and worn structures, to restore and maintain with two kids under six, and fifteen minutes further away from work. But we did. And I never probed.

I never asked about what the conversations were like between Mom and Dad at that first place to make them, him, want to leave the home he had imagined, designed, plumbed, and nailed himself with his father, my grandfather, the one I never met. I assumed there were rational conversations about the move, but maybe not. Maybe there were furious arguments when my brother and I weren't around. Or maybe it was an easy, mutual decision they discussed and agreed upon in bed. My wife and I made many of our "big" decisions in bed at night, when heart rates had slowed, and the day had mellowed. I assumed my mom and dad, and every other couple, did the same. *Should we have a baby? Should we have another one? Do we move? What about college? Should I retire? Do you still love me?* Yes, those kinds of discussions and decisions.

The ranch was spectacular. From a kid's point of view. It was full of magical potential. The key word being "potential." And the inventory of that potential was long: a live orchard of apple and cherry trees; an in-ground swimming pool and barbeque pit; barns for horses and kids with playful imaginations; fields for riding and roaming; and nearly two acres of grassy space for mini-biking, baseball games, and under-aged Skylark practice. Did I say magical?

Oh, and it butted up on one side, fenced by where the orchard flowered, against a horseshoe-shaped subdivision of homes with small yards and plenty of kids to pass the hours with, sunup to sundown in the summers and until the cold or the twilight stopped us the rest of the year. Or until Dad called for us to come home for dinner, placing his fingers against his tongue and whistling with a sharpness and volume we could hear wherever we were on our property or others'. He never screamed or hollered. Just whistled. And we came. Quickly, obediently, regardless of which pickup game we were in the middle of, or which swing set we were hanging from. We learned early on

71

to not challenge Dad's authority or his command. That included his wordless calls to dinner.

On the north edge of our property grew a row of enormous trees with spring-green hedge apples the size of softballs and heavy as lead, whose welts and bruises lingered for days. Beyond those towering trees were more houses with deep yards and driveway access off a ribbon of Illinois Route 6 that snaked through town. Our only reason to venture that direction was to cross the busy highway to get to the truck stop on the other side.

The Beaufort Truck Stop was a small, dingy concrete block diner with a large unpaved parking lot for semi-trucks and a handful of counter seats and tables for their drivers. And besides selling greasy hash browns and parchment-like pancakes to its starving eighteen-wheeled clientele, the truck stop kept a small supply of goods on hand for retail purchase such as milk by the quart, eggs, and a small inventory of Hostess. You didn't shop there, you bought there. I remembered buying there. Maybe two or three times. It was not our restaurant or market of choice, but it never closed. Ever.

The main road directly to our east, Rural Route 2, was a narrow strip of partial pavement that separated our property from the public high school's football field and black-cinder track. Our "ranch" was more of a carve-out of confined land and fields on the edge of town than an expansive re-creation of *Bonanza* or *Gunsmoke*. In fact, the gravel access lane to and from our farmhouse T'd at the main road directly opposite the Beaufort Cardinal's west goal posts. We were literally close enough to watch a game from our roadside mailbox, and Dad would sometimes walk us down and take us into the stands to watch one on a Friday night or Saturday afternoon if he wasn't coaching his own games in Mennawa, which he often was. He loved football, and it seemed he couldn't get enough of it, to Mom's chagrin.

From the end zone, RR2 proceeded south to an abandoned quarry and equally desolate clay pits. The quarry, visible from the main road and fairly shallow, was where I learned to ice skate, and learned rule number one—*wear skates that fit.*

Dad's initial effort to teach me to skate required me lacing up my mom's bright-white figure skates once we got down to the quarry. As small as she was, and as oversized as I was for six or seven years old, I still wasn't able to fill out the ankles in her skates. I wobbled and fell continuously on our first outing, defining a hideously epic fail. My ego was bruised almost as much as my butt, not only by my total inability to stand and move on the chipped, lumpy ice, but by having to wear "girls' white" skates.

I loved my dad for not laughing or judging me during that short, horrible effort, but I loved him more for taking me later that day all the way to the sporting goods store in Mennawa for a brand-new pair of "boy black" skates that fit. Like a glove. And for my little brother, too.

Outing number two the following morning was truly like night and day. After inching ourselves down the rugged side of the quarry, Dad laced up my brother and me in our new skates. They hugged my thick socks and felt like they belonged this time, unlike the flimsy white ones the day before. Snuggly laced, we stood up and steadied each other, then launched ourselves across the cloudy, frozen pond of ice. Literally, night and day.

Both of us zoomed hesitantly around the quarry, accumulating confidence by the minute. My brother was a little slower, as expected, but had a knack for it right away. And even though it was miserably cold out, we didn't feel any of it. The adrenaline, the newness, the thrill warmed us that morning. It was a moment to remember. We laughed when we fell, and we helped each other up. We raced and fell some more. And Mom and Dad skated with us. Laughing, falling, freezing together. As a family.

"Gotta have the right tools to do the job right," Dad said to us when we finished our excursion, smiles on our faces, snot in our noses, and more bruises on our butts. That motto served him well.

"Can we get hockey sticks and a puck?" I asked Dad, ready to conquer the NHL.

"Yeah, can we?" my brother added.

Dad looked up as he unlaced us and smiled, happy with our success and his own.

"Sure, we'll go tomorrow."

And we did.

From then on, with skates and sticks as our tools of amusement, that iced quarry kept us busy each winter while living on the ranch.

South beyond the entry to the quarry, Rural Route 2 became an all-gravel, arrow-straight artery into the dusty horizon, where other tiny villages, genuine farms, and fertile fields of corn, beans, and potatoes hid. Our trips in that direction were few and forgettable. The "real" action was north of the quarry, on our ranch and in the tangent burg of a few hundred, mostly white, small-towners. That was our world.

#

"Stop fighting! Now! Get over here and help me if you want to swim in this thing!" Dad yelled.

I bucked my brother off my back and told him to stop. We were in the final stages of our typical brother-on-brother cageless cage match when Dad screamed at us. The main event that day was taking place in the grass between the sandbox and our concrete in-ground pool, the one Dad was working to make functional when he heard my brother crying and screeching. And me laughing.

That was our standard fight formula—my brother and I would argue over something meaningless, like who'd get the last can of pop, then I would smack him, kick him, or inflict some sort of physical pain on him until he cried and became uncontrollably enraged. Then I'd fall on my stomach and let him pound me on my back while I laughed and further fueled his fury, until I'd had enough and threw him off. Or until Dad came. And when Dad came, all hell broke loose.

"He started it," my brother bawled, lying face up in the grass and shrieking at the sky through his own pool of tears.

"No I didn't, he did," I obviously countered.

"Both of you, get over here now!" Dad demanded.

Fortunately, Dad's hands were gloved and occupied—and unable to pull out his belt. His belted responses to our undisciplined antics were the worst, normally telegraphed by him removing it and folding it in half, then with a hand holding each end, he'd push the folded belt together between his hands, causing it to separate into opposing bell-shaped straps. Then he'd pull his hands apart quickly until the belt tightened and SNAPPED loudly back into place. He'd repeat the snapping as he walked toward us—or came up the stairs, or chased us if we ran. It was the sound of a for-sure ass beating on its way. And not always butt-meets-belt.

Sometimes, the primary target was the back of the leg, beneath our butts, where it stung even more. Those lashes were usually reserved for the most violent or egregious fights we had, or whenever we ran. The belt also made its painful appearance on days when Mom tried but couldn't control us, usually when Dad got home from work, to remind us she was the boss as well. We understood, but somehow managed to frequently forget and fought like the brothers we were.

I got off the ground and walked quickly toward the pool, maybe twenty feet away. Seeing that, my brother—still red-faced and sobbing—jumped up and followed me. I could tell he still wanted a piece of me as we approached Dad, who, thankfully, was separated from us by the six-foot-tall wire mesh fencing that guarded the pool area. Dad was red, too, with fire in his eyes. He held a five-gallon bucket full of leaves, animal carcasses, and other gunk he'd pulled out of the algae-caked pool. His sleeveless, ribbed muscle-shirt was soaked with sweat as he stared at us through the fence.

"I'll stop working on this goddamn pool right now, if you can't behave yourselves! We'll never swim here! Do you want me to do that?!"

Dad was thoroughly perturbed with us. Thank God for that fence.

The pool was the first restoration project our team of four, almost four, tackled on the ranch. The built-in pool sat on the south edge of our big grassy lawn and east of the orchard, along with its adjacent barbeque area and the second renovation project, the large summer house. The pool was a quick walk from the farmhouse and sat almost midpoint between the house and orchard. It was the area of the ranch that accounted for most of Dad's memories of the happy times there, and the pool itself was a no-fight, DMZ for my brother and me. My memories of the pool, and of my brother in it, were always playful and peaceful. And full of bright sunshine, like those of the big snow.

"No," my brother and I responded in harmony.

"Then come around and help me clean this!"

Dad was still pissed, but focused on getting the pool in shape. And focus was definitely needed. Along with a lot of bleach. And cement patch. And paint. And chlorine. And wire brushes. And sweat. And beer. But over the course of just a few sunny days our first summer, from dawn to dusk, our team of four—*almost* four—transformed what initially was a squalid, cracked, concrete hole full of dead leaves, acorns, decaying birds, rotting squirrels, contented frogs, and putrid black-green water into a clean, clear playground of respite and wet fun!

As we heeded Dad's request and circled around to the ramshackle pool gate, both of us dreading the likely handling of slimy, smelly muck and decomposing varmints, we heard the voice of an angel come our way.

"Who wants watermelon?" Mom shouted as she walked toward us, unaware of the sibling terror we'd just executed or the command Dad gave us.

"I do!" we yelled, again in harmony, smiling and sprinting away from the toxic rectangular swamp and into the thick, chilled slices of pink watermelon Mom had plated for us.

We knew in that moment she wasn't just carrying our juicy summer favorite, she was carrying the reins of the family on that platter. And her calling us over to chew rind and spit seeds trumped Dad's demand for muck bucketing. So we were safe, for a few minutes. Mom to the rescue, all five-foot-two, 110 pounds of her.

#

And Dad deferred to her, too. For as long as I could remember, he always deferred to her and did whatever he could, within reason and at times beyond his means, to make her happy. He bought her the ranch, and her prized horses. He raised and tended goats for the milk that supposedly calmed her stomach. He put up with her unwieldy family and the drama they perpetuated, which was a huge give on his part considering his only real remaining family was his low-maintenance Polish mother and her distant siblings.

In my young eyes, it appeared to be a very one-way relationship, but when it worked, Mom and Dad also appeared to be a good team and happy with each other. She was a petite but rugged tomboy who preferred her wavy, red hair pulled back in a ponytail, unlike most of her girlfriends who adopted more contemporary, puffy, sprayed sixties-styled coifs. She didn't mind getting her hands dirty maintaining the ranch, and she enjoyed activities that most moms seemed to avoid: shooting guns, hunting rabbits and squirrels, catching and cleaning fish, breaking and grooming horses, and wrestling her sons in the grass.

My memories of those times were vivid, especially the time she took my brother and me squirrel hunting along Deer Creek, about thirty minutes southwest of our house.

#

Mom's brothers and cousins hunted there inconspicuously, gaining access to the creek and the woods that lined it via a long narrow dirt road off a stretch of gravel, barely-two-lane, county highway. We walked those thick woods for hours one summer afternoon, which seemed like days for our short legs and skinny arms hauling our .22 rifles in the hot sun and stagnant humidity without seeing a bird, let alone a squirrel we could shoot at.

As we neared the end of our wildlife-less journey, and the start of our long, hungry, sweaty walk back to the car, wherever the hell that was, we wandered into a clearing near the water. To our surprise, sitting in a shaded spot on a wide stump with his back to the creek, was a distant "uncle" of my mom's. He knew her and she knew him, and they greeted each other like family, minus any hugs.

We received a brief introduction. He was much older with a lean, tanned face full of stubble, his greasy hair tucked under a soiled farmer's cap. A toothpick wobbled out the side of his mouth. And though he was clad in loose jeans, work boots, and a grimy, long-sleeved flannel shirt, he wasn't sweating and didn't look nearly as worn by the day as we were. And to make matters worse, he had five or six dead squirrels piled up next to him near the stump.

"Wow, that's a lot. Been here long?" Mom asked, pointing to his furry bounty.

The hunter smiled at us and tongued the toothpick to the other side of his mouth. "Hour. Maybe less."

"Where did you find all those squirrels? We haven't seen anything today," I blurted out amazed, dejected, and feeling as lifeless as the squirrels in the pile.

The hunter's shiny rifle rested in the crook of his elbow and forearm as he took a sip from the can of Hamm's he held in his other hand.

"Right here," he replied. "I just sit here and wait for them to come to me."

Brilliant, fucking brilliant, I thought to my young self! I likely didn't actually use the f-word in that thought at that time, but I would have if I'd known to. Anyway, Mom's Uncle Einstein was *fucking brilliant,* I must have thought.

"Mom, can we do that?" I pleaded.

"Yeah, can we?" my brother piped in.

"Well, it's," she stammered, "it's getting late, I'm hot, and we need to eat supper."

"Please, Mom!" my brother and I asked heavily, like-minded in our desire to kill, or at least shoot at, something before we went home.

The hunter smiled as he watched us beg, then gulped down the last of his Hamm's, tossing the empty can into the brush next to a couple other dead soldiers that had kept him lubricated in the heat.

"Fifteen minutes. That's it. No more. We'll find a spot on the way to the car," she relented.

We smiled. The hunter smiled. Mom smiled.

"Good luck here. I guess we're gonna find us a spot," Mom waved to her uncle.

"Tell your mom and brothers I said hi," he replied and waved back.

Mom took the lead and walked briskly through the woods, following the creek bank, while we looked for an optimal squirrel-killing spot to park ourselves.

"Does the fifteen minutes start now or when we find a spot?" I asked, wanting to clarify her promise.

"Let's just get there," Mom chirped back, eyes forward.

It was clear she was mentally and physically done with hunting for the day, and was ready for a highball and something to eat. But she'd promised.

Shortly after, we found our own clearing, but no stumps. We stood facing the same direction to avoid shooting each other, looking up at the canopy of tree branches above us, waiting for our prey to arrive. And we waited. And waited. The rifles got heavier, and heavier. And we got thirstier, and thirstier. And nothing arrived.

"I'll look for some empty cans, and we can practice shooting them before we leave," Mom called out, signaling it was time to go.

Fifteen minutes easily had elapsed, but she wanted to give us an opportunity to bag our own game. It was probably closer to a half hour, just standing there, parched and hoping to see any movement at all in the trees, while also hearing intermittent pops, probably from her uncle taking down more squirrels as he sat on his ass. She kicked aside some tall grass and looked around the foot of the trees until she found two rusty beer cans to shoot at. She stuck them onto some low hanging branches or bushes, and my brother and I took turns aiming and firing our single shot rifles. I remembered finishing and being frustrated and upset about our day, but also how happy I was she cared enough to stay out with us and give us the chance to be hunters.

"Can we do that again?" I asked as we loaded the rifles and ammo belts into the trunk of the car.

"Sure. Next time we'll get us some squirrels. And maybe we'll bring our fishing poles, too." She sounded ready to come back.

But at that moment, it was time for a Seagram's and ginger ale. On ice.

#

Dad joined us to finish the watermelon. He could spit the seeds the farthest. Then the four of us—almost four, depending on how much help my brother actually provided—got to work as a team to follow Dad's instructions on fishing the crap out of the pool so he could pump out the filthy water and begin the process of bleaching, scraping, and repairing its concrete skin.

We worked especially well together after Mom's refreshments, including a beer she brought for Dad. When they clicked, Mom and Dad were a productive, fun-filled duo. They were bowling partners, and horseback riding partners, and spirited co-hosts of parlor games, pool parties, and horseshoe matches. It was fun to see them having fun together, a fulfilling reaction I'm sure most kids have when they see their parents in sync and firing on all cylinders.

It was even more satisfying in our case, it would seem, as their mutual interests and energy had to cross a generational gap of nearly twenty years between them. Dad was Mom's high school math teacher before they got married. She was seventeen years old when they wed, a month away from turning eighteen; he was thirty-four, his next birthday coming two days after hers.

As a kid, I never dwelled on that weird, awkward dynamic. Some might call it creepy. Or crazy. I just thought of Mom and Dad as being Mom and Dad. Age was irrelevant, unimportant. To me. And when I was old enough to better understand the significance of that dynamic, to unpack that corner of the duffle bag, there were more things to worry about and deal with than something I had no control over and couldn't change. I was developing my own judgments based on what was in front of me in the seventies and eighties, not on what was decided and done before I was born. Their differences in age, and values, and perspectives shaped what I'd become, but they were still just Mom and Dad to me. Not teacher-student, sailor-teenager, man-child.

On the ranch, I never saw their age difference manifest itself in a bad way, or in any way. I may have been too young to see it. Or Dad may have worked hard to mask it, to be the energetic, active guy for Mom, or at least the younger guy at heart. Their friends treated them as friends, not an anomaly or a sideshow. They bowled on the same team together. They drank at the bar together. He'd grill steaks; she'd grill chicken. I'd ask my dad to fix the minibike and my mom to wrap

Christmas presents. Mom taught me cursive; Dad taught me algebra. Dad supported Mom's decisions, and vice versa. Regardless of their vast difference of life experiences, their life, our life, together was normal to me.

Or was it?

How could it be?

#

Katie eased her way back into the ICU room, trying to not disturb my dad or me. She was half successful.

"I'm just going to give him another dose. Is there anything I can get you?" she asked quietly as she crept toward the bed and saw me stretch my eyes at her. The pain of seated slumber kept me from turning my head fully in her direction.

"No, thank you. I'm good," I lied to her about my actual state.

Coffee, Visine, and a king-sized bed would have definitely improved my response. And don't forget the sugar and hazelnut creamer. But none of that would come from Katie as she moved along silently and effortlessly to glove up, log in, scan, inject, log out. So I didn't ask.

In the corner of my eye, the blackness outside was submitting to sunrise. Likewise, I was submitting to the warm womb of my jacket and calmness of Dad's hand. I pulled out my phone to check the time before slouching back into place on the chair: 91 percent battery, 6:35 a.m.

I closed my eyes and headed back to the ranch, as Katie finished her pain assassination and slinked out of the room with ninja-like grace.

HOUR 7: The RIDE

I wanted it all to be *normal*. And to me, it was. Only if you know what is abnormal would it not be. And I didn't.

Normal was that renovated swimming pool, transformed from a 12,000-gallon cesspool to a crystal-clear hillbilly spa by the four—almost four—of us. My brother and I learned to swim there, and my mom, in her leopard-skin one-piece, washed down hot summer days with Old Styles and her friends there. My dad smiled non-stop in that pool, splashing and laughing like a kid. Like *us*. And like us, he sported a crew cut that sliced through the water and dried quickly in the sun. Only fun was allowed inside that fence.

Normal was the summer house. Once the pool was functional, we shifted our focus fifteen feet west and replaced all the loose and torn screens and rotted planking on the otherwise solid structure, and painted the inside and outside a sharp redwood hue. Rickety doors on each end were pulled shut by long springs to keep the flies and mosquitos hungry. Metal folding tables and chairs filled the airy space where we gobbled up the grilled steaks and chicken, hot dogs and burgers, and Mom's homemade potato salad. And plenty of watermelon. It was the hub for the summer yard parties, triangulating with the pool and charcoal barbeque pit to generate hours of beer-soaked fun for the adults and a base for us kids to cool off and replenish well-spent calories.

Normal was the minibike—that yellow, overweight, five-horse Montgomery Ward's XE525 special, with a cushy seat, fat waffled tires, front headlight, and annoyingly loose chain. It made its way home with us one Saturday—along with an ugly, bright-blue, glittery helmet—after a random, and expensive, trip to Mennawa. I couldn't recall what possessed him to buy it, but Dad swept up the last big box on the floor that day, along with that gauche fishbowl of a helmet.

#

"Do we really have to wear that helmet?"

I was beyond excited about the minibike and couldn't wait to get it home, but I also dreaded zipping around on it like a bobble head in front of my friends. The minibike was cool, very cool. The helmet? Not at all.

"Only if you want to ride the minibike," Dad confirmed.

I knew I couldn't change his mind, and I really wanted that minibike.

He continued, "The only time you don't have to wear it," my heart raced, "is when you're giving your brother a ride, then he has to wear it." Thud.

He traded me one uncool thing for another.

By a hair, my brother was too small to manipulate the minibike himself, evidenced by him jumping on the display model in the Wards' showroom and looking incredibly awkward and off-balance, stretching his arms and legs as far as he could to reach the handlebars and floor. So one of us would have to take him with us whenever it was his turn to ride. *Very uncool.*

"Okay, fine. Can we ride it tonight?" I pushed Dad for action as he and the guys from the store loaded the heavy box into the bed of the pickup truck.

"Let's get it home first and see what your mom thinks," Dad said, as the three of us climbed in the Ford's cab to go home.

I couldn't tell if he was curious what she would think about him buying the top-of-the-line model, or about buying one, period. In either case, he wasn't committing to anything. Yet.

My brother sat in the middle of the cab and held the sparkly helmet while we quietly poked each other's arms, hinting our excitement about the minibike but not getting too carried away. Yet.

"Guess what Dad bought us!" my brother yelled to Mom when we got back to the ranch and climbed out of the cab.

It was late in the afternoon, and she had already started making supper when she came outside to greet us.

"He got us a minibike! It's in the box!"

My mom looked at the box with a smile and walked toward my dad. He put his arm around her shoulder and smiled with her. Apparently, she approved. Everyone looked at the box sitting in the back of the pickup as Dad anticipated the conversation.

"Let's eat first, then we can put it together," he said.

That was Dad—never mañana, never wait till later, never procrastinate if it could be done now. He wasn't impulsive; he just liked to get stuff done.

We were all excited and ate in record time that evening, then raced outside to assemble the minibike before night fell. It was the dead of summer, so we had time. And Dad had a couple martinis at supper to celebrate the purchase. A cold can of Old Style followed him to the truck where the heavy box was too much for us to unload at once.

He peeled off the shirt he'd worn into town—getting down to his signature sleeveless undershirt—jumped onto the truck bed and ripped through the box, then handed us the smaller components, which we put on the ground, under Mom's supervision. The last to go was the frame and engine, which Dad eased to the ground himself off the back of the truck.

Mom rewarded him with another Old Style. Dad was happy. And getting juiced.

After about an hour and a half, and a few more cold ones, Dad put down his tools and the instruction manual.

"Go get the gas can," he puffed, not caring which of us got it.

I sprinted into the barn and retrieved the grimy red gas can. It was time to fill up the newly assembled minibike and give it a whirl. The sun was setting on us, but there was still plenty of daylight to check out our new toy. And Dad was merrily buzzed by the gin martinis and his six-pack dessert, to the point where it would have been impossible to stop him from taking it out on its maiden voyage before nightfall.

"Are you going to wear the helmet?" I asked as I handed him the can.

"No, I'm just gonna take it for a little spin to make sure it runs okay," Dad slurred back excitedly as he filled up the small tank.

We all hovered around him with big grins, Mom and her Old Style included.

"That's a good-looking minibike. You guys better take care of it," she told my brother and me as we listened to the tank fill with gas and enjoyed that pungent petrol aroma, like we did when filling up the riding mower.

"You better say thanks to your dad."

"Thanks, Dad!" we screamed together.

Dad pulled the rubber nozzle out of the tank and smiled at us as he sat the can on the grass. His smile was warm. So was Mom's. We were all happy to have a new plaything on the ranch. My brother and I were the happiest, of course, but Mom and Dad were happy to see us so thrilled—and that they'd provided it.

Dad slung his leg over the thick, Naugahyde seat and sat back to get a view of the minibike from a new perspective. The chrome handlebars were shiny, the yellow frame was un-nicked, and everything that was black gleamed. He took it all in, then reached down to prime the 5-hp Tecumseh engine, before pulling its cord to start it. After two or three hard tugs, the engine roared to life! As did we!

Dad listened to the sound of the engine as it idled, like he'd done hundreds of times before with cars, mowers, and Navy cargo ships. He knew the hum of a properly tuned engine, and how to tune it if it wasn't. New plugs, gap the plugs, adjust the governor, clean the carburetor, treat the carburetor. Some of the above. All of the above. He was a wizard with an engine.

"Good luck, honey!" Mom yelled to him as the engine rumbled in a thick purr.

Dad looked over at the three of us and smiled widely, then twisted the throttle to let the Tecumseh know he was ready to go. Fueled by martinis and Old Styles, Dad really thought he was ready to go.

In a flash, the minibike tore away from us as Dad tried to control its speed and direction. Mostly its direction. We were no more than thirty to forty feet from the barn when we had assembled the minibike with Dad, and he covered that distance in an instant as he revved the throttle and steered wildly. The energy and spunk of the brand-new, well-tuned Tecumseh had taken Dad completely by surprise. And his reaction time, and balance, was definitely blunted by the celebratory cocktails he'd imbibed prior to the initial ride.

That was obvious as he barreled toward the side of the barn, unable to stop. The barn helped him with that. But fortunately, or not, a combination of speed, braking, swerving, and uneven dirt lifted the front tire of the minibike as it hit the barn, and he rode it vertical up the asbestos siding until it tipped to the ground on its side. Dad dismounted the minibike by sliding off the back of the seat with his arms extended, still trying to control its speed and direction.

Our anxious pre-ride excitement quickly changed to terror as we watched Dad thoroughly out of control and completely out of character, the minibike taking him for a ride instead of vice versa.

"Martin, are you okay?" Mom yelled half-frantic as she raced to him, only a step ahead of us.

The engine continued to run as the minibike laid on its side.

"Son of a bitch got away from me. Faster than I thought," he declared sheepishly as he wobbled over and pressed the kill switch to stop it.

I wasn't going to mention the helmet to him.

"I'm sure it's fine, but I'll look at it tomorrow before we take it out," Dad said, implying the good news that we'd be riding it soon.

"Let's put it in the garage for the night. Boys, grab my toolbox and clean up the yard."

The good news continued, as he smiled while commanding us and laughed with Mom as they walked the minibike toward the house. He was shaken and embarrassed by his two-wheeled escapade, but it was nothing a martini and plump olive couldn't solve.

#

That minibike was normal. Racing it around the high school track was normal. So was sliding it into a tree in the wet grass and tearing up my wrist. And like the Superman scar on my forehead, the lifetime scar of exhaust-pipe-burnt flesh on the back of my hand from constantly re-sprocketing the chain was normal. That stupid disco helmet was normal. It was all normal to me, regardless of how *not normal* my parents' relationship was to everyone else.

My mom's hypochondriac mother was the first to tell me about the age difference between Dad and Mom, and some generalities of their high school engagement. I was sitting in my grandma's tiny kitchen at her green Formica table as she fed me hand-picked details of their meeting. Even at my young age, I quickly figured out the difference between seventeen and thirty-four. Yeah, that and the teacher-student stuff seemed weird, but they were Mom and Dad to me. And my grandma wasn't overtly agitated by their odd dynamic, like you'd expect most mothers to act under the circumstances.

In fact, it was probable that in my grandma's world of divorce, health anxieties, and deeply dramatic relatives, she was truly delighted to have an employed, athletic, college-educated, war veteran as a son-in-law, regardless of him being only a few years her junior and old enough to be her daughter's father. And as I learned later in life, there was plenty of strangeness on her side of the family already, so a little or a lot more wasn't such a big deal. My grandma's accepting behavior, if not downright pride to have Dad in her family, was likely another reason I considered the pairing of Mom and Dad to be normal.

My mom was a spitting image of her mom. They shared the same flowing red hair and penciled eyebrows, and both carried themselves with a don't-mess-with-me attitude. When pressed, they'd say their ethnicity was more "Heinz 57" than anything else—basically a mix of everything, including a splash of Pequot Indian. Their family hailed from Vienna, near the southern tip of Illinois, a rural speck of Mom's heritage I'd heard described occasionally at grandma's table. And their interest in hunting and guns, and ability to laugh raucously at dirty or off-color jokes, was common between them as well. At one point, they even worked together in the same rat lab at the nearby Werner pharmaceutical factory. There was no denying they were cut from the same cloth.

What I didn't see early on was any sharing of my grandma's severe hypochondria. Her affliction was so intense, so melodramatic, so ingrained in her persona, that many—including my mom, my dad, my uncles, her ex, everyone—not only made harsh comedy of it, but made decisions to engage, or usually not engage, her because of it. Every group event, birthday party, Thanksgiving, Easter, you name it, with my grandma seemed to revolve around her ailments of the day. Her feet. Her breathing. Her knees. Her migraines. Her sinuses. They were all-consuming, as was the attention she demanded from everyone to support her and her symptoms. So much so that joking, teasing, and spot-on impersonations, mostly from Mom's witty and merciless brothers, became the main theater at family gatherings.

And during a normal day or evening, you were taking a huge risk when answering an unexpected phone call for fear it was her. If she was on the other end of the line, you would subsequently be locked in for what seemed a lifetime to hear her graphically lament her swollen limbs, shaky bowels, or allergic reactions. At times, we literally set the phone on the counter and played with its long curly cord while she talked incessantly about herself, picking it up minutes later and inserting a "Hmmm" or a "Really?" into the one-way conversation before putting it back down. She was none the wiser of our shenanigans and rambled nonstop to whomever dared answer the phone. Caller ID would have been a blessing back then.

Alternatively, my dad's widowed Polish mother was an entirely different story. I suspect she realized how atypical my dad's and mom's marriage was but preferred to look the other way rather than risk her relationship with her only child. *Living* child. My dad's older brother had died in his twenties from a long-term muscular disease. And my grandfather died a couple years after I was born. So besides her many sisters, most of whom were first-generation immigrants like herself, my dad was her lifeline.

My grandmother lived by herself in a small apartment, above the tavern she had run then rented out, in the brick building she owned where my dad grew up. He cleaned spittoons and poured drafts in the family's bar as a kid, and taught us to play shuffleboard and pool there once we were old enough to see over the tables. An Old Style sign hung out front. The building was a ten-minute walk from the house my mom was raised in. My grandmothers practically lived next to each other but rarely talked. They came from different worlds.

My dad's mother had a classic European immigrant story—crossed the Atlantic by ship, landed at Ellis Island, learned French and English in addition to her native Polish, started a small business with her immigrant husband, raised their sons with her extended family, and survived the Depression, multiple wars, and the cultural prejudices that came her way. She was a strong, quiet woman who accepted my mom and the decisions my dad had made, but likely not without reservation, evident by how she despised the Polish jokes my un-PC uncles would test on her.

My dad was a good son to his mother, bringing her groceries and repairing the building and tavern when things broke. In return, she watched after my brother and me whenever Dad needed help, and entertained us with her accordion playing and a decent set of Hot Wheels. Her homemade chicken-and-rice soup and fluffy cheesecake were to die for.

I never asked her what she thought about her son marrying one of his students. Or what her family thought. I never asked, and she was probably happy I didn't. I never saw my grandmother overjoyed or excited in Mom's presence, and vice versa, which perhaps said it all. But unlike my mom's family—whose acceptance of my dad and the abyss of age was likely the tradeoff for a model mate—my grandmother's and grandfather's approval of the otherwise scandalous scenario was one of familial love and hope for their by-then only child.

Then again, it was a different time.

So different, almost nothing was normal. Or everything was. My parents—what they did, how they acted, what they valued—were part of that very different time of the sixties and seventies. So was I.

But it wasn't always so obvious to us on the ranch how different things were around us. At least not to me. And Mom and Dad kept our small-town life small. Very small. We spent hours as a family at the bowling alley on the north edge of town, digging cheddar cheese out of a crock, playing pinball between frames, and eating plastic-wrapped, oven-toasted ham and cheese sandwiches. Dad let us roll dice at the bar and open "tickets" to unlock free beers for him and Mom. She liked a shake of salt in her drafts.

We learned to bowl without gutter guards and keep score by hand at Daisy Lanes. And if the Cubs were playing, we'd park ourselves at the bar and watch. Usually the entire game. Sometimes we'd bowl when the other team batted. Double headers were marathons of Slim Jims, 7-Ups, Old Styles, and a John's pizza. Channel 9, Home of the Cubs, seemed to play continuously on the one fuzzy TV behind the bar.

It's that TV, and dozens of Jack Brickhouse "Hey Heys," that introduced and sucked me into the team during their fateful 1969 campaign. I spent a huge slice of my summer, when not in the bowling alley, collecting and trading the Topps cards of Ernie Banks, Ron Santo, Fergie Jenkins, Don Kessinger, their Cubby teammates, and any other major leaguer attached to the rigid pink sticks of chewing gum they came wrapped with. And had the Cubs fulfilled our heated dreams that season, rather than melting away to the Mets after Labor Day, those cards would have been golden, though maybe still boxed and rubber-banded for posterity. But we survived that tragic season, and a few more like it, thanks to our family time at the bowling alley. Which was normal. To us.

\#

"I'm going to put Nick in the barn," Dad hollered to me, "Open the gate."

"Can I ride him in? Please Dad?" I offered. Begged.

Mom and Dad had just finished riding their horses in the north field, giving turns to their intoxicated friends on a warm, clear summer evening as the sun set. It was the culmination of a day-long pool party for my parents and five or six other couples who were their friends. Some were from the subdivision and around town, while others were from Mennawa like Jim and Nancy, one of Mom's friends from high school. Jim drove a bread truck, and Nancy was a stay-at-home mom like mine and the rest of the women at the party. They were a nice couple who lived in a pink house with two kids around my age, and they were fun people but never too rowdy.

And there was Don and Linda from the subdivision next to us. Definitely the most boisterous couple, they always had something to say, and both had energetic laughs. Their bi-level house had grass-green shag carpeting throughout, and they had three boys; the middle one, the loudest, was my age.

And Brenda and Larry were there, too. They lived a few blocks from us in Beaufort, and Larry worked in a factory. Brenda was nice enough, but her husband always seemed to be a know-it-all pain in the ass—like their young daughter. But at the party that day, there were no kids around besides my brother and me. It was parents only. And our job was to keep the metal wash tubs stocked full of beer and ice for them.

The sunny day made use of all the amenities the ranch had to offer. Swimming and floating in the pool. Grilling in the late afternoon. A competitive and unruly Jarts tournament that eventually calmed into a series of mixed couples horseshoe games. Mini-biking through the orchard and around the iron horseshoe stakes. Horseback riding for those who wanted to show off their skills, or preferred pairing up to ride with a partner, capped off the day. Many of the guys tried their hands solo, while a few of the women rode double, usually with Mom or Dad. The Hamm's, Old Style, and Miller made everyone a rodeo star. My brother and I did our job well that day.

When we moved to the ranch, Mom seemed to already have some experience handling horses, but she also took some riding lessons after we got our first horse—her horse, Apache. Apache was a glistening, chestnut brown quarter horse with a black mane and a need for speed. He was a medium height gelding, just the right size for my mom. A white streak separated his dark eyes, which always seemed to be looking for mischief or a place to run. Mom adored Apache. She always felt confident and in control when riding him. The lessons helped, too. And she and my dad went to great pains to make sure she looked the part, with cowboy boots and hat, a hand-crafted leather saddle and wool Navajo blanket, and form-fitting riding apparel. And a red bandana. She loved clenching the riding whip between her teeth as she leaned into the wind.

My dad, on the other hand, was all thumbs initially when it came to horses. He listened to my mom and asked a lot of questions. He loved to learn, and riding and caring for horses was an education for him. Dad wasn't into speed as much as Mom was, but they would canter together in the north field, or in our big corral which was south of the orchard and gated between the two barns.

Dad's horse was Nick, a huge, muscular palomino stallion that lumbered along when Dad rode him. Nick was a mature, intimidating beast, with a powerful stature, but he was easy to ride and care for. He was a gentle giant in every sense, and he was kind to me when I rode him.

But most of Dad's horse-related time was spent finding and hauling hay, alfalfa, and oats back to the ranch, shoeing the horses, and keeping the tack room organized. He delegated the manure shoveling, watering, and feeding to me when he was busy elsewhere. I scooped gallons of oats from the oat bin Dad built, which was also a paradise for mice, and loaded and emptied tons of manure with our coal shovel and wheelbarrow. The horses were fun, but I learned the work to maintain them and keep them healthy was filthy and mountainous. Dad taught me that. Or we learned it together.

Dad looked down at me from his mount, his answer delayed. That was a good sign. Or maybe it was the Old Style. "Okay. Come around, and I'll help you up," Dad said. I could sense exhaustion in his voice. The sun and events of the day weighed on him, along with the beer. He was tired, but this was an easy reward for me helping to keep the party fueled. He wasn't much of a rider, so he may have had enough of Nick for the day, too. In any case, I was ecstatic.

Besides a smattering of small trees near the main road, the north field was mostly flat and clear, and was out of range of the equine magnetism of the barn, making it ideal for riding. It was fenced entirely with barbed wire, some of which I helped Dad repair, with the exception of the long, wooden southwest gate near the house and parallel with the lane. Most of the adults rested on the gate that day, beers in hand, and watched and giggled as riders crossed back and forth across the field.

They had already opened the gate to let Mom and Apache head back to the barn, so I squirted through and headed toward Nick. His dusty gold coat was wet with perspiration. I circled in front to his left side while my dad kept him still. As Dad dismounted, I hustled over so he could boost me up onto the massive steed. I was only eight or nine years old at the time. Nick was wide, and my feet struggled to reach the stirrups, but I grabbed the reins tightly and gripped the saddle horn with all of my might. I was ready for an easy walk to the barn, and so was Nick.

"Do you want to take him for a short ride around the field?" Dad asked me out of the blue. He must have been having a good day.

"Yeah, sure! We'll go slow. I'll be careful," I replied.

Oh man, I thought to myself, *this is going to be great!* Riding Nick was like riding on a huge float in a parade. Even if we just went in a couple of big circles, I'd be happy. I already was.

Dad shut the gate behind him as I sat high up on Nick. As always, I was a little nervous atop the big animal but knew how to balance and maneuver him around. And Nick always complied.

"Take your time out there. I'm going to help your mom at the barn, and I'll be back," he called out confidently.

My brother stood by the gate and watched us between the horizontal planks, reaching out to try and touch Nick. He was majestic to my brother. Attainable only with Dad riding in the saddle behind him.

95

But before we could get moving on our walk, I heard two loud noises, both at the same time. And then we really got moving.

"YEE HAA!" was accompanied by a thunderous slap to Nick's backside, both coming from that drunken asshole, Larry. I couldn't see him, but I could hear him laugh as Nick bolted in a full-speed gallop straight across the field toward its north edge.

My chest swelled with shock and fright. My knees squeezed Nick as hard as I could, and my eyes opened wide as my back straightened in surprise. My hands clutched the reins and the horn without mercy as I teetered about in the saddle. I quickly realized what people meant by "holding on for dear life," as Nick picked up speed.

But as quickly as my day turned to horror and my stomach displaced my lungs, I caught my breath and my balance, and I leaned forward with Nick as he gained speed and charged toward the fence line. I had yet to take control of the big guy as he barreled ahead, his coarse white mane entangled in the reins, but my momentum was in sync with his, and I felt his power and velocity in tandem with the saddle.

And it felt great! Dangerous and exhilarating, daring yet familiar. So I let go of the horn and grabbed the reins with both hands, while loosening the vice grip my knees had on his ribs. I wanted to go faster. I leaned closer to Nick, inhaling his musty scent, and lunged into the gallop as he flew across the field. I felt the rush of warm air in my face and the strength of the horse in my thighs, and I wanted more. Nick was ready to release some stress that day and, I guess, so was I.

For a few incredible seconds, in a manic run that could have ended in disaster, I was, mostly, fearless. And numb with excitement. As if I was riding a four-legged roller coaster. It was way more thrilling than the inanimate minibike, that's for sure.

As we neared the barbed wire fence, I slowly pulled back on the reins and felt Nick respond to my tug. He was still traveling faster than I'd ever been on a horse, but I could tell he was ready to ease up with me. I pulled back harder and leaned left as we decelerated, both eyeballing the fence post in front of us, and abruptly finished our sprint. My heart was still pounding from the assault of adrenaline as we turned and started to walk back toward the gate. I reached down and patted Nick's thick neck, and repeatedly told him he was a "good boy!" He truly was.

Holding the reins tightly, I pulled back on them frequently to keep him from accelerating again, though I could tell he was gassed and uninterested in another run. Across the field, I heard the adults all hollering and whistling at me, not sure if they were congratulating me for staying off the ground or hooting about the impromptu performance, or both. Either way, I wasn't looking forward to getting back to the gate, even though I was pretty proud of the "off the ground" accomplishment and was chock full of head-to-toe glee from the ride itself. I didn't know what to expect from them. And I sure as hell didn't need any more of that drunken asshole, Larry.

But as I got closer, my anxieties dwindled as I heard their shouts.

"Great job!"

"Well done, Lone Ranger!"

"That was great!"

I exhaled. And smiled wide. Dad smiled, too, at the gate. He must have doubled back after hearing me take off, instead of going to the barn with Mom. But he wasn't hollering or whistling. Just staring at me and smiling, as he clapped in approval. He looked proud.

I'd seen that look before when he coached, when his team executed in the game what they'd rehearsed dozens of times in practice. That quiet, positive pride. He opened the gate and came to greet us as Nick pulled up to the crowd.

"Are you okay?" Dad asked, looking up at me, though he could tell I was fine as we smiled at each other.

"That was so fast! Did you see me?" I was looking for verbal confirmation of his clapping.

"I did," Dad continued to smile as he helped me down. "I'll walk him to the barn. Why don't you get a Pepsi for you and your brother?"

As we escorted Nick through the gate, the adults continued to praise our dash across the field, including that drunken asshole, Larry.

"Nice job, young guy. You looked like a real jockey up there. Kentucky Derby!" Larry complimented, trying to make nice.

But it didn't work. I looked up at his sweaty face and bloodshot eyes and said nothing. I was pissed. And Dad stared him down with a look I hadn't seen before. He didn't say anything to Larry, at least not in front of me, but his look said it all. It said he'd be happy if Larry *took his scraggly mustache and crooked tooth, and his hair-sprayed wife, and got the hell off the ranch.*

And by the time Dad got back from taking Nick to the barn, they were gone. And we got our Pepsi.

Just another normal day for us.

#

Dad rustled in the bed and woke up, and woke me, with a scratchy yelp, "Can I get some water?"

"Sure thing, here ya go, Dad. Did you sleep okay? How's the pain?"

I wiped the semi-crust from my eyes, grabbed the cup of water, and held the straw to his lips as he sucked gently for some comfort. He seemed alert and his eyes darted around the room as it filled with natural light. The sun was rising, and in the corner of my eye I caught it splashing delicately on the river outside his window.

It was 7:29 a.m.

HOUR 8: The DECISION

D ad's need for refreshment, and the onset of a sunlit morning, were my cues to exit the uncomfortable hibernation into which I'd twisted myself. And to evaluate the moment. And to find a bathroom. For the past few hours, I had confined myself to roughly six square feet of space next to my dad's bed, holding his hand as we both went into a sleepy low-maintenance mode, his more painful than mine. I had rested, but not really rested. Same for him.

But as the day began to break, and my hips and joints settled and ached in the armchair, it became obvious a change of pace and stretch of my still-tired limbs was needed. Along with a bathroom.

I carefully turned my head and looked east out the big windows, avoiding any quick movements that would strain my stiffened neck and any brightness or glare that would trigger a migraine. I was prone to those sickly headaches, which were usually brought on by sudden flashes or changes in light, and I'd learned over the decades to guard myself from them by being intentional in my glances and focus. And by the liberal use of sunglasses. I was surely cursed by the same genetics that saddled my dad with macular degeneration and his mother with glaucoma. It was just a matter of time for me. My hope, or foolish plan, was to pin my optical salvation on some new technology that would come along by the time my vision truly needed it. Before the Titleists disappeared.

It looked as if it was going to be a clear, sun-filled day as I cautiously squinted outside from my place in the chair. Across the river and alongside it, traffic had come to life, as I could see a few cars moving north and south on Roosevelt Drive. I shifted my gaze slowly back to the bed, as I wasn't yet ready to take in the full muddy majesty of what was flowing freely and unfrozen next to us. I had seen the river up close and personal many times before. So many times before. I just wanted to get a gauge on what January had brought us and what I, and maybe my wife, would have to deal with without having to open my phone and consult the weather app. My take was positive. The lack of anything remotely arctic in January was very positive. Knock on wood.

My desire to find a bathroom drove me to sit up and get my feet under me. I was still cozy inside my jacket, and I could feel the warm perspiration under my arms as I started to move about. I took a quick pull of water on the straw my dad had sipped from, before putting the cup back on the table.

"The pain's really bad," Dad moaned quietly as he scrunched his shoulders and tried to reposition himself for some relief.

He wasn't making much progress. The tubes around his head, up his nose, and in his arm didn't help.

"Oh, my back. It really hurts. And my lips hurt. They're so dry."

"Dad, I'll go get the nurse. I've got to find a bathroom, too. I'll be right back," I told him.

I was getting frustrated with the continual reappearance of his back pain, and equally as antsy with my need to pee. It was time to leave and resolve both.

I let go of Dad's hand and pushed the chair away from the bed with a weird, cockeyed shove. The chair was heavy, but my arms and legs were still just coming to life and not yet at 100 percent strength. And, like my migraine defense, I had become, over the years, very intentional to avoid any sudden or awkward twisting that could tweak my back or knees and temporarily linger as an annoyance to daily life. It was definitely a middle-age thing, and I could remember when I first thought to myself, "Hey, you're not twenty-five anymore." Of course, I was way past twenty-five when that thought first came to me.

And it didn't come to me when we tore apart and rebuilt the deck on our house in my late forties. I expected those days and nights of pain that came from hauling lumber, auguring post holes, kneeling and nailing, and making the angled and herringbone cuts by hand with a circular saw. I didn't have the power tools my dad had, so a certain amount of physical grief would accompany my less-than-professional execution—a fact I accepted.

And it didn't come to me as my brother and I, also in our forties, built a jungle gym for my kids in the backyard of my house. He was a carpenter and liked working with his hands, and his body was used to the physical distress that came with the day-to-day tasks of roofing, framing, and finishing. I wasn't, and like the deck work but on a smaller scale, I felt it. But I knew what I was getting into and expected the soreness and strains.

And it didn't come to me as I hung over the edge of our eight-foot-deep exterior sump well one early February day to replace three dead pumps that failed to control a rising river—the same one outside the ICU windows—near our summer house not long after 9/11. The repeated lifting, lowering, adjusting, adapting, and testing the pumps and hoses—ungloved and laying in the snow—would have made it a good time for my body and mind to tell me I was getting too old for that kind of exertion. My dad certainly told me, as he stood out in the cold and handed me tools while his nose weeped nonstop in the numbing chill. I knew it would be a dirty job, which I'd pay for with some physical misery. And I did.

No, it didn't come to me on any of those occasions that I wasn't twenty-five anymore. It definitely should have, but it didn't. It came to me one morning at 6:40-ish a.m.—waiting for an elevator in the lobby of my office building, four or five years back—in a very un-heroic, unproductive, weak-sauce way.

It came at the end of my normal morning commute, having left the house precisely at 6:00 a.m., then walking to the Metra station and catching the 6:12 train into the city, which delivered me a few blocks from my office and the Dunkin Donuts next door to it. For many years, the DD's "extra-large, cream and sugar," and the perky, pre-dawn ladies behind the counter, Deepa and Judy, started my day with a healthy amount of caffeinated cheer, regardless of the weather I'd endured the previous half hour or the corporate storms I'd endure the next eleven. I had become so routine I didn't even need to place my order anymore, as my arrival through the door or presence in line put the coffee in motion without a word and with just a glance. And when I became a user of their pre-order-and-pickup app, my mornings became even more efficient, though I missed the pleasant "Have a nice day!" after paying then rejecting my receipt.

I really didn't have to get there while the donuts were still warm, but the early-bird routine suited me. It allowed me a peaceful mile-and-a-half of exercise and pre-Microsoft Office meditation each morning, though heavy snow or rain could put a major crimp in the peaceful part. It also allowed me to grab a decent seat on the inbound bi-level train without too much jockeying; however in later years, the reduction of cars and our close proximity to the city usually had me squeezing into a seat next to a sleeping construction worker in their safety-sorbeted T-shirt of lime green or mandarin orange, or a less lucky commuter who'd been riding east the past hour. I'd try not to jostle or wake them, so they could enjoy their last eighteen minutes of bumpy calm.

And the early arrival also allowed me a head start to the day in the office, before most others arrived or came online, to catch up on the West Coast emails from the night before or the UK messages from that day. And it let me scarf down a warm cup of microwaved instant oatmeal, which paired perfectly with the coffee. Minus the 7:00 a.m. conference calls to deal with a train-wrecked project or to accommodate an Atlanta or New Jersey calendar, I could usually get myself sufficiently amped up and prepped to face the day in that precious time between 6:45 and 8:00 a.m.

But the real benefit of commuting early, and the key alignment with my personality, was that I didn't have to deal with the general population of humans that I did in the evening on my reverse trip home. The end-of-day all-about-me'ers were the antithesis of the diligent, harmonious morning crowd: think indignant, obnoxious, tunnel-visioned, and righteous. Think obtuse and clueless. That was the evening posse. And my assessment never failed to be confirmed regularly by someone balking on a busy Metra stairway, full of hungry homebound bodies, to update their playlist or thumb through their latest novel. Or who inserted their lazy ass in the line exiting the train after sitting on it while everyone else waiting to leave had to stand. One could easily tell which way my allegiance fell. Morning crew ruled.

I was carrying my twenty-four ounces of Dunkin dynamite when it came to me. Balanced by my pleather briefcase, circa 2001 and showing its age, I passed the two likeable but vigilant security guards, flashed my company ID, and headed to the elevator bank serving the lower altitude floors. I used to have the northeast corner office on thirty, the top floor, after being abruptly displaced years earlier due to another department's urgent relocation in the building. The penthouse floor was our consolation.

It was a grand space with nice furniture and an impeccable view of Lake Michigan, especially at sunrise and when the Blue Angels practiced for the Air and Water Show each August. It was once the office of a senior executive before they eliminated all the local senior execs in favor of Texas-based royalty. Which was fine with me given the comfy, high-backed swivel chair and walnut desk I inherited for ten-plus years.

But after another "restacking" of the building, I found myself in a more typical office on the ninth floor, with ergonomic poly-plastic furniture and a less prestigious view facing west toward Wacker Drive and the Chicago River. It was fine. It was good "working" space. And I had brought the comfy chair down from thirty to give it some pizzazz. So I pressed the button to head to my corporate cockpit and buckle in for the day's ride.

As I stood there transfixed on the lighted up-arrow, waiting for one of the eight potential elevators to arrive and whisk me vertical, my mind drifted to my agenda for the day. With little variation, it was normally a parade of continuous and contentious back-to-back conference calls, one-on-one phone meetings with direct reports, lunch at my desk à la homemade nut mix washed down with a sweetened flaxseed potion, and various offline acts of Wording, Exceling, and PowerPointing related to said conference calls. Mix in some virtual training sessions and mindless web surfing to chill out between calls, and that's what kept my family fed. I was an experienced cog in a big wheel and worked hard to be proficient and professional. We enjoyed eating.

It didn't take long for the elevator to chime and signal it was ready to take me to my destination, politely interrupting my lobby trance with its familiar ping as the doors opened to an elevator car directly behind me. I stood with my feet planted and jerked my head around to see which car arrived.

That's when it came to me.

My thoughtless and casual twist, done hundreds of times as a kid playing sports, and as a young adult goofing off, generated a tingle in my neck and a sharp twinge in my back, enough to paralyze me for an instant, just long enough to really wake me up for the day. A flash of pain darted up my spine and poked my shoulders ruthlessly. As I hobbled into the elevator, my back cramped in agony; careful not to spill my coffee, that's when the epiphany arrived. *I was not twenty-five anymore.* If I couldn't twist my head without incurring three weeks of daily hell, shampooing with my neck on fire and sleeping stiff like a corpse, I definitely wasn't twenty-five anymore. Nope. It was time to act, and move, like the fifty-plus, gray-haired middle manager I'd become. Or at least it was time to recognize that I couldn't act, and move, like I was twenty-five. There's a difference.

I stood up slowly and maneuvered between Dad's bed and the armchair, easing out of my heavy jacket to feel some relief. I caught the table with my forearm as I removed the sleeve and it bounced loudly, nearly spilling the cups of melted ice and lukewarm water. They wobbled and settled, but the racket startled Dad.

"What's that?" he asked, opening his eyes in my direction.

"Nothing. I just hit the table. It's good," I told him.

"If you're hurt, they have doctors here," he quipped. Even in pain he was a smart ass.

"Thanks, Dad. I'll be right back. Don't go anywhere," I countered with a smirk.

I walked toward the sliding glass doors and pulled the curtains back. As I slipped out the doors and squinted into the bright lights of the ICU floor, I noticed Dr. Bhatta heading my way. He hurried a little when he saw me.

"Hello. I'm doing my rounds now. Would you like to listen to your father's case?"

He was polite and direct, and caught me by surprise.

"Uh, sure. Thanks," I said somewhat hesitantly, half not sure what he really meant, and half focused on finding a bathroom ASAP.

"It will be a few minutes while I get the team together. We'll be right there," he said as he turned to leave.

Oh yeah, the painkiller. I almost forgot.

"Doctor, my dad is still having a lot of pain, even with the half-hour doses. Can you increase them for him or give him something else?"

"Um, uh, yes. I'll check him now before we meet," he concurred, a little taken aback by my ask, and made a quick left into my dad's room.

"Thank you."

I appreciated him making the immediate effort, as he disappeared behind the curtain.

On to objective number two.

I spotted Katie a few feet away, standing hunched over her workstation, and called to her.

"Hi. Hello, where can I find a bathroom?"

She tilted her head at me and smiled, staying hunched over and leaning on the desk with both hands.

"Hi. Yeah, there's, uh, there's one in the visitors' lounge down the hall. I'll show you."

She moved with ICU-like urgency and way more energy than I had, and swung her hips around the desk as she turned and sling-shotted herself ahead of me.

"It's just down the hall and to the right, through the big double doors." She talked into the air directly in front of her as I tried to catch up.

"Oh, okay, I think I can find it. Thank you," I said, wanting to let her get back to her duties. And to my dad.

"Okay, let me know if there's anything you need," she replied with a smile, slowing quickly to a stop as I passed her and headed to where I'd initially entered the ICU.

Oh yeah, the dry lips. I almost forgot.

I spun around—well, not really spun, I wasn't twenty-five anymore—I, more like, stopped fully and turned my entire body to face her. She, however, had definitely spun around and was already heading back to where I'd found her.

"Katie?" I called out.

She stopped and spun again, looking at me with eyes wide open and forehead raised while waiting for my reason to stop her.

"My dad said his lips are dry. Do you have anything he could put on them?"

"Sure. I'll find something and bring it to him," she said as she smiled, spun again, and got on her way.

Katie was making the day's burden manageable for me, and it came without attitude or delay. I was truly appreciative and tried to let her know it.

"Thank you, again," I said, really meaning it.

I wondered if the nursing schools had added formal "customer service" training to their technical curriculum. If so, Katie must have passed with flying colors. She was well on her way to getting my contribution towards improving the hospital's Yelp rating or Net Promoter Score.

Or was it just her personality, her desire to turn a typically tense, life-altering ICU experience into something less clinical or dire for the patient and the family? Something they couldn't teach you in school? I didn't know, and I couldn't recall my mom studying anything other than anatomy and CPR.

While we were still on the ranch, shortly before we left Beaufort, my mom had decided to become a nurse. Dad supported her decision. She took a brief program at the community college and earned her LPN license. She was diligent in her studies and serious in her goal, at times asking me to quiz her for a test or be her practice dummy for taking a temperature or finding a pulse. She was proud to graduate in her crisp white uniform, with a gaggle of new nurse friends, and we were proud of her, too. She was almost thirty when she posed for Polaroids with her certificate, and we celebrated at home with a thick chocolate sheet cake.

Her first nursing job was a part-time position in Chester, about twenty minutes directly west of the ranch, assisting an older Indian doctor in his musty, Victorian home, which doubled as an office for the rural patients he treated. He dressed splendidly in a suit and tie, with a bright white shirt that accentuated his brown skin and slicked-back silver hair. He presented himself professionally and looked like a banker or lawyer, but the stethoscope hanging from his neck said otherwise. Mom took us there a few times for simple treatments or checkups, and I remembered the dark wood trim and creaking floors of the tired interior, along with the dated wallpaper and translucent glass of the exam room door.

It was a strange divergence from the typically bright, sterile medical facilities we were used to seeing. The vintage, wrap-around front porch also contributed to that difference and showed its age in worn planks and peeled paint, in stark contrast to the shiny brown Mercedes sedan the doctor parked in the driveway next to it.

My mom left the doctor's practice within a year of starting there and found another position at Havenshore's competitor and our birthplace, Regents. The two hospitals were oddly situated diagonally across the river from each other in a clustering of routine and critical care support for the entire county, their campuses linked easily by a short drive or a long, scenic walk across the bridge. Mom's tenure at Regents spanned a variety of units but was also short-lived.

Brief as it was, she always talked fondly of the friends she had made at the hospital, along with those she went to school with at the community college. And I never heard her complain about her work. I suspect the tasks and patients challenged her, in a good way, and their interactions energized her extroverted personality. I know she didn't learn that in her training. It came naturally to her. Probably the same for Katie.

Objective number two had become number one, as I made my way through the double doors and into the comfortably appointed visitors' lounge. It was well lit, and much brighter than when I had first passed it on my way in, with plenty of seating, tables, artwork, magazines, and a big screen TV waiting to be powered up. But it was still empty and quiet. I suspected visiting hours hadn't begun yet, which got me thinking of the privilege of being at my dad's side the past few. The Yelp rating climbed again.

I looked around for the bathroom and saw an open door in the back, near a water fountain. Double relief. I made a beeline to the fountain. The water was cold and clean. *Hospital clean.* My throat thanked me.

I flicked the light on in the visitors' bathroom. It was huge and outfitted with all the required accessibility features built into most healthcare facilities. I shut the door and quickly knocked objective number one off the list, issuing an exuberant exhale. Mission accomplished.

As I stood at the sink washing my hands, I looked at the matted gray hair and tired eyes abusing the mirror. *What happens next? Who needs to be involved? Is this how it ends? We just saw the guy a week ago, and he was doing great. I've got the video of him dancing in his walker with my daughter to prove it. And he was on a glide path to the veterans' home and a bigger audience there. Shit, am I ready for this? That goddamn stent!*

I dried my hands and used the damp paper towel to wipe down my oily face as I exited the bathroom. I took another cold slurp from the fountain and pulled out my phone to check the time: 8:03 a.m.

Out of habit, I held the "home" button as Touch ID unlocked my small, 16 GB world of photos, emails, and a handful of news and political websites. And my laundry list of alarms—regular reminders to do things, check things, start things, fix things, say things. My wife and kids hated my reliance on them. But like the Outlook reminders I used to keep myself in line when I was working, my phone alarms kept me sane and on my toes. And unlike other task and to-do apps, an alarm would annoy me until I responded to stop or snooze it. And unlike me, it never forgot.

I tapped the Safari icon to get a quick snapshot of the day's news. My signal was pretty strong in the visitors' lounge, so sites painted quickly. Mostly anti-Trump stuff from the mainstream outlets. Stories about newly legalized weed in Illinois. Democratic primary crap. College bowl game results. I closed the browser to check emails. The usual unsolicited, overnight stuff was there. Kohl's deals. Target specials. Costco closeouts. I started clicking to delete them.

Shit! The meeting with Dr. Bhatta! I completely forgot.

Totally distracted and neglectful.

Should have set an alarm.

I jammed my phone back in my pocket and scurried out of the visitors' lounge, through the double doors, and back toward my dad's room. A small group of people in white coats and blue scrubs had gathered in a loose circle. I slipped into the perimeter near Dr. Bhatta, who was flipping through some notes and fortunately hadn't yet started his review. None of the others in the circle seemed to notice or care about my tardiness, and generally didn't seem very attentive.

Katie chatted softly with a couple other nurses while a tall, slender woman with graying hair and a pastel-colored medical coat approached me.

"Hello, I'm Marcia, I'm the ICU social worker for Mr. Grojnecki. Are you his son?" she asked.

My bad hair and street clothes were dead giveaways.

"Yes, hi," I replied, shaking her hand firmly and trying to eke out some early-morning people skills.

"I'll come by shortly to talk with you and your father. About his options, once he's stable."

She had a kind smile and a friendly demeanor. Probably job requirements for being a healthcare social worker, which I assumed meant she was the person who talked with patients and families about issues that doctors and nurses weren't trained for. Or avoided. I repeated her name in my head, so I could recall it later. *Marcia, Marcia, Marcia.* I was bad at names and used every trick possible to get better at remembering them.

"Okay, thank you, that would be great," I said, happy for any and all help, from anyone.

Dr. Bhatta started talking.

"Patient suffers from a rupturing aortic stent, with treatment currently focused on pain management. Expecting advice post-consult from patient's cardiologist this morning. Thank you."

And that was it. Done. I'd placed more complex orders for Thai food takeout than what I'd just heard, but if that's what was necessary to rally the troops to help my dad, then so be it. *Whatever.*

"I increased your father's dosage. That should help. We'll see what Dr. Mahanti advises when he sees him. He should be here early this morning," the doctor confirmed, looking at me with his own tired eyes and anxious to move on to his next patient.

"Okay, thank you, doctor. Hopefully that helps," I said, actually hoping. He turned and walked away, and I headed back into my dad's room.

Surrounded by cords and tubes, and color-coded monitors and machinery, my dad looked ironically tranquil in the bed. His eyes were closed, and he faced forward, his head elevated at thirtyish degrees. I was glad he seemed so peaceful, but it was an eerie sight nonetheless. His pale skin and partially open mouth made me look twice. I glanced at the monitor to verify nothing was flat as I sat back down next to him. He felt me arrive.

"The doctor said he's going to give me more painkiller for my back," he said, opening his eyes.

I put my hand on his shoulder and leaned into him,

"Yes, I talked to him. Hopefully it helps. He said Dr. Mahanti will be coming by soon to see you."

"Oh, that's good. Did we just see him?" he asked as he gripped me tightly with his thumb.

"No, it's been a while since we saw him. The doctor we just went to was your regular doctor, Simonson," I reminded him.

"Right. We cancelled the appointment with Mahanti, right?"

He was spot on and was keeping it all together. He had a knack for that.

"Yes, I cancelled it and set it up for February, remember?" I wasn't sure he would.

"End of February, right?" He was spot on again.

"Yes, sometime at the end of February," I confirmed.

One p.m. on the twenty-seventh, to be precise.

"Dad, try to get some rest now, okay?" I rubbed his bicep and tried to comfort him to sleep.

"Can I have some water? My throat hurts," he asked.

I let go of his arm and reached around myself to get the cup. I put the straw to his mouth, and he sipped quickly. He was thirsty like I had been. He turned his head away from the straw when he was done. It reminded me of when our kids were infants and had finished feeding on my wife or on a bottle. They just turned away. Satisfied and fulfilled.

And as if she saw or heard us, Katie popped into the room to provide more comfort to Dad.

"Hi, Martin. I've got something here for your lips. And the doctor changed your dosage, so I'll give you that, too. I'm sorry you're still having so much pain," she said, both helpfully and helplessly.

Katie pulled out a stick of hospital-issued Chapstick and glossed my dad's lips in a style resembling more makeup artist than nurse. He gladly complied. When she finished, she handed it to me for future applications.

He massaged his lips together to feel the balm, then mumbled weakly, "Thank you."

Katie began logging into the workstation next to Dad, when Marcia pushed open the curtain and walked slowly toward his bed.

"Hello, Mr. Grojnecki. My name is Marcia, and I'm the social worker here. I just came by to talk with you about your options once you're well enough to leave the ICU. Is this a good time?" she asked.

"What?" Dad seemed both startled by the newcomer and unable to hear much of what she said.

"She's the social worker, Dad. She's here to talk about when they move you out of ICU."

I spoke directly at him, continuing to hold his hand. Marcia's presence didn't seem to register with him.

"Can I sit next to you?" Marcia asked me as she pulled a smaller chair next to the bed.

Then, like *The Gong Show*, the curtain opened again.

"Good morning, Martin! It's Dr. Mahanti here. How are you feeling?"

The big room seemed strangely crowded by the six of us there, including the resident accompanying Mahanti. It felt like a PTA meeting was about to start.

"Oh, hi doctor. The pain is really bad," he replied to the cardiologist and installer of that goddamn stent.

Dad liked Mahanti and enjoyed seeing him for checkups in his office on Havenshore's first floor. I liked him, too. The doctor would always make my dad feel welcome during his visits and would spar jokingly while examining him, but he was also very direct with his feedback

113

and instructions, which my dad liked. Mahanti was surely a few years older than me but didn't look it with his smooth, dark skin and full, still-black hair. The resident that trailed him had similar features but was decades younger than both of us.

The doctor looked across the bed at me, and I nodded politely, greeting him with a quick, tight grin. He nodded back with a solemn, serious look of condolence. The resident stayed quiet and anonymous.

Katie moved to the foot of Dad's bed and listened with Marcia and me as the doctor talked pleasantly with Dad.

"You know, Martin, what we've talked about regarding this stent, if it were to rupture, right?"

He moved closer to the bed and put his hand on Dad's shoulder, and looked at me periodically as he talked, basically talking to both of us. His tone was serious, and he spoke clearly and loud enough for Dad to hear him. And for me, too.

"I know, doctor," Dad said with some despair, resigned to the fact that the hypothetical had become reality—the reality we'd discussed a few times over Dilly Bars and Dean Martin.

"We can go in and replace it, but there's a risk you might not be able to handle the procedure or the recovery. It's a very big risk with no guarantees."

The doctor's voice softened, almost cracked, and he looked at me directly.

"Or we can try to make you as comfortable as possible with the painkiller."

He stopped there, also resigned to the reality of the non-ideal options he was proposing.

But I knew what he was saying. *We can try something to keep your father alive, but it has a very small chance of success and could be very painful and debilitating. Or we can pump him full of drugs to ease the discomfort until he dies from that goddamn stent.*

114

I didn't want to hear it, but I knew what he was saying.

My dad knew it, too. "Doctor, I've had a good life. I don't want surgery or anything like that. Just make the pain stop. Please," my dad pleaded.

"Are you sure, Martin?" Mahanti asked as he fixed his eyes on my dad and grabbed his hand. I squeezed the other one.

"Yes, thank you for everything, doctor," my dad said, his voice sincere but quivering. *He had decided.*

"Okay, Martin, we'll try to make you comfortable here," the doctor offered, still holding Dad's hand.

I could see the sadness in Mahanti's face. He undoubtedly was at the point in his career where he had mastered the technical aspects of his specialty, or knew who to go to if he hadn't, and the process of diagnosing and treating patients was one he took seriously but did so with a routine and professional ease. But this moment was less about a doctor and patient than about two congenial men brought together by one's ailment, then fated to be separated by it as well.

Unable to give my dad good options, and realizing this would be the last time they saw each other, the doctor was clearly moved. It was obvious he cared about my dad and was disappointed he couldn't save him.

"Your father's a tough guy! You're lucky to have him!" Mahanti exclaimed to me, trying to lighten the moment and exit on a high note.

Before I could agree with the doctor, my dad chimed in.

"I'm the lucky one, doctor. I have a good son and a beautiful family. I've had a good life. I wouldn't do anything different."

I held back my tears as Dad held my hand.

"That's really great, Martin. You're both lucky. I'll go talk to Dr. Bhatta about your pain. Good luck, my friend."

Mahanti rubbed Dad's shoulder again, then reached across him to shake my hand.

"Thank you for everything, doctor," I said, grateful that he had helped to add some memories and playful years to my kids' Papa.

Mahanti turned and talked quietly to the resident as they left the room. My dad closed his eyes to rest.

Katie and Marcia heard the exchange and also knew what it meant.

"There are a number of hospice services we work with here. I have a list you can choose from if you're not already working with one," Marcia explained as she opened a small binder next to me.

Katie moved back around to the workstation to log in and inject Dad with some needed relief. His eyes remained closed as Marcia talked. I was hoping he was dreaming of better things.

I was confused by Marcia's offer. I knew what hospice was, as other older friends and relatives needed the services of drug-induced comfort in their final days, but I didn't know the process of acquiring it. And I didn't know the process allowed me to shop around.

Marcia saw I was perplexed and continued to lay it all out for me.

"If you don't have a specific company in mind, there are five or six hospice companies that work with Havenshore for patients that need those services. Sometimes the patient is moved to another wing of the hospital, and sometimes they receive hospice at home. I can have a hospice representative come by from one of the companies and meet with you to discuss your father's situation and get the paperwork started if you like."

I was still absorbing the conversation between my dad and Mahanti, and the consequences of Dad's decision, and hadn't really mentally transitioned to the whole hospice thing yet—let alone to deciding who was going to ease him out of this world.

But Marcia was getting the ball rolling. She flipped to a page in her binder, protected by a plastic sleeve, which showed a list of hospice companies I could choose from. The names all looked the same to me. Marcia paused as I viewed the page. I looked up at her stupidly. She looked back at me like I was.

"So is there one here you'd like to work with?" she asked, wanting me to select someone to take care of my dad and fill him full of opioids.

This seemed like a big decision that needed some reflection and discussion. *Hell, I spend more time picking out grapes at Aldi,* I thought to myself.

Marcia could see I was confused by the proposition.

"All of them provide basically the same services, especially at the stage your father's at," she said, trying to help me along in a soothing, friendly voice.

The fog finally started to clear for me as I could see she wanted to get someone engaged to handle the messy hospice details with me and take over my dad's care from the ICU. Marcia was doing her job to get that baton passed. And I was quickly becoming resigned to my dad's decision and the process that came with it.

"I, I, I have no idea. Do you have any recommendations?" I asked as I stared at the list, not really digesting anything I was looking at.

Marcia was somewhat hesitant to point me to any specific company, but relented when she could tell I was treading water.

"We work a lot with these two. They're both very good."

She pointed to the first two on the list.

I focused on them and the key words in their brief descriptions: *caring, kind, comfort, professional.* It was a crapshoot for me.

Marcia, thankfully, jumped in, pointing to the second one.

"I think I can get you an appointment here today with this one."

"Okay, let's go with it," I confirmed, realizing I spent too much time evaluating grapes.

Marcia pulled out her phone and sprung into action.

"Hello, I have a patient in ICU in need of hospice, and his son is here at Havenshore and would like to meet with you today. Is there a good time for you today?"

Marcia looked at me with the phone to her ear.

"Does 11:00 a.m. work for you?" she asked me.

I looked up over her shoulder at the big white clock and assessed the time, not that it really mattered. Just habit. Twenty years of project management will do that to you. It was 8:43. The damn second hand stayed in motion, undeterred, apparently missing the conversation with Mahanti.

"Sure, that's fine, thanks," I replied to Marcia.

She relayed my confirmation to the hospice person on the other end and finished the call.

"Anne is the representative who will come by at 11:00. If anything changes, she'll get back to me, and I'll let you know. I'll also give her your phone number, if that's okay?"

I nodded.

"She'll have much more information to share when you meet with her." Marcia had done her job well and passed the baton.

"Is there anything else I can help you with at this time?" she asked, closing her binder.

Dad was still resting quietly.

"No, thank you for your help."

I shook her hand as we stood up from our chairs, trying not to wake him.

"Good luck with your father. And if you do have any questions, I'll be around here all day."

Marcia exuded warmth and compassion. And efficiency. She exited the room as Katie tended to my dad. The PTA gathering had dwindled to three.

"I really think that was the right decision," Katie remarked as she took off her gloves and logged out of the computer.

Her unsolicited statement surprised me.

"Hospice?" I asked, assuming that's what she meant.

She looked at me across the bed as she grabbed the side rail with both hands.

"Yeah. I was a cardiovascular surgery nurse before I came to ICU a few years ago. A lot of patients your father's age don't make it through that kind of surgery. To replace the stent. A lot of them bleed out on the table. And the pain your father has now is horrible. In my opinion, hospice is the way to go."

She spoke matter-of-factly and was confident in what she said next.

"I would have made the same decision."

The elephant fell off my shoulders. Sure, it was Dad who made the decision to give Mahanti the afternoon off in lieu of some extra-strength narcotics, but I carried the burden of letting him. At least that's how I felt. And the weight of that was excruciating. *Who knew? Maybe Mahanti could actually thread the needle and fix that goddamn stent without much collateral damage. Or maybe Dad, in another age-defying feat similar to his alley jog, could master the challenge of recovery. Or maybe there wouldn't really be much of a challenge to recovery.*

Who knew?

I didn't. But Katie did, or at least had a pretty good idea of it. Damn sure better than mine. Her third-party reflection couldn't have come at a better time.

"Thank you. It really helps to know that," I said, grossly understating the benefit as the pachyderm landed next to me.

I took a deep breath and inhaled the newfound clarity.

"We talked a few times about which way to go if it ever came to this. He didn't want the pain of just surviving."

"I'm sure. Yeah, I'd definitely do hospice if it were my father," she said, finishing the conversation and turning to leave. "Is there anything I can get you?"

She'd done enough. In a good way.

"No, I'm good. Thanks Katie."

My dad continued to sleep, so he was good, too.

As she left, I pulled out my phone to start updating my family on the path forward. Then I stopped.

After the stimulus of the last hour, I decided I needed some time alone with Dad, and he may have needed some with me. Minus the phone. Minus the PTA crowd. Minus the elephant.

I peeked before I shoved it back in my pocket. It was 8:57 a.m., 73 percent battery.

HOUR 9: The ORNAMENTS

I sat and looked at my dad as he slept. The painkiller was an obliging acquaintance. But it masked the fleshy hourglass he had become since Mahanti left. Sedated and content, my dad appeared as if he could exist under the influence indefinitely, though it definitely was not the existence he preferred.

As I watched him rhythmically inhale the oxygen strapped to his nostrils, I envisioned his final days hospicing in another room in the hospital, in basically the same state of induced bliss, until the stent collapsed or exploded. He was mentally strong and functionally fit, excluding the tiny mesh sleeve securing his aorta. So if he could endure the last few hours of pain and hospital fatigue, he could surely make it a few more days until my wife had an opportunity to see him and our kids could fly in and reminisce with him over Dilly Bars. I anticipated that's how I'd proceed with Anne at 11:00 a.m. That was Plan A.

Or—the mortal grains of sand could already be rushing through his gently breathing hourglass like the river unimpeded outside, though finite in number and unforgiving when they run out. Which could be minutes or hours away. Or seconds. I didn't know, but wanted to believe we had more time together. Not in the ICU. Not just the two of us. We needed to agitate about spring training and the Bears' next draft pick. He needed to tell the kids more stories about the Navy and about working in his parents' tavern as a kid. My wife needed to

121

feed him another batch of homemade cookies to piss off his diabetes. He needed to know how much he meant to us and how much he'd be missed. How much I'd miss him.

Needless to say, I wasn't a fan of not-Plan-A, so I looked forward to my meeting with Anne as the stent stretched its limits and wreaked havoc on him from the inside out.

I looked at my dad, wondering where the painkiller was taking him. I imagined, and hoped, it was someplace, or places, warm and cheerful. And thrilling. Places that made him feel alive. Made him feel virile. Made him laugh and excited to be there. I thought about the times he held dear to him. The ones he told us about.

Was he in the post-Pearl Harbor Pacific, somewhere between San Diego and Hawaii, basking in the sun with 250 other sailors, happy and brave but ever vulnerable aboard that relatively helpless aircraft transport ship in the unending ocean?

Or was he in Vegas, at the Golden Nugget or the Sahara, where he could cultivate his longtime vice in the desert, and gamble on slots, or blackjack, or the horses, and drink all the Old Styles and martinis he could handle?

Maybe he was back in college, at Eastern Illinois, frolicking with his Phi Sig frat brothers and his football teammates, doing what college kids do, or what they did, back when they were war veterans before they were freshmen.

Or maybe he was somewhere in that decade between the late 1940s and late 50s, after college and before my mom, a period that Dad never talked about, and I never prodded him to.

I looked at his stubbled cheeks, spotted with age, and rubbed his thumb with mine as I thought about his stories. But with experience to inform me, though frayed by the almost fifty years that had passed, I thought mostly about the times from our six or so years on the ranch, and where in that span the painkiller could be depositing him. He liked to recall how *fun* those years were and hoped I'd recall the same. And I did. Yes, there were the horses and the minibike and the bowling alley. And the pool and the parties. And the snow pile.

But as I watched life quietly leave him, its pace throttled by that goddamn stent, more memories came to life for me. As if they'd been tightly tucked away in boxes like Christmas tree ornaments, then eventually opened and their details remembered as they were untangled and hung for the last time.

I remembered the drive-in movies. In the gigantic turquoise Buick. Mom and Dad would stuff us, pre-pajamaed, into the backseat with pillows, blankets, jackets, and an empty Folgers coffee can to pee in, and head about a half hour northwest to the outdoor theater on Route 12, near an interstate exit to Mennawa. Mom would sit close to Dad and hold the buttery popcorn, and my brother and I would take turns jamming ourselves into the raised compartment by the back window, *just because*. And even though the double-featured flicks we watched were more my parents' flair—like *Bonnie and Clyde, Barbarella, Love Story, Patton*, and *Rosemary's Baby*—the four of us trapped in the car together for hours under the stars was incomparable! *They Shoot Horses, Don't They?* was my favorite. Always, we slept on the way home, usually starting our slumber midway through the second film. Mom emptied the coffee can in the lot before we left and stayed close to Dad as he drove us back to the ranch. The simple path home on 12 east to south Prairie Highway made for an easy delivery of his tired troops.

#

"DAD! MOM! They won't come out! They won't come out!" I screamed in panic, convincing myself with each passing second my six-year-old life was on the line and the end was near.

"HELP! They're stuck! They won't come out! DAD! Dad, come here!"

"What the hell is going on up here?" my dad yelled as he bounded up the stairs two at a time, recognizing my despair and the urgency it required.

"Are you okay?"

"They're stuck! I can't get them out! Dad, I'm scared!" I cried, the tears and terror completely justified and accelerating with each scream.

"What is going on? Did you hurt yourself? What the hell?"

Dad wanted to help, but didn't know where to start besides looking for bloody wounds and rightfully taking a quick glance at my brother, and around the bedroom we shared, for any makeshift weaponry he may have used on me.

"Ooooh, Dad! It really hurts! Pleeeeease!"

I bawled in horror, not knowing what to do and fearful of how it was going to end, if it ever did. The disaster that struck me couldn't have been worse, and my dad seemed helpless as he made his initial diagnosis. Mom was absent from the second-floor pandemonium.

My little brother, however, sat cross-legged on the floor a few feet from the chaos and laughed hysterically, half afraid of what was happening, but fully loving that it was happening to me.

"What the hell did you do to him?" Dad raged, ready to give his belt a workout on my brother's butt.

"Nothing. I didn't do nothing to him," my brother gasped during a pause in his laughing fit.

Dad refocused his attention and growing irritation on me.

"What's wrong? Tell me! What did you do?"

The towheaded hyena pointed at me and nearly teetered over, screeching in glee, "He put magnets up his nose!"

"What?!" Dad asked, confused by the two of us.

He looked down at the worn-out carpeted floor between my brother and me. A small pile of brightly colored plastic letters littered the musty gray rug. Yellow B, green T, blue A, red M, and other tinted representatives from the alphabet were sprawled in front of us, *minus* their small, rectangular, nostril-sized magnets intended to hold them to the metal radiators.

"What the hell did you do?"

Dad's curiosity landed squarely on my overpopulated nose. "Let me see. Look up!"

"We were just playing," I sobbed, inhaling only through my mouth as I tilted my head up so Dad could view the damage. "I can't get them out." I reached up to attempt another one-finger extract but was immediately slapped down.

"Don't! Don't touch it. You'll jam them up there further," Dad cautioned.

I sobbed harder.

The hyena continued cackling, enjoying the moment as he peered around my dad to get a gander up my nose. He recoiled as Dad turned and sneered at him.

"Let me get a flashlight. Don't touch anything!" Dad said as he dashed toward his bedroom a few feet away.

My brother smiled and shoved his finger up his nose mocking my predicament.

"Look up again!" Dad commanded as he returned with the stainless-steel lamp to examine the depth of the problem.

"Jesus Christ, what the hell were you two doing?"

"Just playing," I cried softly through my mouth.

But I had no clue what the hell we were doing. It was just another semi-destructive thing boys do when they have too much time on their hands. Like burning up ants with a magnifying glass. Or tearing night crawlers in half. Or using those metal radiators as a Crayon canvass, something my brother had done previously, which earned him some up-close-and-personal time with the belt. I was the hyena then.

"I need to take you to the hospital. I can't do anything with it. Get your shoes on and get in the truck! I'll be there in a minute. Let's go!" Dad hurried me along.

"You stay here with your mom," he barked at my brother, who continued to smirk and drive his finger up his nose.

I carefully walked down the stairs and sat on the bottom step to put on my PF Flyers.

"What did you do?" my mom asked as she walked toward me from the kitchen.

"He shoved a bunch of goddamn magnets up his nose," Dad yelled from his bedroom. "Get him in the truck, I'm coming down."

Mom had kneeled down next to me, also wanting to get a peek up my beak.

"Oh honey. I'm sorry. Don't touch it," she was more sympathetic than Dad but also unsure how to resolve the situation. "Hurry out to the truck now. Don't get him mad."

It was too late for that.

My crying had stopped as I hustled through the kitchen and garage to the Ford sitting in the circle drive outside. It was a blistering sunny day, and the oven-like heat held captive in the truck cab billowed out on me as I opened the passenger door and carefully climbed onto the hot vinyl bench seat. I pulled the heavy door shut behind me. My head throbbed with pain as the combined impacts of crying, screaming, embarrassment, and tiny magnets rammed up my nose had generated a first-class headache, bringing a new element to my condition. Along with the stifling cab, it was all too much.

I reached over to roll down the window and get some air in the truck so I could breathe. As I cranked the handle, I looked up toward the naked sun that was roasting the Ford, and me in it. With a slight tingle in both nostrils, and pressure welling between my eyes, I reacted to that brief but intense glimpse of brilliance and unleashed a vicious, all-relieving sneeze!

In an instant, with my eyes closed and my head whipping forward at a hundred miles an hour, a half dozen or so small magnets were dislodged by the blast and strewn throughout the cab in front of me. Almost simultaneously, Dad opened his door to jump in the truck and haul me to Regents. The facial explosion stunned him.

"Are you okay?" he wondered aloud, poking his head cautiously into the cab.

I sneezed again, with less force. And less shrapnel.

"I think they're out!" I responded with a full smile and an empty nasal cavity.

My dad smiled and started laughing as he pointed in front of me, "Look."

Some of the magnets that burst out of my nose had attached themselves to the steel dashboard. It was unclear which letters they belonged to. I counted four of them stuck to the glove compartment and started laughing with Dad.

"Let's go tell your mom. C'mon."

Dad was immediately in a much better mood as I jumped out of the truck and circled around to him. He rubbed my head and cradled my shoulder as we walked to the house, laughing together.

#

I remembered that story from the ranch as I stared at my dad and the tiny oxygen tubes in his nose. The small jets, resting atop his scruffy mustache, were welcome armament to battle the stent and sustain him. *No sneezing allowed*, I thought to myself.

And there were other fun times on the ranch that Dad liked to remember when we were together. Animals played a role in some of them as we had plenty of space on the ranch to accommodate the rabbits my parents got us for Easter, and the litters of German shepherd puppies that were regular tenants in the multipurpose barn.

We also had interesting times with snakes—like the elusive, little green grass snakes that were fun to watch but difficult to capture, and the thicker, longer garter snakes that seemed to pop up everywhere. They were slower and easier to snag, usually by applying a foot to keep them still on the ground, then pinching them behind the head to put them in a jar. Or in a bucket. Or to chase my brother.

The snakes were harmless. I wasn't.

#

And there was the time, at one of my parents' pool parties, where a few of the guys were standing in the circle drive laughing and knocking down beers with my dad in the afternoon, when one of them noticed a black streak stretched across the white gravel lane, down by the main road. Hovering nearby to replenish their Hamm's and hear dirty jokes, I squinted and peered east at the streak. It was a good seventy-five yards away and looked like a shadow from one of the small trees in the north or south field. Until it moved!

At that point, the well-oiled crew got excited to go investigate what was at least six feet long and laying in the sun. My dad yelled for me to get a baseball bat and my brother. I hurried into the garage and grabbed a wooden bat leaning against his Craftsman table saw, then shouted for my brother. Some of the women ran out of the house and over to the circle drive as well. My dad carried the Louisville Slugger and was the only armed member of the group as they walked quickly down the lane toward the streak—careful not to spill their beers, Dad's included. The ladies followed. My brother and I stuck close to our dad.

As we neared the streak, it began to move slowly, undulating from left to right. The group slowed, too. My brother and I followed my dad as he crept up near the tail end of the massive boa constrictor. Or cottonmouth? Or kingsnake? We didn't know, but it was enormous! Definitely as long as the lane was wide, and thicker than my prepubescent forearm.

With no fanfare and all his might, Dad raised the bat and brought it swiftly down onto the snake until it lay bloody and gutted halfway across the lane. There was no cheering from the spectators, just comments of awe regarding the size of the snake and the beating Dad gave it. A good ten minutes of post-pulverizing analysis took place near the reptile's remains before the group retreated toward the house, smiling and sipping and ready for refills.

Moments later, Dad walked back down the lane with his trusty coal shovel and hurled the spoils into the south field. I went with him to watch. He wasn't looking for kudos or glory from his performance, but it was clear he was pleased with the outcome, as were the flies swarming the scaly carcass. And it was clear to me, in those few lumberjack-like strokes, how raw and unemotional my dad's fury could get.

#

Unfortunately, the last thing I would see from my dad as he lay in the ICU bed was fury. Fury would have been welcome. Laughter would have been welcome. Anything but the pain and finality that was dominating the morning would have been welcome.

But as I thought more about the times we shared at our semi-rural haven—trying to remember the impulsive, boisterous fun we had there—I began excavating memories that weren't so positive. Sure, I'd found a lot of treasures as I recalled the playful joy we shared on the ranch, but along with the treasures came some cigarette butts and empty beer cans—the ugly stuff of life that is buried with the beautiful.

Some of the ugliness was a function of the tumultuous world that paralleled, or piloted, our life in Beaufort. My parents experienced the sixties and early seventies without filters, but my brother and I were exposed to them in a dimmer light. As elementary schoolers, we saw tidbits of the turmoil and tension that surrounded us—war, racism, civil rights protests, riots, assassinations—but what *we* saw were crumbs of the heftier issues that ravaged the adult world we knew, or cared, little about.

As we ran home from the subdivision at night for tin-foiled TV dinners or Spaghetti-Os or a ketchup-bathed meatloaf, some of the houses we passed on our way back toward the orchard were void of kids our age. Those homes were typically silent and somber during the day, dark at night except for a single lamp or a kitchen light. We ignored their fences and yards, and the adults that lived there whenever we saw them. They were of no interest or use to us in our world of tag, hide-and-seek, or right-field-out. But instead of contributing noise and laughs to the neighborhood, many of the homes contributed more than we knew or understood at the time, displaying Blue Star Banners in their windows. Some of the service flags had one blue star, some two, signifying one or two children serving in the Vietnam War that raged while we played.

I didn't realize the significance of the flags, or notice the flags themselves, until we'd lived there a couple years and Dad recounted stories about his time in the Navy. His World War II was vastly different from the unpopular conflict in Vietnam, but they had many things in common including the comradery and sacrifice of young men and women, and the toll it took on their families. Dad noted the flags in the windows one night and told us what they were for. I paid attention and thought about those quiet houses differently from then on. I recalled our closest neighbor, in proximity only, having a banner with a single star as we sprinted home one evening, then two stars when we ran past it the next day. I recognized the change, but I really didn't understand how those parents must have felt about their teenage soldiers—proud, scared, hopeful, anxious, never knowing what waited in their mailbox or who was knocking at their door. I never saw a gold star—reflecting the ultimate sacrifice—in the subdivision windows, and was thankful for it.

Day after day, Vietnam was one of those stories that chewed up time on the television and pages in the newspaper—but its impact on the simple, snake-chasing, worm-ripping lives of my brother and me was random and muted. Much like the effects of the protesting and rioting of the sixties.

#

"When are you coming home?!" my mom pleaded angrily into the phone. "You better not stay at your mom's. Don't leave us here alone again!"

She slammed the handset onto the cradle, hanging up on my dad. The ringer inside the avocado-colored wall phone jingled loudly. My nerves shook me in response.

It was late afternoon, but not yet dinner time. And it was Friday, which usually meant we'd be eating at the bowling alley or Italian restaurant, rather than Mom's usual fare of Hamburger Helper, a Spam surprise, or something frozen in foil from Swanson's. Cooking was not her strength, and she never claimed it to be. She preferred to spend her time diddling in the yard, sunning at the pool, or tending to the horses, versus toiling in the tiny, dimly lit kitchen with aging cupboards and overly friendly cockroaches. The kitchen I nearly burnt to the ground at our first house was much nicer, before and after the flames—flames which were innocent and accidental, unlike the combustion surrounding us that Friday.

She was already well past her first highball of the day, the bottle of Seagram's parked on the counter near the sink, as she picked up the traumatized handset and attacked the rotary dial with seven forceful spins. She alternated sips with drags on her Marlboro as she waited for an answer, then started the conversation excitedly when she got one.

"Hi, it's Lori. Yeah, I'm okay. Is Larry home yet?"

131

I assumed Mom was talking to her friend Brenda across town. I sat at the dining room table as she stood by the counter across from me and fidgeted with a ceramic ashtray, her volume increasing.

"No, I just talked to him. He hasn't left yet and it's getting pretty shitty over here. I can hear a lot of shouting. And bullhorns."

She paused, listening to Brenda's response, then answered anxiously as she pulled the phone cord around the counter and got up on her toes to look out the kitchen window above the sink, checking side to side.

"No, nobody's come up to the house yet. Thank God."

She faithfully returned to her cocktail and cigarette and continued chatting with her friend about the day's events.

I was nervous because she was nervous—nervous enough to pull out her shotgun and load it after picking me up early from school. She stood it against the wall in the kitchen, arm's length from her other best friends that chilled and smoldered on the counter.

With my brother in tow in the big Buick, she had picked me up from kindergarten before lunch. The entire grade school was released early that cool spring day. None of us six-year-olds knew what was happening, or what had happened. For us, it was a Friday like any other—everyone was tired of being in school the whole week, having dealt with the daily drudgeries of sit-straight story times, communal naps, and milk runs to the big cooler by the cafeteria. And Saturday morning cartoons were right around the corner, so we were already mentally checking out for the week when we were told the day would end before having to decide if we'd spend our three cents on white or chocolate. But for everyone else, it was a different kind of Friday, the first one in April 1968, the day after Martin Luther King Jr.'s assassination.

And America was on fire, physically and emotionally. Some of those emotional embers were being stoked that day at the local high school as it simmered directly across the lane leading to our ranch. The school was somewhat integrated, mostly white, and pulled students from a variety of towns in a fifteen mile or so radius. Some students came from potato, gladiola, or livestock farms, and some had a common French heritage, while many of the black students were bussed there from tiny, destitute communities like Hemmer and Robertsville. Beaufort High School was the township's public default for those who preferred it or couldn't afford the tuition of the Catholic school in Mennawa, making it likely that I'd be walking down our lane for my post-elementary education rather than taking the long ride west to Sacred Heart HS.

But on that day, the high school I saw on the way back home, peeking above the dash and keeping my head low, was no institution of higher learning. It wasn't the usual single-building campus where teenagers crisscrossed paths on the sidewalk or front steps, or jumped in and out of big yellow school buses parked under massive oaks on the main street. There were no kids running around in cardinal red PE uniforms in the recreation fields behind the school, near our property, chasing each other or looking bored waiting for a teacher's instruction.

No, what I saw, what I remembered as the cause of our early exit from school that Friday, was a hotbed of screaming outrage, littered with signs and garbage, and young people who, on that day, were activists demanding answers—not students waiting for them. And in my much younger, uninformed eyes, I saw mayhem and anarchy, contrary to what my dad expected from us. And I saw anger and resentment from the noisy teenagers paying no attention to streets or traffic, but doing anything they could to make people pay attention to them. Some were black; others were white. All were incensed.

A small squad of local police cleared a path for my mom to drive down RR2 and get to our lane. By the time we got back home, we were all scared by what we saw, never having witnessed that kind of bedlam before, and wondered if the angry mob would be coming for us. Mom headed straight to the basement for her shotgun and called our dog into the garage. The highballs and Marlboros followed.

#

At the time, as a pre-teen in the late sixties and early seventies, I didn't really understand what was going on, and neither my mom nor dad took the time to talk about it. I'm not sure they understood the gravity of the events other than what they absorbed on the surface: Cars and buildings on fire were bad, as were the people who torched them; broken windows and ransacked businesses were bad, as were the people who trashed and looted them; cops being confronted and opposed was bad, as were the people who challenged and provoked them.

Or maybe they did understand, and just shielded us from what we, and they, couldn't control. Generally though, we weren't a family that sat down and dissected or debated things. We talked about the What, but never the Why, or the Why Not.

And as a young family, we never discussed how we felt, nor how we felt about each other. Hugs didn't happen. Ever. Accomplishments got a smile or a nod and disappointments got a frown or a belt. There were commands and instructions and expectations, but most came without dialog and perspective. *"Because I said so"* was a typical reasoning I accepted, and got used to, without challenge. And whatever I learned about the world outside of the grade school classroom that wasn't a functional skill or an experience my dad could impart to me, came from *Laugh-In* and *Jeopardy*, and from a few older kids in the subdivision.

Likewise, the knotty topics of prejudice and racism weren't discussed, nor were they topics of education for us. They were behaviors. They happened without introspection or analysis in our sphere. Like breathing and bathing. There were no second thoughts to stereotypes, "which were made for a reason," right? I was supposed to laugh at, and embody, the snide jokes my classmates aimed at me, right? As a "dumb Polack," it was miraculous I could ace a test, or my dad could be a teacher, right? I was supposed to believe the disparaging daggers hurled when a black player struck out with men on base, or someone of color raised their voice to have one at all, right? I grew up with a thick skin and impaired vision. Breathing, bathing, and berating. It just was.

Yeah, it just was. But my dad never took the bait, at least I never saw him take it. And the bait was set often, especially when my uncles were around. Their prejudices ran deep and thick like river mud, and were tattooed loudly in their voices. Even louder when there was alcohol in the room. No one, not friend or foe, escaped being the target of their caustic comedy; and when together at family gatherings, the toxic whirlpool they whipped up spiraled even faster. Infused with highballs, Hamm's, and anecdotes of my grandma's hypochondria, the madcap events defined wrong in every way possible. Adjective, adverb, noun. Breathing, bathing, and berating. It just was.

In that respect, my dad and mom differed enormously in what seemed to be a clear result of nurture over nature. He had seen firsthand his Polish parents' immigrant experience and their struggle to survive and prosper. He served in the Navy where the enemy wasn't the other white, black, and brown sailors who were protecting their country and fellow soldiers. He coached and played on sports teams where competence and commitment counted more than color. He played the violin at an early age, and three months before my mom was born, he played Big Boy Roberts alongside a number of young female actors in the high school production of *Lindy Lou*. His biases weren't obvious, other than a strong prejudice against all things lazy and undisciplined. To him, to us, *merit* mattered.

In short, my mom wasn't any of that. She didn't have that broad

135

exposure or the positive experiences with others unlike her. And whatever wrongs she thought were right were reinforced by family who saw life with the same narrow lens. Far different from my dad who, as imperfect as he was, knew and accepted there was more to people than meets the eye.

My dad wheezed, startling me and bringing me back to the January morning that welcomed us earlier. I peeked at the wall clock. The second hand rotated with continued arrogance. It was 9:43 a.m.

HOUR 10: The RIVER

My disdain for time began to subside when, without prompting but as scheduled, my phone sprang to life for the day. The repetitive radar alarm jolted me more than usual, and I quickly reached for the smooth outline of my phone vibrating in my front pocket. By feel, through the denim, I instinctively pressed the power button on top of the phone to shut it up and snooze it for another nine minutes, hoping it didn't wake my dad, and giving me time to investigate what I'd just postponed. Dad wheezed a little more but remained pacified by the painkiller as I pulled out my phone to see what I'd missed. I had a good idea.

And I was right; the clock app was reliably reminding me to send "three things I'm grateful for" to our family text group. It was a habit I started a few years back after listening to one of those high-paid, high-gloss speakers who appeared at an annual meeting in Dallas while I was still working. And though it was one of just a few positive takeaways, besides the frequent-flier miles I got from that and other annual meetings, it was a nugget of advice that hit home, and I latched onto it.

In the job I was in, and in the environment that I had created for myself, much of my day was spent on the negatives—project jeopardies, missed deadlines, headcount reductions, idiots on the train—which, like weeds in a flower bed, were suffocating the positives around

137

me. I was an old peony being strangled by thistles, and I knew the Einsteinian definition of insanity. Recalling and identifying some of the good in my life and sharing it with family seemed to be cheap therapy and easy to execute. *Something different. Worth a try.*

So I launched my new habit, partnering with my phone to keep me on task: 9:45 a.m., Monday through Friday. I gave my wife and kids a break from me on the weekends. Results of the new routine came quickly. Those morning alarms reminded me to think—and to think differently—while my mind was still fresh and not fully accosted by the workday's dilemmas. They reminded me to acknowledge and intentionally recognize something positive that happened in my life, regardless of how big or small, and to share it with others who might just do the same.

I became explicitly grateful for the haircuts my wife gave me without appointment. And for hot Dunkin coffee waiting for me after trudging through the snow. And for an oil change that didn't turn into a brake job. Some days were chock full of relevant events, others more scarce. And on the days when the thistles grew tall and thick, I was forced to rethink if they were weeds at all. *Or did I just need to look a little closer to find the flowers they hid?*

I stopped being pissed that it rained during my entire walk to the office and started being grateful that my pocket-sized umbrella was always in my bag. I stopped harping about some, not all, of the nitwits on the train and started being grateful I wasn't married or related to them. And as I sat there in the ICU and slid the green pixels to shut off the three dozen or so alarms destined to interrupt the time with my dad, I stopped fretting about that goddamn stent and the pain it was inflicting on both of us—and started being grateful that I was there to hold his hand as he started his descent.

Having calmed the assembly line of self-imposed reminders for the day, I checked the corner of the screen for the amount of juice left in my phone, not to be confused with the juice left in me, which had been drained by too little sleep, too much emotion, and a serious deficiency in caffeine.

As my biological needle approached E, the phone displayed a perkier 62 percent. Given its age, however, I knew it would need a charge if I stayed for the afternoon. And I definitely would need a charge of my own but figured I'd meet with the hospice nurse at 11:00, then head down to the hospital lobby afterwards to find some food and coffee for a midday revival.

As my dad slept, I cycled through my usual app rotation to get started or caught up with the day, picking up where I left off after my trip to the bathroom. Email first, deleting whatever I could that wasn't my wife's domain. Then news sites again. Then a brief check of the stock market to see if the day was green or red. Fortunately it was the former to start the new year, and keep me retired.

I tapped the weather icon reflexively. But then squinted out the windows at the bright, clear day. The morning alongside the river was peaceful and gorgeous. I didn't need a "robo-rithm" to echo that for me. I clicked the power button before the app could load and slid the phone back into my pocket to save some %, and to keep Dad company as his battery drained helplessly without recharge.

As I settled back into the sturdy armchair, feeling every smooth edge of its rigid frame on mine, I heard the muffled, familiar two-note chime of glass. A text from my wife had arrived in my pocket. Eventually, I would have texted or called her to give her an update to the "I'm okay" message I sent her when I had parked in the then-empty garage and the morning was dark and less informed. She deserved it.

Over the decades, she had become invested in my dad, and he in her. Almost forty years had elapsed since they first met, from college to marriage to kids to solitude to illness to the call on the cordless. Long enough, and loving enough, for the "-in-law" suffix to lose its relevance between them. He was happy to have a daughter in his life, especially after my mom and brother passed. And she treated him as a father from day-one, but even more so after hers passed unexpectedly some fifteen years back, prematurely severing a growing friendship between our fathers, both high school teachers and purebreds—one Irish, the other Polish. And like me, both lucky to have my wife on their side. Yes, she deserved an update.

But neither of us were panicky or machine-gun texters, the kind who disgorge their thoughts or emotions as soon as they realize them, usually in rapid-fire succession of incomplete phrase followed by incomplete phrase until their collective droplets of wisdom or anxiety cascaded into a digital stream of frenetic consciousness. I pulled out my phone to read her text.

You ok? How's your dad
doing? Call me if you have
a minute

Though her tone was subdued, I was sure she was thoroughly concerned and curious but also figured if I hadn't called or messaged her earlier, then no news was good news. But I wasn't so sure the news was good. It was less news and more update. An update on what we'd anticipated and talked about for years, especially since his bout with pneumonia. An update on his seemingly inextinguishable mortality, which nearly outlasted his entire immediate family's, including mine. An update on that dream-killing call on the cordless. I responded to her.

I'm fine. Tired. He's sleeping now.
Lots of pain. Going down the hospice
path. I'll call you in a min. Love you!

My dad continued to sleep through the various noises that monitored him and kept him in the unwinnable game to outlast the stent. I stood up to stretch and call my wife. My body needed it. I had told myself I would put some steps on my Fitbit at some point while he rested. Probably after meeting the hospice nurse and heading downstairs for something to eat and drink. Not only was I feeling the effect of being coffee-less, but I was starting to get the tight pangs of dehydration in my head to go with a tad bit of morning hunger. Thankfully, New Year's Day was pretty uneventful and sober, else that dearth of liquids and nutrients would have amplified everything not good about the day so far. But as I told my wife, I was *fine*, just tired.

I tapped my favorites, then my wife's cell, as I took a few steps toward the windows, expecting to secure a better signal and visually release myself from the sight of my dad slipping away while encumbered by the tubes, wires, and gravity of pain tethering him to the bed.

It wasn't a fair fight. And he was losing.

As the phone rang, I squinted then stared at the river below. Unlike my dad, it flowed without restraint.

"Hi, are you alright? How's it going? What can I do?"

My wife's effortless, butter-soaked voice hit the spot. A welcome relief to the beeps, wheezes, and hospital-speak of the past few hours. And our phone connection was clear. She sounded as if she were next to me. I moved nearer the windows to get closer to her.

"My dad's sleeping. They've got him on a lot of painkillers. He said he woke up at night and went to the bathroom and felt a lot of pain, so he called 911. We saw his cardiologist already this morning, and my dad doesn't want surgery. So, hospice. I'm meeting with the hospice person at eleven."

My summary was straightforward but sounded cold in retrospect. Fairly common for most of my phone conversations. My dad and I had that in common. We weren't talkers on the phone, possibly a behavior resulting from interactions with my mom's mom. But he, like my wife, and unlike me, was an extrovert and would happily talk to anyone who would listen, or was within earshot of him. It was annoying when I was a teenager but a cute trait as he aged.

"Is he comfortable? What did they say about hospice?" my wife asked. I stared deeper into the river as she talked, mesmerized by its energy and aware of its power. The guy behind me used to be full of both, but no longer. As the years passed, he had done a better job of accepting that than I did.

"Not much. Could be here, could be at his house. I'll find out more in a little bit and let you know. He's okay, in and out with the painkiller. Able to talk but pretty groggy."

"Do you want me to drive down there? I can take the rest of the day off and be there by noon or so. The roads seem to be fine. I'd really like to see him in case something happens."

She truly cared about him, and I knew it. So did he.

"Let's wait a little while and see how he feels, and see what the hospice nurse thinks. I'd hate for you to drive down here and have it be too late, you know, if he goes while you're on the road. Or you just sit here for the rest of the day. Let's just wait."

I didn't want to put her out. And the whole situation seemed to still be unfolding. At least it did to me.

"Well, I'd really like to see him. So let me know what you think after you talk to the hospice person. Have you gotten anything to eat there?"

She was the consummate Irish-Italian combination of mother, wife, and self-taught chef, sculpted beautifully in a slender silhouette with dark chocolate eyes and thick cocoa hair. The more I aged, the less she did, or so it appeared. Her zest for all things life-affirming was an added attraction on top of her health-conscious figure and desire to stay busy.

She was a rambunctious lover, lively talker, and a compulsive do-er, never sitting to sit and not afraid to get her hands dirty, though she invariably "cleaned up well" and was always styled to live; apparel of every type was her friend, following each curve as designed. An only-daughter and tomboy amongst brothers, perpetually ready for the next family gathering or party with friends, she was an equal mix of affectionate, social, and outspoken—spiced with a splash of benign volatility. She hugged with a vengeance and taught me to do the same.

For her, life meant relationships, and her passion to be helpful and help others was surpassed only by her ferocity to protect her kids. And her sleep. My dad and I were fortunate to be in her circle of kindness and ever-thankful for her focus on family, becoming extra thrilled when it was manifested by her love of the kitchen.

"No, not yet," I replied. "I'll grab something after I meet with hospice."

"Okay, don't forget. And I told the kids your dad's in the hospital. I didn't want them to be surprised if something happens. They all want to come see him."

"Thanks. I'll text everyone later when I know more."

"Sounds good, but if you want me to come down and be with you, just say so, okay?"

"I will. Thanks."

I paused to collect myself. It meant a lot to hear her offer—to feel not alone with my dad, even though I was. And as much as being alone never really bothered me or my dad, it felt better to know I wasn't. My lungs tightened and my stomach caved as I stammered, "I love you."

"I love you, too. Get something to eat. And let me know what hospice says."

"Okay, bye." I had to let go of her before my composure crumbled. Another five seconds would have been too much. I tapped the red button on the display and was alone again with my dad.

I slid the phone back into my pocket and looked aimlessly at the river, careful to avoid a dizzying glare. It was the first time I'd really assessed how it had permeated my life, even though I'd never been a river rat growing up nor spent any consistent time on it or its shores. I didn't know its deep or shallow spots, where all the boat landings were, or the best places to catch catfish or carp. Not until we bought a summer place to bring our kids closer to my dad, and I needed to follow water levels and flood stages, did I learn its 130-mile path started in Indiana and flowed leisurely southwest in a series of shallow channels before dipping near our summer house and V-ing northwest through Mennawa for the final, and more playful, third of its journey. Like many things growing up, unexplored and taken for granted, the river just was.

It was there, running past Dove's Park, just out of eyesight to my right, as I looked out the ICU windows. The Park was the place my mom and grandma would take us as kids with a loaf of bread to feed the ducks and pass the time on the swings. Distractions there along the west bank of the river were plenty, and it was cheap fun. On special days, we'd stop for small twist cones at a Dairy Queen next to the park. No Dilly Bars, unless, on a rare weekend occasion, Dad happened to be with us.

It was there, running past the Booster Club's tent on Labor Day weekends, when super-charged powerboats raced past with their rooster tails jetting out behind them while we helped my dad and other coaches pour beers and count money for his high school's athletic fund. As gleeful grade schoolers, my brother and I looked forward to the end of summer to tie on the change aprons and hang out behind the makeshift counters with Dad and his friends, absorbing their stories and cuss words amid the deafening roar of boat engines and over-served crowds.

It was there, running calmly on a sun-drenched senior skip day as we canoed through the state park to celebrate graduation, before heading our separate ways to college. Or jobs. Or whatever life had in store for us. The coolers of Strohs and Olympia we tied between the canoes balanced us when we stood to relieve ourselves of their iced and illicit contents, sometimes falling in as we emptied more cans in the heat, but always with a laugh. And never with a life jacket to constrict our fun.

It was there, running rampant past our summer place, especially when the river swelled with energy generated by torrential rains or the quick thaw of knee-deep snow. And when less lively, we put the river to use tubing behind our family-sized jet ski or watching the reflection of Fourth of July fireworks on its quiet surface. Or fished it for bluegill and sunfish off our dock, the dock my dad helped me rebuild as he was pushing eighty. Or just watched it glide listlessly past Roman's Pier as we gobbled up a grilled cheese or one of their signature pork tenderloin sandwiches—Dad's favorite.

It was there, running briskly over the dam, across the street from Sandy's—a downtown restaurant for special occasions—when my dad offered to give us a break and babysit our almost-one-year-old first born, a strong, colic-riddled baby with a penchant for his mom. As we left Dad's house for a nice dinner out, he smiled confidently as he held our son who on cue started wailing for my wife as soon as she turned her back. Surely, the two could manage each other while we were sharing a surf and turf dinner and a couple glasses of wine by ourselves, right?

Fast-forward an hour and a half as we returned to my dad's house to find him still carrying our son, both of them beet red and dripping with sweat as they greeted us at the front door—our son exhausted from crying and screaming in Dad's arms, my dad flustered and spent by the little guy's inconsolable writhing and raging. As our son lunged immediately toward my wife, my dad happily guided him to her like pouring a slimy fish back into its native waters. Though he loved our son and all our kids with every ounce of himself, my dad was thrilled to disengage with the infant at that moment and wipe his own sweat-soaked face with the burp towel we'd left him for other reasons. For the next nearly thirty years, my dad recalled that story frequently when our son was with him, the latest just a week before the midnight ride to the ER with that goddamn ruptured stent.

It was there, running reliably under the Jury Street bridge, near where my dad would take my mom fishing in the early evenings, as she craved obsessively to set up her lawn chair and pole on the east bank, and to crack open an Olympia as the river brought a familiar, mellow peace to her isolated life. From the ICU, I could see the area, diagonal from Dove's Park, where they baited their hooks, cast their lines, and challenged the darkness in the company of one or two other friendly fishermen quenching their after-dinner thirsts and hoping for a nibble.

My mom's unsolvable nutrient deficiency, coupled with her alcoholism, left her body and mind weak—but her tenacity never subsided. She was adamant about her evening fishing trips—and her need for beer, Scotch, and frozen pizza with squeeze butter. Her surliness and pessimism compensated for the loss of agility and decline in overall health that welcomed her to her forties. My brother and I watched her perilous transformation as we navigated our erratic teenage and college years, seeing the increase in valleys versus peaks as she aged. More often than not, we enlisted our friends to help and comfort us, rarely relying on each other.

My dad was patient and accommodating as Mom sank, a loving but frustrated caregiver and spouse, unable to stop her descent—much like I was unable to stop his. When she passed—her body depleted and heart diseased—the emotional anchor he had towed during her last ten years was gradually released, returning to him both an energy and a calm that had been buried from us for so long. It was five years later when our son innocently broke that calm as we dined tranquilly at Sandy's.

And that same river was there running freely along the south end of the hospital, just yards from the ICU, when we spread my brother's ashes at dusk in its swift but placid current one warm Saturday in late May 2009.

A month prior, I had received a call at home on a beautiful Sunday evening as we celebrated the day with a cheap, chilled Riesling, while simultaneously trying to blunt the anticipated grind of the coming work week. I was upstairs at the time, heading back down from our bedroom, when the cordless rang. The infamous *bad-news cordless*. Everyone else was outside enjoying the unseasonable weather as I detoured to the side of the bed to check the caller ID before intending to ignore it and rejoin them.

But the unusual sight of "Clark County" in the small display stopped me. Curious, I looked harder as it rang again, then picked up the handset, unsure of where Clark County was or what prankster was on the other end. I sipped the sweet white and inquired, "Hello?"

There was no prankster. Just a foggy, twelve-minute conversation with a polite, professional officer from the Clark County Sheriff's department informing me my brother had taken his life in the desert and left a note with my name and number to contact once he was gone. Her words were solemn but direct, and the information they carried rushed over me as I sat still on our bathroom floor, absorbing the shock of her initial message, unable to fully capture the details that followed.

\#

"I'm sorry, can I grab a pen and paper before you go any further?" I asked, feeling hollow but responsible for all that would come next. My project management tendencies had kicked in.

"Sure, of course," she replied.

I had already peeled myself off the floor to grab a pad of Post-Its and a pen from my dresser, wondering again if it could be an elaborate prank, but mostly believing the worst had happened. I sat back down on the cool tile floor, prepared to take notes.

"Thanks, please tell me again what happened?"

I took another sip.

She proceeded to give me everything I needed and answered all the questions I could think of at the time. She was kind and patient, and by the time she'd finished, the fog was transcribed on a half dozen or so stickies forming a messy yellow mosaic on the floor:

Shot himself in his truck

Found him in the desert

Not sure exactly when he did it, but recent

Found note with my name/number

They've only contacted me

Call the morgue re: what to do with his body

Pick up other personal effects at sheriff's office in Vegas

By the time she offered her condolences and wished me the best, and gave me her number and the morgue's, I had already played through in my head the scenario of his final, desolate moments alone and tried to remember our last conversation, which was difficult to do. He was distant, literally and figuratively, but so was I. Each of us could be blamed for not knowing the other's business.

But I always felt the goodness in life that had come my way, by work and by fate, somehow came at his expense—or without an extra scoop for him. Life hadn't been easy for him, and luck rarely seemed to be on his side. And though we tried to help him get started when he was finding himself in his twenties, and his friends were always there to offer a hand and a smile, his wick never seemed to light, or stay lit, no matter how hard he struggled to spark it. Many people loved him, or tried to, but in the end, it wasn't enough to keep him from taking that last, long drive to end whatever horrible misery had finally extinguished his fire.

The days and weeks following that unwanted Sunday call whizzed by with a flurry of activities—phone calls, faxes and emails, taking time off work and coordinating kids' schedules to fly to Las Vegas with my wife to do all those things you never want to do because you have to: clean his apartment, deal with the cat he left at the shelter before his desert drive, assess whether his blood-soaked truck could be salvaged, forward his mail to us, notify his banks and creditors from our hotel room—which was off the Strip and not nearly as plush as our Mandalay Bay accommodations when we renewed our vows there on a more pleasant trip five years earlier, meet with the helpful deputy to get the few personal items he had with him at the end, and retrieve his cremains from the funeral home director who processed his body.

None of it was easy to stomach, no matter how easy all the actors in the process made it, and they all did. There was no lack of sympathy or empathy from anyone we encountered, in person or over the phone. My limited faith in humanity skyrocketed during those weeks after the Sunday call. But as easy as others made it for us to wrap up the life of my forty-five-year-old little brother, the first two tasks of the journey were the most emotionally wrenching—telling my wife what had happened after I hung up with the deputy, then making my own lonely drive later that same night to tell my dad the news.

I set the cordless down next to my Riesling as I left the bathroom. Both had warmed during the twelve-minute discussion, but each was quiet and still as I ambled numbly downstairs. The shell of me moved itself as tasks and priorities raced through my head, jockeying for attention among the random thoughts and typical survivor questions ping-ponging between my ears, most beginning with "why?" None eventually answered. My wife was in the kitchen, whipping up another

149

sure-fire gourmet creation of hers as I shuffled in. I closed in on her as she sensed something wasn't right.

"What's wrong?" she asked. My face must have telegraphed the news. She put down the knife she'd been gracefully wielding on some unlucky vegetable and stepped toward me. I hugged her hard and stuck my face in her thick brown hair, smelling the oils and spices that hovered around her.

"My brother killed himself. The police just called," I mumbled in her ear, unable to catch my breath as I cried softly on her shoulder and squeezed her as if I needed her to be part of me. She squeezed back. She always did. Like when I told her my mom had passed twenty-some years earlier. And when I told her I had cancer.

"Oh no. No. Oh, I'm so sorry."

She was caught completely by surprise, surely thinking my sullen expression reflected some kind of news about my dad. But it wasn't. It was almost worse.

No, it *was* worse.

And telling her that, confiding in her that my brother picked the ultimate, irreversible solution to a problem, and that I couldn't help—wasn't asked to help, didn't ask to help—solve it, was like falling on a football, knocking the wind out of me like I'd never breathe again. And just wondering so hard, *why?*

That sunny April Sunday turned dark in minutes, even as the sky remained bright into the evening. And as soon as I pulled myself away from my wife's warmth and security, confirming she would break the news later to our kids, I headed back upstairs to ready myself for the drive south to tell my dad. The deputy didn't know of him nor have his number, and I told her that I would inform him myself.

It had been a while since we'd been down to visit my dad, and I suspected he would be surprised by me just showing up at his door unannounced. But I wasn't going to tell him what had happened by phone when I was only an hour away. There's no roadmap, or "How To," or user guide for telling a parent their child is dead. And I wasn't going to read a book or search the web for any shrink-wrapped therapy or wisdom before getting in the car.

My only, and very remote, point of reference was when, in the early nineties, at work, we had to notify hundreds of managers on the same day that they were being terminated. And I was part of the planning team to make it happen. At the time, mass layoffs of managers were a big deal, even bigger since the company had never laid off anyone before. So the recommendation for executing that unannounced axing was to deliver the message to each person as directly as possible, and where possible, utilize two people to do it—one, usually the supervisor, to deliver the unexpected termination news and leave the scene quickly, and the other to stay behind and talk the typically-shocked manager through their benefits and next steps. Bad cop, good cop. It worked well. That Sunday night, however, I would be both.

I put on a decent shirt and some jeans, imbibed the Riesling warming in the bathroom, brushed my teeth, went downstairs, hugged my wife and assured her I was okay to drive, grabbed the keys, and jumped in our van—a roomy, red Ford Windstar that held the five of us comfortably. No pen, no paper, no Post-Its. I memorized enough of the story to tell my dad that it was down to the two of us, and I would handle the burden of what came next, if necessary—if he wanted me to.

The next hour-plus in the minivan was a blur. Mental role playing of what to say to my dad, mixed with voicemails left for my boss and coworkers to alert them of the coming days' unknowns, mixed with memories of my brother on the ranch and when we last saw him at our house on the river, mixed with horrible thoughts of that horrible act in the desert. The drive to my dad's was endless, but I was there before

I knew it. Sunset came and went. Of course, the evening's darkness closed in on me as I knocked on his front door to deliver even darker news.

Picture an almost-eighty-five-year-old man going from delighted surprise, to complete dread, to inconsolable sadness in a matter of seconds. There was only one way to tell him, much like how I told my wife; direct, no sugar. The honesty was painful. The guilt, insufferable.

We cried together. We hugged each other. We postulated the "why" at his kitchen table, our eyes red and swollen as I sat in front of him and held his soft, smooth hands. Without pause, he asked me if I could deal with all the arrangements, the paperwork, the logistical and mental messiness that came with a long-distance gunshot to the chest. In no uncertain terms he told me he just couldn't do it.

It was then that I first realized that as strong and as confident as I remembered him to be, and thought he still was, he just wasn't anymore. And he needed my help.

He got up slowly and made his way around me, toward the bathroom to his antique safe, the one in his broom closet covered with old newspapers and Kroger bags, the one he transported from both the first house I remembered and the ranch—the short, stocky safe weighing a few hundred pounds of solid steel with a silky-smooth combination dial that responded faithfully to alternate twists of 22-72-52-90. He opened it and pulled out a bundle of heavy-bond pocket folders for me to take, each a tad larger than a business envelope—the same documents I grabbed from my dresser as I headed to Havenshore because of that goddamn stent. Neither of us knew what legal approvals or validations would be needed in Vegas or elsewhere, so he gave me what he thought was important or potentially useful. It was his way of helping.

I took the folders, hugged my dad hard, and made the lonely drive home in the dark to see my family. The weight of that conversation had been lifted from my shoulders but quickly settled around my ankles as I engaged the cruise control and contemplated what I needed to do next. The to-do list and project plan that I built in my head was mostly a list of unknowns—and mostly generated by what I'd seen in movies, heard at the office, or watched friends manage for their loved ones. And it meant a few days in Vegas at places and with people that weren't remotely part of the typical "few days in Vegas." The weight had settled, but I had to carry it for my dad. And for my brother. At least that's why I suspected he left my name and number for whomever found him. Hopefully out of confidence and not out of spite.

The month of May was long and drained all of us. Actually vaporized us. The elation and celebration of our oldest's high school graduation and college plans were muted by my brother's news and the refocusing of emotion, time, and attention on all that came next to understand—*attempt* to understand—what had happened, and to close the tragic final chapter in his too-short story.

Completing the task required us to deal with the cremains we chaperoned back from Vegas, tightly packed in my roll-on, next to my shaving kit and dirty clothes, in a thick, translucent plastic bag—and much heavier than expected. I couldn't help but wonder if it was truly my brother or just a random mélange of ash and chips from the funeral home oven. Pushing my pessimism aside, I generated the necessary belief we got what we paid for in our $1,200, and the remains were his. *Him.*

My brother sat securely in a small cardboard box in our extra bedroom when we returned from Vegas. Near the printer. Determining what to do with him, how to pay our last respects, required thought and discussion between my dad, my wife, and me, though my dad's contribution was limited to a "whatever you want" each time he was asked. I recalled the happier times with my brother, and most of those were from the ranch when we were kids, usually when we played and swam in the concrete pool. Every vision I had of him in that pool included a wet, wide-eyed smile or laugh with his thin, straight blonde hair matted to his head or his crew cut glistening in the sun like my dad's.

So we decided water would be his final resting place, and the Mennawa River his cemetery. I was sure he'd approve. Maybe that's why he left my name and number. I hoped so.

With the hospital butted up to the river, it was a near-perfect place—quiet, safe, plenty of parking and riverbank access—for all of us to say goodbye to our son, uncle, and brother. I had crafted a brief eulogy a few days prior at the office, during that quiet time in the morning, after the oatmeal and before the chaos, and emailed it home.

Rather than try something spontaneous that captured the moment as we spread his remains, I focused my effort on writing a few words that would hopefully take my dad back to some happier times, while reinforcing to our kids that their uncle did experience some joy and playfulness in his life, regardless of how sorrowful his end. I printed it out next to my brother, and took both with us as we drove south and picked up my dad at his house that warm Saturday afternoon at the end of May.

As usual, my dad was thrilled to see the kids, and vice versa. They joked back and forth on the short drive to the hospital in the spacious Windstar. The mood cooled as I parked "Ruby" in the open outdoor lot near the river, south of the ER and not far from a walk path that paralleled the west bank. We emptied the van en masse, while the octogenarian exited slowly from the front bucket seat. The air was calm, and the evening was peaceful, as we looked for a shaded refuge close to the water. We spoke quietly to each other as we approached a small clearing near the path, collectively becoming mindful of why we were there. Our journey resembled the short treks from parking lot to church, which for us were few and far between. But on that

Saturday, as the birds and insects quieted, and the river purred with power next to us, I knew we picked the right place for my brother's Mass. We were in the right pew, in the right church that day.

We gathered in a close circle and held hands. My brother rested in the box at our feet. I pulled the folded eulogy from the front pocket of my pants, took a deep breath as I peered at it below my glasses, and verbally limped into what had been excruciating to type:

When we were little, my brother and I learned to swim in the in-ground pool on our farm. But he was primarily an underwater swimmer, and he did so with his arms pressed firmly to his sides and his feet kicking him forward. He glided smoothly around the pool, while the rest of us envied his ease of motion. When he was in the pool, he seemed to belong there, and he was at home underwater, maneuvering everywhere with speed and confidence. He was a blonde-haired seal...a towheaded trout. I remember him happy, playful, and smiling in the sun whenever he was in that pool. Out of the pool, we were antagonists and holy terror together as young brothers, but in the pool, we were happy kids full of laughter and mischief.

I couldn't continue. My lungs froze. My jaw locked, and my abdomen clenched. I cried in short gasps, unable to read anymore. As brothers, we weren't close, but I couldn't summon the strength to say goodbye to him forever. Not even in my own words.

My wife cradled me around the shoulders as I reached out with the wrinkled paper to our oldest son, hoping he'd take it and finish what I'd started. In a moment of unplanned maturity and love, he tackled what I couldn't and finished the sendoff with a tear-tinged eloquence; he made my brother and me so proud:

This evening we will spread his ashes in the river. When doing so, I'll think of him smiling at us and being happy to be back in the water—water that brings

155

us life, health, strength, energy, freedom, and peace. The same elements that he may have been searching for but could not find when he chose to end his life too early for us to understand. And though he may not have accepted our offers to help him while he was with us physically, I doubt he would decline our love and support this evening in returning him to a place where he was truly happy and full of joy, and where he can always be with us. May he rest in peace and swim forever in our hearts.

Amen.

I hugged my son hard and thanked him, but nowhere close to what he deserved. Our small circle of sadness cried softly in each other's arms, no doubt creating a modest spectacle on the walk path, but also not caring if we were. That moment together—and the warmth my son had generated with his voice—were needed to help us heal, regardless of where we were and who was watching.

But sharing our grief was just the first act in completing my brother's journey that evening, so I picked up the bag of ashes and headed toward the river with everyone, looking for a place to spread him safely. In a somewhat precarious spot on the bank, my wife and I leaned out with the large bag and spilled my brother into the river, as my dad and kids watched curiously, with heavy hearts. Our effort was less than elegant, as most of the ashes were swept away in the water, while some settled on the bank below us; but we accomplished what we set out to do, returning my brother to a place of comfort and allowing us all to say our goodbyes.

Yes, the river was there running.

#

"Hello?"

The voice behind me was faint but startling. I turned around quickly. It was Marcia, the social worker, stepping halfway into the room.

"Hello. I'm sorry," she said, "the hospice nurse now has another appointment at eleven. Is it okay if she comes by between one and two this afternoon?"

Of course it was, but I looked at the smug wall clock anyway. It was 10:41 a.m.

"Sure, that's fine," I replied, reassessing my game plan to find food and coffee, sooner than later.

"Thanks. Is there anything I can get you?" Marcia asked.

"No, I'm good."

"Okay. If there are any other changes, I'll let you know, but Anne will be here around one. Good luck."

"Thanks."

As Marcia pulled the sliding door closed, I pulled out my phone to update my wife on the change in plans.

Meeting with hospice changed to 1p.

Will keep you posted.

She responded seconds later.

Ok. Love you! Eat something.

I pressed my thumb on her text and tapped the heart that popped up. I loved her message, but I loved her more.

Before putting my phone away, I searched my text strings and found our family group messages. It was that time.

Grateful to be with Papa. He's resting

comfortably. Love you all!

I paused and looked at my dad to confirm, his mouth partially open, snoring with some effort, but he generally seemed at peace. *Send.*

Within a few seconds of each other, four hearts popped back at me, filling the room with enough love for the both of us. We really weren't alone.

HOUR 11: The MOVE

Without much effort, the battery in my phone had dropped to 44 percent. The morning's digital stress, as simple and unanimated as it was, had sapped the energy of my old device as predicted. *Not to worry*, I thought to myself as I leaned over and reached into my jacket pocket for the lightning cable I'd brought with me.

But then—*Crap!*—I realized immediately—*Crap!*—I hadn't brought a plug head, having relied on the port in the car. *Crap!* Again, not to worry, as I was sure that somewhere amongst all the glitzy electronics that beeped and whirred and pulsated in the ICU room, keeping my dad alive and Medicare minions busy, I would find a USB port to partner with my cable to bring more life to my aging phone.

I scoured the equipment surrounding my dad. There was no CPU for the computer which was cabled to the wall. None of the monitors or other state-of-the-art apparatus housed the rectangular hole I needed, nor did the feature-filled mechanical bed my dad occupied. As I moved my fruitless search to the electrical outlets on the wall, I was confident someone from the hospital staff would poke their head in during my investigation and of course assume the worst: "Hi. Sorry. No, I was looking to plug in my phone, not pull the plug on my dad," I was prepared to respond.

My dad continued to sleep comfortably as my frustration built. If awake, he would have given me plenty of advice and direction on where to look and what to do, regardless of not knowing a USB port from a hole in the ground. He thrived on thinking he knew it all, but also liked to feign sage-like ignorance of some mundane or made-up phenomena like, "Why do I always find something in the last place I look?" or "Why does my beard grow faster in the summer?" In his mind, he was Edison, Ford, Rockne, and Plato all baked together in a big Polish casserole. I was kind of glad he was asleep for this one.

Then I spied it—an unspoiled USB port in the TV cable box waiting patiently for my lightning cord! I pulled out my phone to quench its electro-thirst, AND! Nothing. The familiar, muffled *pong* that confirmed commencement of my fatigued phone's lithium-ion replenishment didn't *pong*. I checked the connections. Nada. Phone to box to wall. Juiceless. I triple-checked. Dead. Perfect for the ICU. On par with the day. I lost. The room won.

As much as I wanted to play around with the gadgets and figure out the power puzzle, I also wanted to sit with my dad. I was down to 40 percent, which was enough for a few more hours, assuming I stayed away from videos or phone calls. I turned off Bluetooth and put it into low power mode, shoved the phone back in my pocket, and sat down next to my dad—who was in a low power mode of his own. He seemed a little restless as I reached for his hand. Reflexively, he squeezed me with his thumb as I gripped him lightly, trying not to wake him but to let him know I was back by his side.

As I settled myself in the chair, I put my other hand on his forearm to balance my position and looked at his weary face. I'd seen that face before, usually when he hadn't slept well and woke up just before I arrived with his groceries and goodies from my wife. That look always worried me and caused me to think his decline was imminent. Those visits were short and disturbing.

But then a week later, he would be as feisty as ever, eager to complain

159

about the Cubs, bitch about the Bears, or cut a rug with my daughter. Those were the visits, more often than not, that made me think he'd live forever. Or at least long enough to regale the veterans' home with his naval stories and exaggerated feats of athletic prowess.

Unfortunately, the sands of Dad's forever spilled quickly onto the pillow as his crippled hourglass emptied unabated in front of me. It was disturbing.

I slid forward in the chair and leaned over the bed rail, still holding him with both hands.

"I love you, Dad."

I needed to say it, not knowing if he heard me, but needing to let it out. I should have said it to my mom and to my brother, but I didn't. Maybe it was the river and my reflections that drove me to tell him. Or that we might not have another phone call to end with those words. Like we'd always done since my brother passed. Whatever the reason, I was glad I did.

"Heaven!" my dad blurted out, his head coming inches off the pillow with eyes wide open, staring straight at the wall in front of him, as if he were somewhere else. I grabbed his hand and arm tightly, half scared for him, and half for me.

"Dori!" or something like it, came out of him next. It sounded like my mom's name, Lori. His head fell back to the pillow, but his gaze was locked.

"Dad, hey, Dad, it's okay. I'm right here; I'm right here," I said, still stunned by his outbursts. "Are you alright?"

He turned his head slowly toward me, gradually waking but looking stunned and unsure of who I was and where he was. His glazed and bloodshot eyes stared past me. I assumed the painkiller had sent him deep into some dreamscape. *Inception* level-three deep. It was either that, or this was the end. I perked up with a new, caffeinated-like attention.

Then he blinked.

"My throat's dry. Can I get a drink?" His voice was faint, and he was still waking up. But he was back to the present.

I reached around me for the Styrofoam cups, grabbing the one with the straw, and held it to his lips. He sipped mightily until he couldn't.

"Oh, gosh, the pain is really bad," he said as he turned his head away from me, drops of warm water trickling down his whiskered cheek and neck.

"It looked like you were having a nightmare or something. Do you remember?"

I wanted him to talk a little, tell me what he was thinking, or seeing, that jolted him nearly upright.

"My lips are dry. Can I get something?"

He was uncomfortable in about every way possible in that bed.

"Sure. I'll put it on," I said as he twisted toward me again so I could apply the balm.

"Oh, my back really hurts."

Extracting the details of his dream, his vision, would have to wait.

"I'll go get the nurse, Dad. I'll be right back."

I put the Chapstick on the table as I stood to go find Katie.

Before I could push the chair away from the bed, and without summons, she arrived. As if she heard him. Or knew I was coming to fetch her. The coincidence was eerie.

"Hi Martin. I'm so sorry, I'm late for your medication. Are you feeling more pain?" she asked.

Katie was still operating at an energy level beyond what my dad and I could muster together, but I could tell her shift was wearing on her. The tight ponytail had loosened around her temples, and her scrubs showed the expected work wrinkles from twisting, pulling, bending, and injecting. But she continued to smile at my dad.

He, however, was unable to reply in kind.

161

"My back hurts a lot," he groaned. "It's really bad."

Katie held his hand as he grimaced.

"Well, let's get you something to take care of that," she said.

He was still important to her, and she wanted him to know it.

"He just woke up a few minutes ago, and started complaining about the pain right away," I recounted to her, talking across his torso. "Is it possible to give him a stronger dose?"

"I'll give him the current dose now, then I'll see if the doctor will up it again."

She held Dad's hand as she talked to me in a softer, more casual tone. "Or maybe they'll put him on an IV drip."

"Great, thank you," I said.

She was being as helpful as possible, but I could tell she wanted to do more. Holding his hand while he suffered was all I could really ask for.

"Okay, Martin, let's get you feeling better!" Katie's voice bounced with promise as she pulled away and logged in to the computer to start slaying some pain.

"Dad, when she's done, she'll ask the doctor for a stronger dose next time," I said, confirming for him while also reminding her.

"Make it a double," my dad jested in total seriousness.

Katie smiled at him as she pushed the syringe plunger with a steady, controlled ease. Mercy mission accomplished.

As she wrapped up and logged out of the computer, she reached for Dad's hand again.

"Okay, I'm going to look for the doctor and ask about your next dose. Can I get you anything, either of you?"

"No, thank you. You're an angel," my dad said with conviction.

What had he seen in his dream?

"No, I'm good. Thanks," I said, as Katie patted Dad's hand patiently, then pulled away.

"I'll be back later, Martin. Get some rest."

She exited the room and pulled the curtain closed behind her. My dad's eyelids followed, closing as she vanished through the doors.

I could only imagine what my dad may have been dreaming when he lurched awake earlier, or what he was hallucinating by way of the opioid cocktail served to his veins, but I assumed it was related to my mom. It had been over thirty years since they were together. Many more since they enjoyed each other. They had gone through some rough times, like all couples do, but they kept at it, trying to make it work in spite of their finances, their health, their families, their cultures, and whatever else got in their way during their almost-three-decades partnership.

Sometimes their effort was fruitful, many times not. Or somewhere in between. Her stubbornness and his desire to please her, or to be the "man of the house," was their recipe for quasi-success. Or limited failure.

When Mom chided him to come home during the rioting at the high school near our ranch, Dad complied as expected, for her safety and ours. But since he wasn't there immediately or when she felt she was in danger, his effort rated a C-minus at most. And she wouldn't let him forget it. In fact, the main thing I took away from that day had nothing to do with injustice or oppression, or the grim shouting from furious teenagers, but it was my mom's command, "Don't leave us here alone again!"

The operative word being *again*.

I had suspected the "first time" was during the big snowstorm of '67—when we trampled the milky-white deluge while constructing our fabulous Frosty, gnawed greasy Slim Jims, and zoomed down the snow pile into the brights of the old Ford. That day of wintery escapades was irreplaceable, in reality and memory. The night before, however, Mom and Dad had filled the drafty, old farmhouse with everything that wasn't that day—anger, cursing, and plenty of Marlboro 100s.

I looked at my dad snoring softly and helplessly, hoping the narcotics were doing their job, as I tried to recall that fateful January night on the ranch. The horizontal version of him was much different than the one from that evening. As the digital monitors chirped above, confirming his medicated calm, I closed my eyes to wander back half a century. To a time less tranquil.

#

"We could have died here!" my mom cried, leaning back against the kitchen sink.

"You were fine! You were all fine! There was nothing I could do," my dad snapped. He kept his distance but didn't back off.

"You could have come home!"

"The goddamn roads were closed. There's two feet of snow out there! Three or four with the drifts."

The fury they whipped up in the narrow space had them both red-faced and yelling at peak volume in between nervous drags on their cigarettes. My brother and I stood close to each other at the foot of the stairs, where the dining and living rooms met, and peeked around the corner in terror as our parents exploded in the kitchen. My brother began to cry.

Hearing the whimper, my dad turned toward us, his forehead clenched and eyes fixed in our direction.

"Get up to your room! Right now! Go!"

I pushed my brother aside and hurried up the creaky stairs as he followed, still crying.

"It's okay, just get in your bed and stop crying. He'll hear you," I said as we finished our climb and turned into our room.

My brother hustled to get under his blankets and turned on his side to watch me as I crouched at our open door to continue listening. We were both able to hear the steely argument directly below us, muffled but clear and full of venom, as cigarette smoke polluted the house beyond its norm.

#

I opened my eyes and looked at my dad, still dozing peacefully despite the tubes and repetitive ICU clatter doing their best to wake him. I realized I was remembering things I had buried miles away and years ago. *Had I buried them or just forgot they happened, clearing my buffer so I could fill it with thoughts not so sour?* I wanted to tell him. I wanted him to validate or correct me. I wanted him to fill in the gaps. I wanted a lot right then, but it wasn't happening. Not with him pumped full of painkiller and cognitively AWOL. I closed my eyes and went back to crouching at our bedroom door, before the buffer cleared again.

#

Mom continued her tirade. "Do you know what I've been through here the past week?"

#

Week? I swore we'd only been snowbound in the house a couple days. Did it seem like a week to her? Was I just on the dayless calendar of a five-year-old? Was it both?

#

"I know, I know," my dad said.

I could hear the lighter flint snap as it tried to fire another Marlboro.

"No! No, you don't know! While you were at your mom's, eating homecooked meals, I was here in the goddamn blizzard with nothing!"

"The first night I slept in Mennawa, at school. We couldn't get out either!" Dad said.

"At least you were with your friends! I was here with the kids, goddamn it!" Mom was still heated. "You could have called."

"Son of a bitch! The phones didn't work; the lines were all down!"

"But why didn't you come home?!"

165

My mom was angry, and she wanted some answers.

"They only plowed some of the city streets, so I went to my mother's. I barely got there. The radio said the roads out of town were blocked and there was no way out, so I stayed there."

"Yeah, you stayed THERE! While I was HERE! I trudged through the goddamn snow, to the goddamn truck stop, to buy goddamn milk and Twinkies! With two kids! You left me here with nothing!"

\#

That horrific white day, long forgotten, or suppressed, barreled back into my consciousness. Mom had bundled up my brother and me, and led us to the truck stop on the other side of the snow-packed highway to find food. What would have been, in the summer, a casual fifteen-minute walk past the pool, north through the open field and past the tall trees with the heavy hedge apples, seemed to be a haunting, hours-long expedition as I held Mom's gloved hand in my left, my brother's in my right, and we all fought the blowing snow and wind in our faces while plodding our way to the truck stop. I was scared. We were all scared. Was it life or death? No. Did we know that then? Hell no. If needed, there were plenty of houses nearby, though quiet and muted by the blizzard's ivory shards that blew hard around us. But at the time, in that wind-whipped sea of snow, the truck stop was as close to the wilderness as it was to Route 6. Thankfully, it was open. The cinder-blocked space was cold and quiet, frigidly spooky as the wind swirled around it outside. And thankfully someone was there, maybe stuck like my dad was at his high school in Mennawa. They sold my mom whatever she could afford and carry home in a single brown paper bag. We didn't dawdle, staying just long enough to thaw and compose ourselves before heading back in our three-person chain. The journey home was somewhat less laborious, as we followed the chunky path we had created earlier. But it was no less tense than our original trek. When we finally got back to the chilly peace of the farmhouse, Mom fired up and drained a Marlboro before any of us could get our coats off. Then fired up another one as she emptied the bag.

I remembered why she was so pissed.

#

"There was plenty here for you," my dad said.

I could hear him slamming the cupboard doors shut after opening them to show my mom what they held. Or didn't.

"You left us with *nothing!*" my mom said, convinced of our destitution. The lighter flint snapped again, as did Dad.

"Bullshit! I got home as soon as I could. Hell, tonight was the first time Jake could get his truck out! Cost me forty bucks to get him here to plow the drive!" Dad said, referring to one of his friends from the bowling alley who plowed snow in the winter and sometimes helped him with hay for the horses.

"Well, I hope you got a lot to eat at your mom's, 'cause there's not much left here."

"I'm not hungry. I'll take you to the store tomorrow for groceries. I'm gonna have another beer and go to bed." Dad was tired, and tired of arguing.

Mom persisted. "I'm not shopping! I've done all the goddamn shopping I'm gonna do this week!"

"Fine, I'll do it myself! Like everything else around here! Son of a bitch!" I could tell Dad was heating up again.

I heard the distinct sound of a bottle cap hitting the counter, followed by my dad's hefty footsteps heading through the dining room toward the stairs. I backed away from the door frame and slowly pushed the door almost closed, then crawled quietly to my bed which was closest to the door.

"Is he coming?" my brother whispered.

From the hallway light that seeped into the room, I could see my brother was still turned toward me, under the blankets but face exposed. And full of fear.

"Shut up," I said, in a harsh hushed tone.

167

I scurried to get under my blankets with minimal commotion. It was not the time to have Dad in our room uninvited. We both looked at each other and held our breath as he reached the top of the stairs.

"Get to bed, you two," Dad said sternly. He knew we were awake. He always knew.

A few steps later, we heard his bedroom door shut. I could still see my brother's face as his eyes closed in the pale light and we sighed together with relief. Then Mom's footsteps, lighter but just as tired, gave away her position in the house as she climbed the uneven stairs. Her image blocked the light momentarily as she passed our door on the way to their bedroom. A second later, and with a loud click, she flipped the light switch to darken the hall, blackening my brother's face and everything else in our room.

The knob on their bedroom door rattled as she opened it, then again as she shut it firmly behind her, obviously not caring if we were asleep. And we weren't. The ensuing argument and garbled shouting we heard through the wall made sure of that. At least until we were too tired to listen and wept ourselves to sleep.

Within hours, though, the magic of the next day's snow pile made it all seem like a dream.

#

I opened my eyes again and looked at the weakened man lying in front of me, his pain numbed but ever-present. Those smoky memories, unearthed replays of wretched times long forgotten, served no purpose in the ICU that morning other than to make me wish I had more time to talk with him. To ask him what happened. Not necessarily about that night at the farmhouse, or the snow-drenched days before it, or the following year with the bedlam and the bullhorns, but more generally, what happened between him and Mom?

Sure, those events shaped how they felt about each other, and themselves. I remembered, as a teenager, Mom hoarding and hiding everything from Johnnie Walker Red to Campbell's soup to Reese's peanut butter cups in every nook and cranny of our house because of, as she said, "that blizzard on the farm." Her neuroses to over-inventory drove their bank account down and the tension between them through the roof.

But there had to be something more.

Something that made her reliant on the chalky, flavorless Maalox antacid that sat next to the Seagram's on the farmhouse kitchen counter.

Something that made her want to go back to school and become more independent.

Something that ultimately drove them to leave my brother and me in California while they flew back and prepared to separate. And move again.

#

During the summer before I entered fifth grade, we boarded an Amtrak train in Mennawa and took a rare family vacation to visit my mom's father and stepmother in southern California. Ventura. For my brother and me, the train ride was interesting and swift—and resulted in memorable trips to Disneyland, the beach, Hollywood and its studio lots, and the quarry where my burly, leathered grandpa piloted mammoth, boulder-hauling trucks. We picked lemons and oranges off the trees in the small back patio of my grandpa's house and tasted Jack-in-the-Box burgers for the first time.

And when we ran out of tourist sites in the LA area, my parents squeezed in outings much further north up the Pacific Coast Highway to the opulent Hearst Castle and kitschy Trader Vic's in San Francisco. Flashy, umbrellaed Mai Tais for Mom were required, regardless of time and distance. It was a two-week vacation full of newness, postcard-perfect weather, and attractions we'd only seen on TV.

And then they left.

My uncle, Mom's younger brother, appeared at my grandparents' house a couple of days before our vacation was to end. He was a handsome character who was always quick with a joke and loved to impersonate friends and family equally—almost as much as he loved brunettes, cold beer, and steaks medium-rare. Carefree in every sense of the word. My brother and I loved being around him, and he treated us without regard to our age.

Dad, however, wasn't as enthused about our uncle as we were, skeptical of his impulsiveness, rowdy behavior, and influence on us. But my uncle's willingness to participate in my parents' plan ensured he'd always have a place at Dad's table.

That plan, orchestrated behind our backs, consisted of my brother and me staying with our uncle and grandparents another week with the promise of "more fun," while Mom and Dad flew home to work through their issues and ultimately their mutual separation. Actually, the plan likely started long before we jumped on the Amtrak and headed west. And our parents' desire to be without each other, to put their co-generated anguish on pause, was camouflaged with precision by all parties during the entire vacation, including the week after they left us.

Our Ventura hosts and their smiling faces treated us to more beach, more ocean, and more Jack-in-the-Box fare. Meanwhile, Mom and Dad were back on the ranch undoubtedly yelling, cursing, and smoking like chimneys while they divvied up responsibilities and struggled to be civil. Back in California, we were none the wiser of the deception being waged and the outcomes being concocted on our behalf.

What the camo hid, and what we learned after being escorted home by our uncle on our very first plane ride, was that our life on the ranch was quickly ending. The long drive from O'Hare, and a detour to drop off our uncle near Mennawa, gave us time to tell our parents of the additional fun we'd had in their absence. We told them about the

James Bond movies at the drive-in. We told them about the baseball game at Dodger Stadium and showed them the miniature bats our uncle bought us. We told them about the jellyfish that washed up on the beach, and all the citrus we plucked without them. But as soon as we got to the ranch, it was their turn to tell us something.

Even before we could empty the single, aqua-paneled suitcase that accompanied us on the flight to Chicago—the same suitcase my brother had fractionally filled a few years earlier with nothing but his Batman underwear and plastic baseball mitt, then dragged down the gravel lane bawling in an effort to run away from home after another senseless fight I'd won—they brought us into the living room of the farmhouse to give us the gloomy news.

We sat in a tight, makeshift circle of four as my dad told us that Mom would be moving, and we would be going with her. Not staying with him. He was somber but direct. Mom said little. I remembered being surprised by our first, and last, "family meeting," then shocked and confused by my dad's announcement, then angry I'd be leaving my friends and all that was around me. Then saddened by the realization of our parents' new relationship—Mom versus Dad. They seemed sad, too.

"When?"

"Soon."

"Do we know where we'll live?"

"No."

"Can we come back here and visit?"

"No, we're selling the house."

"Where's Dad gonna live?"

"We don't know."

All shitty answers to the few questions that came to me as my eyes filled with loss and the wet residue that tagged along with it. Loss of my dad. Loss of the pool. Loss of the danger-laden clay pits I'd finally mastered, slaloming on my bike. Loss of literally everything I could remember in my life till then. Literally, *everything*.

Suffice it to say, our vacation—and any further basking in its sun-soaked memories—ended there in the living room, with empty stares at its threadbare carpet. And no hugs.

The weeks that followed were an emotional and logistical blur. My mom rented a small, two-bedroom apartment, far from Beaufort and closer to Mennawa. We bought bunk beds for the new place and Mom got a nursing job fifteen minutes away at Regents hospital. We started at a new school within a few blocks of the apartment. Dad stayed at the ranch that fall and visited us occasionally after school and football practice. Sometimes he'd stay late, and they'd talk after we went to bed, but we could still hear them through our bedroom's cheap, hollow-core door. They talked, they argued, they cried. Mostly on the tiny loveseat that ultimately earned its name.

At some point before Thanksgiving, Mom and Dad agreed to reconcile their differences and buy a house near the apartment. My brother and I were thrilled about being a family again, and we accompanied them on their house hunt. Dad preferred the smaller places that needed work. Mom liked the larger, newer homes that carried heftier price tags. We settled on one she liked: a two-story, four-bedroom, brick square with a full basement, front and back yards, and centrally located in walking range of the elementary, middle, and high schools. And a built-in intercom system Dad would eventually use to belt out his version of reveille to wake us for school.

It was a nice house with all the amenities we needed, space for our German shepherd, and a deep closet for Dad's safe. But it wasn't the ranch in any way, shape, or form. In some ways that was good, especially in terms of the work required to maintain it. In other ways, it was disappointing. Or just a stark change from what we were used to and came to know as a way of life.

It was a change we were willing to swallow as the cost of being a family foursome again.

Once we moved, we never looked back. We never went back, either. The ranch, the horses, the minibike, the swimming pool, the snakes, the orchard, the bowling alley—it all became the past. But even with those years and those memories behind us, and the desire to move forward under the same roof, not everything was forgotten. Not everything was new. The brick house and the move just put a fresh coat of paint on a brittle frame. A frame that, over time, weakened and sagged—until it collapsed.

#

"Hello? Excuse me."

A tall, professional-looking woman with a white lab coat and brown skin parted the curtains and walked into Dad's room. Her jet-black hair made her jacket seem whiter.

"I'm Dr. Ramachandran, I'm the staff physician today. I'll be treating your father."

It took me a few seconds to refocus my attention bedside with Dad.

"Hi there. Will Dr. Simonson be coming by?" I asked.

"Well, he doesn't have privileges at the hospital, so our practice provides coverage for his patients here," she said, walking towards my dad.

She pulled a business card out of her pocket and handed it to me, then turned and logged into the computer. I curiously glanced at the card while thinking her presence there was odd—*Simonson's office was right across the street on the medical campus*—but then quickly assumed she was legit as she accessed Dad's info without hesitation. It was a strange, confusing encounter.

Dad stirred as she reviewed his chart on the screen.

"Hi, Martin. I'm Dr. Rama. The nurse said you're in a lot of pain. How are you feeling?"

The tone of her voice was measured and warm as she made an extra-friendly attempt to engage him.

But Dad had to wake up first.

"Who are you?" he asked.

"I'm Dr. Rama. How are you feeling?"

"The pain is really bad, doctor."

Dad sounded like a broken record, in a frustrating way. Whatever they had been injecting in him the past eight hours was only Band-Aiding the hell he was in.

The doctor checked Dad's vitals on the monitor and scanned the IV bag hanging above him.

She looked at me intently.

"He's going into hospice, correct?"

I nodded.

"I'm going to put him on a morphine drip to make him as comfortable as possible. We'll start it on his next dose."

"Good. Thank you," I said.

She turned back toward Dad.

"Martin, we're going to increase your medication to help you with the pain. The nurse will take care of it next time she sees you."

She shifted to the computer, clicked and keyed her instructions, then logged out.

"Okay. Thank you, doctor," Dad said, struggling to express his gratitude.

"You're welcome. You should feel better with the new meds."

She looked at me as she peeled off her gloves.

"Good luck."

She was being positive, but I could tell she knew what was ahead. For him, and for us.

"Thanks."

She turned and left the room. I slid her card in my pocket, doubting

I'd ever need it again.

Her work there was done.

"Dad, is there anything I can get you?"

"Water," he said.

I held the straw to his mouth while he sucked. The irregular sleep in the ICU was tiring for him, and it showed in every pale pore of his face. He was hanging on at the cruel mercy of that goddamn stent, and his body was flooded with enough drugs to soothe a stallion, but I wanted to tell him everything I remembered and ask him everything I wanted to know. There was still so much I didn't understand and had never questioned. But I was too late. It was time to keep him comfortable and make him smile when he could. It was his time, not mine. And the damn clock on the wall wouldn't let me forget it.

It was 11:52 a.m.

HOUR 12: The DRIP

"How are the kids doing?"

Out of the blue, my dad piped up, asking about his grandkids. He always wanted to know how they were doing, but his question surprised me as he labored to stay awake under the drowsy weight of the painkiller.

I played along, wanting him to enjoy every possible positive thought while he still had thoughts to enjoy.

"They're all good, Dad. I told them you're in the hospital. They all said hi and send their love, and hope you feel better soon."

I translated the hearts they had texted, adding a few words to supply well-intentioned meaning to their thumbed sentiments.

"Tell them to have fun while they're young," he demanded.

"I will, Dad."

That was his go-to motto, his parting words of wisdom, whenever he saw them together or individually. No matter what topics they talked about when visiting him—sports, college, music, navy, work, travel—he always wrapped up the discussion, if not the entire visit, with those five words, "Have fun while you're young," and he meant it each time.

"Have fun" was not in his lexicon when we were growing up—when toughness, his and ours, was the preferred feeling to have. But Dad had definitely softened since the time my brother and I were my kids' ages.

Maybe not softened as much as actually developed a level of patience for those things he couldn't change. Or control. Or in response to what his body had begun telling him was doable and suitable for someone in his seventies, then eighties, then nineties.

His awareness of his capabilities and impairments was acute. He realized his once-firm and flexible physique could only do so much, yet he continued to push it as far as it—and his eyesight—would allow. As his body aged, he paid attention to its cues and picked his battles with things that required energy and stamina—like yardwork, shopping, home repairs, and, most importantly, other people. Maybe it was more about tolerance and acceptance—accepting situations and limitations, and others' views—than it was about patience. And maybe it was his acceptance of what he could no longer accomplish but still longed to do that caused him to echo the advice of having fun in youth. I just hoped they'd listened to the Polish Plato.

"Dad, the hospice nurse is going to come by in about an hour. After we see her, I'll let the kids know when they can come and visit you."

In my head, and my wife's of course, we were already making plans for our kids to fly in or drive up to visit my dad. I knew the kids, highly capable young adults, were already planning it as well, without me explicitly telling them what to do or when to do it. They were all pretty good time and task managers, especially for the things that were important like birthdays, holidays, and graduations. And aging grandparents.

"Oh jeez, they don't have to see me like this. I just saw them for Christmas," he said, slightly slurring his words. "You know, you don't have to stay here with me. If you're tired, you can go home. I'll be fine here." He never wanted to be a burden.

"Dad, it's okay. They want to see you. And I'm good here. I might run down and get some coffee and something to eat in a little while. Can I get you anything?"

"Yeah, something to get rid of this pain."

"Well, they don't have that in the cafeteria, but the nurse should be by soon with more painkiller."

Then I thought about the Dairy Queen down the street, near Dove's Park.

"Dad, would you like a Dilly Bar or a chocolate shake from the Dairy Queen? I can go get one for you and be back in half an hour."

I had already bought into my own tasty idea regardless of his response.

"They're not open. It's too cold out."

He was still present, reminding me brusquely it was January, no matter how sunny and mild it looked out the window. No matter how much I could taste that chocolatey, soft-serve shake right then.

I felt stupid, but hopefully the thought counted.

"Crap, you're right," I said, squeezing his hand to confirm his correctness.

He squeezed back.

"Can I have more water?" he asked.

"Do you think you can eat anything, Dad?"

He sipped on the straw I offered him, then pulled away.

"My throat is sore. Just water."

Unfortunately, it seemed that his diet for the day was going to be all liquids, by mouth or IV. I couldn't envision anything by spoon or by hand that required him to chew, or even swallow with effort. The upside was he knew the DQ was closed for the season. I was thankful, and embarrassed, for that.

"Well, hello again, Martin! I've got your new medication here," Katie called out as she entered the room, full of spirit and armed for battle with a full IV bag in hand.

"I hope it's a double," Dad said.

"Oh, it is!" she said, smiling as she logged in and started manipulating tubes and bags. "It'll take me a few minutes to set you up, but it should help a lot with the pain."

"Oh, good."

"Is that the morphine?" I asked.

"It is. It will definitely help his pain, but it will also knock him out. Did you hear that, Martin?" she asked. "You're going to get pretty sleepy with this new medicine."

"As long as it stops the pain."

"He may sleep soundly, or he may be restless or say some weird stuff when this kicks in," Katie said, alerting me to what was in store as the morphine pounded the pain into submission. "People react differently to it, but usually it just knocks them out good."

Dad's droopy eyes followed her as she maneuvered around his arm, adjusting valves and rerouting tubes, then checked her work versus what was in the computer.

"Am I ready for takeoff?" Dad joked.

His low-key comic relief was a breath of fresh air in the cheerless room and brought grins to both Katie and me.

"Yep, ready to launch!" she said, following his lead.

She held his hand as he blasted off.

"Dad, I'm going to grab something to eat and hit the bathroom. I'll be back in a little while. Need anything before I go?" I said as I got up to leave.

"Martin, if you need anything, I'll be right outside on the floor, okay?" Katie made sure he knew he wouldn't be alone.

"No, I'm fine. Thank you both," he said, eyes closing again.

Katie walked out of the room. I followed close behind her and did a quick 180 before exiting. Dad looked as empty as he did when I arrived in the dark, early, morning hours. Even as the midday sun poured into the room, showing off all the utensils and comforts that were keeping my dad and me in the game, it couldn't make him look less empty.

It just spotlighted what was left undrained by that goddamn stent. I closed the curtain behind me. I was drained as well.

"Thanks for all your help with my dad. I really appreciate it," I told Katie as we walked in the direction of the visitors' lounge.

"No problem. I feel so bad for him. I know that pain is horrible. We'll do what we can to make him comfortable. He's lucky you're here for him."

Without segue or further comment, she veered right to the cluster of workstations occupied by other staff members keying in data and jabbering to each other while staring keenly at their screens. I wanted to thank her again, for being kind to my helpless father, for understanding his pain, for taking time to make both of us feel more comfortable when neither of us really was or could be. For making my dad smile. But she was on to her next task, or next patient. Or next blast off.

I hesitated slightly as she left the path we were on, but then picked up stride again and continued toward the visitors' lounge for a pit stop. It had obviously become visiting hours as the lounge blared with Maury, Jerry, or some other laughable reality shtick—and winter coats, guarded by the TV's unmanned remote, were strewn across the otherwise vacant couches. I slipped into the bathroom then quickly slipped out, walking briskly to the elevator to head downstairs for a brief snack before the one o'clock hospice meeting.

As the elevator motor droned during the slow descent, I pulled out my phone to verify how long I had to forage for myself before heading back up.

Crap! It was 12:24 already! Even more concerning was the lack of juice I was looking at—29 percent! There was no time to belly up to the salad bar or get anything that required preparation in a cafeteria. And I needed a plan for charging my phone, since running to the garage and sitting in the car while my ancient device reclaimed some life wasn't going to happen for another hour and a half, assuming Anne from hospice and Dad accommodated the timeline without delay or disaster. As the elevator doors opened, a mild wave of stress washed over me, to pair with the headache and hunger pangs inside.

Until I saw the coffee stand.

I had forgotten about the caffeine refuge, which was dark and lifeless when I passed it hours before. Since that time, as I held Dad's hand and dozed sporadically in the unyielding curveless armchair, the stand came to life and breathed out caramel, hazelnut, and other slow-roasted vapors that melted my sluggishness and coaxed me to the counter without complaint—a counter that also held a small glass-doored pastry case I hoped would partner with the tall coffee carafes to quickly resuscitate me.

Likewise, however, the hospital lobby had come to life for the day, and its occupants had clearly picked over much of what had been baked and frosted. After a more careful inspection, I spied a plump banana nut muffin in the back they had left for me or that had gone unnoticed. Another thing to be grateful for. I was saved. Sort of.

"Hi. Large hazelnut, please. And the banana muffin," I said, anxiously ordering from the young, lanky barista whose readiness to end the morning was obvious as he continued wiping up around the coffee dispensers without a greeting or eye contact.

"We're out of hazelnut."

Damn, I was looking for something flavored to offset the nothingness of ice chips and hospital water.

"Okay, um, caramel, please."

"That's out, too," he said, still wiping and appearing perturbed. Little did he know that if there were two people in that hospital that deserved to be perturbed, one of them was me, and the other was being dosed out of his misery two floors above us.

"Just regular then."

"Large, right?"

"Right. And the muffin."

"Which one?" he said, blowing any opportunity for a tip.

"Banana nut."

He put down his damp rag, poured the plain coffee, and stuck the muffin in a brown bag as I pulled out my credit card.

"$4.10."

I slid my Visa into the small machine and thought about the airport-like inflated price of my modest brunch as I waited for the okay to remove the card and part ways with my surly server.

"Thanks," I said, not expecting a response and not getting one.

Just like his tip.

I grabbed my version of a Happy Meal then stopped to sweeten the coffee and load up on napkins for the dining event. Behind me in a small sitting area was another big screen TV playing the same drivel that was on in the lounge upstairs, but the lure of a few open chairs and the thought of coffee seconds had me finding a seat next to an unsmiling family conversing in Spanish. They seemed distracted with real life and uninterested in a shitty TV show posing as it.

I gulped down as much of the piping hot coffee as possible with my first sip. Even without the artificial flavors, it was delicious—as was the aroma drifting from it. As I dug into the bag to capture the muffin, I could tell by what was falling off that it was at least a few hours old, if not a few days. But as dry and as brittle as it was, it would be the star of my fifteen-minute feast. Not even the moody barista or TV couple arguing about DNA results was going to ruin my meal.

I pulled out my phone to get a perspective on the day in between warm sips and stale bites. All was fine and thankfully uneventful. I'd text my wife and kids after the hospice meeting, hopefully after coming up with a way to charge my phone. With my hunger temporarily resolved, its battery became my next challenge. I was at 24 percent.

I took a final sip and wiped my mouth with the last napkin. The muffin had been destroyed earlier in ruthlessly repetitive bites while deleting useless emails. Then, as I stood up to stretch and make my way back to my dad, it subtly appeared—behind the lobby columns, the hospital's gift shop exposed itself. Like the coffee stand, I had forgotten about it but was joyed to see it again. Back in the day, when we were kids and had our tonsils taken out, or when Mom was ill, gift shops were basically quiet outlets for get well or sympathy cards, or stuffed animals, or points of sale to order flowers for patients. Not much of a product line to pick from.

Nowadays, however, gift shops more closely resembled the Hudson News convenience stores in airports, retailing everything from toothpaste to T-shirts to simple electronics. Which is exactly what I needed—a basic $5 plug head. I shoved my empty cup and crumpled bag in the garbage can, fittingly placed next to the TV, and looked at my phone before leaving the sitting area: 12:54 p.m.

And it *was* his DNA.

The gift shop was just steps away from me and elevator A. I noticed some wires hanging from a chest-high rack and started there.

Bingo! USB charging cables of all colors, lengths, and plug type were hanging from the rack. But I didn't need any of them. I had my own and just needed an adapter. *Rats!*

As I turned toward the register to ask for help, another rack jumped out directly in front of me holding an assortment of random items including the adapters I was looking for. *Perfect!* I snatched one and made sure it was what I needed, then saw the price sticker on its side—$9.95. The airport business model for captive audiences was obviously successful for hospitals, too.

As much as I bristled at that $10 robbery, I really couldn't complain about hospitals, or health care in general. Modern medicine, which consistently became more modern over time, had looked down on our family somewhat favorably in the half-plus century we'd needed it. It was never cheap, nor was it always effective on the first try, nor was it always customer friendly. But thankfully, in our case, after doggedly navigating the labyrinth of insurance providers, employer plans, government supplements, medical facilities, and private loans—and with good ole fiery bull-headedness—it was usually available, attainable, and eventually affordable when we needed it. And there was no shortage of needing it.

#

"If you two don't stop it back there, I'm going to turn right around and go home!" Dad yelled.

My brother and I were beyond excited as we climbed on top of each other in the backseat of the big Buick to see the concrete cliffs of the canyon that was the Chicago Loop.

"What's that?" my brother asked, looking up but questioning the deafening clatter above us.

"That's the L train," Dad said as he turned off Wabash Avenue into the parking facility.

We continued to crane our necks, as did Mom in the front seat, to take in the massive structures and big city bustling around us—everything our ranch's small town wasn't.

Dad pulled the Buick up to an attendant who gave him a ticket and stuck one on the dash.

"How long?" asked the attendant, managing handfuls of cash, tickets, and a gnarly cigarette.

"Just a few hours," Dad said.

"Okay, leave the keys."

"Everybody get their things; let's go," Dad said.

We grabbed our windbreakers and got out of the car, still looking skyward as pigeons perched everywhere.

"Hey, let's go. Pay attention. There's a lot of cars here," Dad warned.

His voice was but one of several noises swarming around us in an urban concert of honking horns, screeching bus brakes, and that omnipresent train circulating above.

We followed Mom and Dad in tight formation as they strode down the wide city sidewalk.

"Stay close. We're almost there," Dad said.

A few steps later, Dad stopped as Mom disappeared into a revolving door. He urged us to follow her.

"C'mon, let's go. We're going to get something to eat before we see the doctor."

My brother and I followed Mom while Dad trailed us through the door into a busy, bacon-soaked diner. He headed for a booth near the counter and sat down with Mom, while I outmaneuvered my brother for the wall seat opposite them. A friendly waitress greeted us and handed out menus, took our orders, and shouted our requests back to the kitchen behind the counter.

Our breakfast arrived minutes later, and the rest of our time in the diner was spent talking and giggling over fluffy pancakes, eggs up and scrambled, greasy link sausages, fresh orange juice, and multiple coffee refills. And plenty of bacon. The four of us left our morning meal thrilled and content with its freshness and variety—and unable to digest any more.

Dad paid, and we left out the diner's side door into an adjacent wood-paneled lobby toward a bank of fancy elevators. As we all marveled at the ornateness of our surroundings, Dad pushed the up button while the train outside rumbled incessantly. Seconds later, the doors opened, and our rural quartet piled into the elevator along with others heading up. The smell of bacon that had woven itself into our clothes was surely evident to them. We ascended smoothly as my brother and I silently traded elbows with each other. Upon reaching our floor, we emptied out into a quiet, professional-looking foyer with marble tile and oak office doors, and Mom and Dad led us down the hallway to our day's destination.

"We're here to see the doctor for some allergy shots for our son," my dad said to the office receptionist.

My brother had been diagnosed in Mennawa with allergies to certain foods, including a weird allergy to ketchup, which required several rounds of injections that could only be administered by a specialist in Chicago. I never quite knew what symptoms drove my mom to get him tested, or how severe was his affliction, but the cost of his testing and treatment wasn't minor based on the comments Dad made each time we drove back from the Windy City.

Our visit that day was the first of a few, all of which included breakfast at the first-floor diner and a brief walk around the Loop to see the sites—and four or five needle pokes into my brother's arms, which he handled stoically, his pained sniveling muted by the constant roar of the train outside the doctor's windows.

As much as those trips were full of prickly discomfort for my brother, they were also an opportunity for family banter in the Buick and diner—where we focused on topics like the Cubs, skyscrapers, Lake Michigan, and the ever-popular bacon. And if we were really good, or Dad was feeling generous, we'd stop for burgers on the drive home at a south side White Castle, picking up a dozen elfin squares of meat-filled grease for about two bucks and change. Onions and pickles included. And ketchup.

#

Aside from typical inoculations and dentist appointments, and our Havenshore tonsillectomies, that was the first time I remembered the health-care system becoming a necessary—and financially impactful—part of our lives. But it wasn't the last time.

Mom needed it for her ulcer, though her daily gulps of Maalox and Dad's goat milking were efforts to dampen the cost and help her manage her condition on the ranch. Years later, as she succumbed to alcohol and her body failed to metabolize nutrients, the visits to doctors and specialists and her hospitalizations increased, as did the bills they generated. Thankfully, as a teacher, my dad had quality insurance, but he still depended on high-interest loans to cover expenses until she passed. And he was meticulous in his accumulation of receipts to get the full benefit of medical deductions on his taxes each year. Every penny mattered.

The health-care system was needed again in a very big way in my mid-thirties when I was deployed overseas to Belgium for work, an assignment I requested and one my wife was excited about. Our young sons, both under five, would come with us for a two-to-three-year change of pace and plenty of chocolate and travel. But shortly after I arrived in Brussels, misfortune followed, and after seven months of misdiagnoses for a variety of incurable illnesses there, I returned to the States for the holidays with my family to receive the crushing and unwanted Christmas gift of a stage-III lymphoma diagnosis from my GP.

We visited my dad and brother to exchange presents and tell them the news—news that included our decision to return to our recently settled home in Brussels for my treatment. Dad cried on my shoulder and I on his, but he understood our choice to power through the dilemma and try to maintain the new normal we'd just created for our boys.

Six blasts of chemo followed by seventeen radiation sessions comprised my Euro treatment. And insurance covered much of it. It also covered my daughter's birth four days after my final session. The subsequent vasectomy, an attempt at mitigating the financial and emotional risk of my unknown remission, was also covered. I kept three folders of receipts for that chaotic year. Every franc mattered.

And we'd definitely needed the system the past ten years as Dad's health slid and critical treatments—like the placement of that goddamn stent and his post-pneumonia rehab—were needed to keep him going. His midnight ambulance ride and the morphine drip were no exception to the need, as would be the hospice treatment I'd be discussing with Anne. Ten dollars for a phone charger quickly became an annoying rounding error.

With that in mind, I completed my gift shop purchase, then made my escape from the overpriced lobby mall, taking the elevator back up to floor 3, then walking swiftly to the ICU.

I entered Dad's still-quiet room and looked up at the stubborn wall clock: 1:04 p.m. *Hopefully Anne was tardy.*

HOUR 13: The REALITY

I pulled the charging cable out of my jacket pocket and introduced it to the newly acquired adapter. The wall outlet next to me was in an ideal spot, and I connected my phone to bring it more life. It *ponged* with approval as I let it rest and recharge on the counter next to me. Unlike Dad, it had no DNR. And responded without complication or wit. *If only Dad could be revived so easily. If only the machines already plugged into the walls around him could give him back just a nano-fraction of the energy he'd generated in his ninety-five-plus years. Maybe a month,* I hoped. *Or at least a week. If only Dad had a lightning plug of his own. If only.*

But that wouldn't be reality.

REALITY. Dad had written it in all caps, about two inches tall, along the top edge of the flat wall-mirror in his cramped, half-bathroom at home. He'd used what appeared to be Wite-Out, or a small brush and white paint—possibly from one of his old model airplane sets. He'd made sure the letters were level and aligned, likely with tape or a straight edge. And as obvious as it was, the lettering was somewhat inconspicuous under the plain, frosted fixture that lit the room, just above the mirror. The reflection of the black-on-white paisley wallpaper opposite the mirror also helped camouflage his artwork to the uninitiated observer. But make no mistake, the defacing graffiti by the artist-formerly-known-as-my-dad was there to stay.

#

"Dad, what the hell is this?" I asked, noticing his unsettling calligraphy as I washed my hands in the lusterless avocado sink.

From his throne in the kitchen, he knew what I was talking about.

"It's what I have to look at every day."

"*Reality*? Did you do this?"

I probed him like he did my brother some thirty-five years back when my dad was less than excited about the crayon catastrophe my brother created on the ranch radiators in our room. I wasn't nearly as pissed as he was then, but I was angrily confused by what would drive an almost-eighty-year-old to vandalize his own wall.

"Yeah. It'll come off with a razor blade. Just leave it."

"But what made you want to write that?

"I don't know. Just leave it. I'll take care of it."

He didn't want me touching it. Or asking any more questions. He was happy with his handiwork, actually proud of it, the product of steady meticulousness at a time when his eyesight started its final spiral toward blindness. Maybe that's why he did it. Just to prove that he could. Or to reinforce what was staring back was not only what he needed to deal with but what was left to do the dealing. I didn't know, and he never talked about "his inspiration for the piece," so eventually I stopped caring. I wasn't going to argue. It was his house. I just hoped his Art Deco sans canvas phase was a one-time event.

Luckily, it was. But *REALITY* never met the razor blade and was still there over a decade and a half later when the kids came by for Christmas a week earlier. They always got a chuckle out of it, never understanding its genesis and just believing it was *classic Papa*. Classic old guy with lots of time on his hands and bored out of his skull, but still clever and able to concoct one-liners to make them laugh. Others who ventured into his bathroom must have wondered about his motivation, as well as his state of mind. I know I did. But I also knew his *reality*. Or thought I did.

#

"Hello? I'm Anne, the hospice admissions nurse. Is now a good time?"

I looked up at the clock. 1:14 p.m. It was.

"Hi. Sure. I'm his son. Nice to meet you."

I extended my hand to greet her as she leaned all the way into the room, then walked toward me. *Anne, Anne, Anne* I repeated in my head as Dad's eyes remained closed, hopefully a sign he was enjoying his drip.

Anne juggled a purple binder along with a couple folders under her left arm as she reached out to shake my hand. Her grip was mild, and she held my hand with a prolonged feeling of condolence. She wasn't dressed like a nurse, more like an administrator. But I got the sense that behind her horn-rimmed glasses, her short, well-styled curls, and her sturdy frame, she'd spent a lot of time caring for patients like my dad. She seemed experienced. It was just a sense.

"Thanks for letting me reschedule today. Do you mind if we sit on the couch to go over a few things?"

I was glad she was taking control of the conversation. I had no idea where to start.

"Yeah, sure. No problem," I said.

I was ready to learn. The couch fit us nicely for my lesson.

"First off, I'm really sorry about your father's health. We'll do everything we can to make him comfortable."

She positioned the folders on her lap and pivoted toward me. She continued with the tutorial.

"Basically, I'm going to tell you a little bit about our company and what we do. Then I'll have you sign a few papers to formally engage us. Once we verify insurance and my director approves, we'll get the process moving. Any questions?"

191

I suspected she only wanted hospice-related questions. Not the obvious ones like, "Why did that goddamn stent have to self-destruct when my dad was still competent and capable in brain and bones?"

Or, "Who's going to be there for me when I need to reminisce about being a kid, about horses and home runs? Had that time of innocence and adolescence become, overnight, just a distant memory to preserve, to shrink wrap and shellac, and no longer an animated experience to embellish and relive with the last person able to corroborate my claims?"

Or, "Would he really not change anything about his life?"

"No, not yet," I replied.

"Just to confirm, are you your father's only immediate relative?"

"Yes." *Sad, but yes.*

At that moment, I realized that I was the only family member, the only visitor, to see my dad there that day. Unlike others in the ICU who had spouses, or siblings, or grandkids visiting—or an entourage of friends checking on them, perusing the lounge magazines or watching *Maury*—for my dad, it was just me.

I wondered what the hospital staff thought: *Does anyone else love the old guy? Does he have a family who cares about him? Who will take care of him when he leaves here? Is this other old guy it?*

Anne ended my wistful paranoia. "And you have power of attorney for healthcare?"

"Yes, do you need to see it?"

"Not right now. We'll need a copy of it later."

She handed me one of the thin, glossy folders.

"So we'll work with the ICU doctors here, and your father's primary doctor, to determine where to best care for him. For some patients, hospicing at home is best. For others, a medical facility is better. There is another floor here at Havenshore for hospice patients. Depending on your father's condition, room availability, insurance, and the doctors' recommendations, we may just move him out of ICU to one of those rooms. Or we may set him up for care in his home. Or a combination. But we'd like to move him out of ICU as soon as possible to start hospice."

I understood her point, made tactfully but with brick-like bluntness. The ICU was a place *to bring people back to life.* A very expensive place to bring them back to life. A place with highly skilled professionals, a heightened sense of urgency, and state of the art equipment intended to save people at death's door. Unfortunately, Dad crossed that threshold a few hours back, going in the opposite direction, and this was the first step to closing that door for good. That was Dad's reality.

"How long before you know which option will work for him?" I asked.

"Do you have a preference?"

Her question sparked new thoughts for me. We'd talked about him going into assisted living, or going into the veterans' home, or coming to live with us in our finished basement. But we'd never talked about where he'd prefer, or where we'd prefer for him, to die. Months ago, days ago, that would have been a choice. Morbid, foreboding, and unsavory to discuss, but still a choice. In the span of a few chilly hours, however, it had become an inevitability. One I had yet to fully consider and only reluctantly come to accept.

"I don't know," I said. "We just want him to be comfortable. His house isn't in the greatest shape for visitors, but he's been using the first floor for a while, so he's good there. Would someone be living with him?"

I should have let Anne finish her spiel before asking my uninformed questions. But until then, no one was living with him, and mentally I hadn't put that option on my own radar even though I could have. Should have. The last time I actually stayed overnight with him was the prior March, when my wife was hosting weekend visitors and I assessed I'd clearly be in their way. Or vice versa. I had already started my weekly post-retirement jaunts to fill up his fridge and meds, and thought it would be a good opportunity to bond with him for a full day or two and share a few meals together. I wouldn't have to hurry and beat the traffic back to Chicago, and I could do some random chores and house cleaning along with finalizing his 2018 tax returns. My dad was all-in and looked forward to our "guys weekend."

\#

"Hey there! Just me. How you doing, Dad?" I shouted, poking my head into his living room.

It was my standard greeting when I arrived at his house, usually interrupting him while he watched *Gunsmoke, Judge Judy,* or the Cubs at full volume in his overworked, crumb-speckled recliner. With his deteriorated vision, it was more like listening and imagining than watching. I dropped my overnight bag in the foyer but held onto the plastic sacks full of his grocery needs.

"Hey," he gurgled.

Dad was groggy, obviously dozing while someone failed to run out a grounder or a plaintiff lodged their post-verdict complaint.

"What are you thinking about for dinner, Dad?"

It was almost four in the afternoon, and I didn't want to miss his mealtime. My growling stomach, deprived of lunch, concurred with the ask. Before he could respond, I turned and headed to the kitchen to unload his treasures. Typically, like a dutiful sidekick, he would shut off the TV, eject himself from the recliner, follow me into the kitchen with the help of his walker, and park his rickety frame in the chair next to the counter to inventory the goods I'd purchased or the meals my wife prepared for him. Each time, he was excited to see what popped out of the bags, regardless of the sameness of their weekly contents. It was fun to watch his childlike interest in that systematic revelation. Sometimes I amped up his anticipation by keeping my hand in the bag, while adding extra commentary and drama prior to the unveiling. He'd stare at the bag while I talked, hearing nothing I said until I exposed the prize. Like a kid.

I heard the walker shuffle on the foyer tile behind me as I set the bags on the kitchen table.

"I don't know. What about hamburgers?" he replied.

"Sure, that sounds good. You hungry? Want me to go now?"

"Let's see what you brought first."

He was a creature of habit and wanted to stick with our routine. He found his spot at the table, while I unloaded the bounty—two bananas, frozen waffles, Fig Newtons, double chocolate muffins, 2 percent milk, and the always-popular homemade cinnamon applesauce. Life was good.

"I can go to McDonalds. How does that sound? Want any fries?"

"Oh yeah. Fries. And a shake. Chocolate. Make it a large."

Dad was excited. He knew he could ask me to pick up a burger or shake anytime he wanted, but even more he wanted not to be a burden. Our weekend together, however, was an opportunity to indulge.

I continued taking his order.

"Hamburgers or cheeseburgers? How many do you want?"

"Just hamburgers. Get me two. No pickles. I can't chew 'em."

Dad had given up on teeth a few years back. Gumming took longer but was lower maintenance for him. Milkshakes and applesauce made sense.

"Okay. I'll be back in a little while," I said, still wearing my jacket from the ride down.

As I pulled the front door closed behind me, I heard his faint reminder coming from the kitchen.

"Large chocolate."

I got in the car and headed east on Center Street to Route 70, then north a half mile to the McDonalds in the mall, opposite the JRL pharmaceutical plant. In the old days, that was the Werners plant. Where my mom and hers worked together in the rat lab. It had undergone a face lift and multiple expansions since then and changed its name a few times after I went to college, but likely it was still testing drugs on white mice. The same kind of docile rodents my brother and I once had as pets on the ranch, courtesy of Mom's insistence and Dad's surrender. They fit in the palms of our hands and would slither up our sleeves to play around our necks and shoulders. Seven of them accompanied me to a memorable second grade show-and-tell, making me big man on campus for the day. I thought about those cute critters every time I drove past that factory.

I hadn't been gone ten minutes and was looking for the drive-thru entrance, when my cell rang.

It was Dad.

"Hey there. You okay?" I asked.

"What about fish? From the fish place?"

I pulled over and stopped to absorb his question.

"You don't want a burger?"

"You know, I haven't had fish in a while. But if you already got 'em, that's fine."

As usual, he didn't want to be a burden.

"No, I'm here now but haven't ordered anything. So you want a fish sandwich instead of the hamburgers?"

I was fine with him changing his mind and was glad he called before I put in my order. I'd had more demanding and complex change requests in my life, the whole of them leading to my retirement. This one would be a no-brainer and make him happy. Or so I thought.

"Well, I don't really want a sandwich. Can I get some perch, like a perch dinner? You know, from that fish place, that one by Arby's?"

That one that shut down five years ago, I thought to myself.

"Yeah, I think that place closed, Dad."

I expected he'd settle for something from the Golden Arches that were staring at me. Wrong again.

"What other places have perch around there?"

His persistence wasn't making my stomach any happier.

"Uh, I'm not sure," I said curtly, trying to preserve the fast in fast food, but also not wanting to disappoint him on our weekend together.

"I'll look for a place on my phone. I'll pick up something and see you in a little while."

I reached for the dash to end the call, when I heard another faint reminder.

"And fries."

I steered into a parking space to search for a perch place to make Dad happy. Local. With takeout. Large shake. And fries. In my mind, if memory served, the probability of success was low to begin with, and diminished with each requirement.

Nonetheless, amid the scented distraction of Big Macs grilling nearby, I poked at my phone for Yelp help, when I noticed what looked like a father and teenage daughter getting into a pickup truck parked a couple spots to my right. I was sure whatever he was carrying in the bag was scrumptious. In serious need of assistance, I lowered the passenger window.

"Excuse me. Is there any place around here that has, like, takeout fish dinners?"

The man looked at me, shaking his head, then glanced across the truck bed at his daughter, also shaking her head.

"Sorry," he said, as he pivoted and threw a look over his shoulder. "They got fish sandwiches in there."

He was preaching to the choir.

"Okay, thanks."

I raised the window and started backing out. I figured I'd do a quick drive up the road to see if I got any bright ideas, thinking maybe Red

Lobster did takeout. Worst case, I'd head straight back to Mickey D's and follow through on the original plan.

"Hey, hey!"

The young girl jumped out of the truck hailing me. I stopped and lowered the window again.

"Culver's has fish dinners. Over on Church Street. Next to the liquor store."

She made my day! Another win for humanity.

"Great! Thank you!"

I appreciated her memory, and was slightly curious if the liquor store landmark was her clue or her father's. Regardless, I was thrilled for a solid lead only a few miles away, and my good fortune netted a couple meaty cod dinners, fries, slaw, and chocolate shakes for the two of us. I loved Culver's but wasn't aware of one in town. I was sure my dad would love it, too.

"The fish tastes greasy. Is it perch?"

Strike three.

"No Dad, it's cod. It's all they had."

"Hmm."

Dad grumbled as he gummed his way through a filet.

"How's your shake?" I asked.

"Too thick."

Dad was politely disappointed in dinner, his heightened expectations watered down like a third inning Wrigley rainout after splurging on box seats.

"Do you want me to go back and get you a burger or something?"

I wanted to make things right, thinking I already had.

"It's fine. Just eat. I'll have a Dilly Bar later."

He didn't want to be a, um, uh, a burden. But that fish dinner weighed us down and punctuated our conversations the rest of the weekend.

Thanks for doing my taxes. I didn't know cod was that greasy, did you?

"The applesauce is delicious. You know, I should have let that shake thaw a little."

"The fries were pretty good. I liked the fries."

And it was likely why, along with my decrepit, un-bunked twin bed, I hadn't put living with him immediately on my radar.

#

"No, we don't provide live-in care for our patients," Anne replied. "But if he hospices at home, we have a team of people who will come in to give him his medication, help with meals, bathing, laundry, et cetera. We also have a twenty-four-hour, on-call service for emergencies."

I began wondering if I needed to order a blowup mattress for my prolonged sleepover, while alternatively hoping they'd approve his move to the hospice floor at Havenshore. And thinking we should have started the veterans' home application much sooner. I felt awkwardly selfish as she opened her folder and continued our session.

"Now, these are the documents I need you to sign. I'll put your copies in the binder here and bring it back to you once he's been approved."

She handed me a nondescript pen, and I proceeded to sign a half-dozen agreements, including a couple with "Medicare/Medicaid" in the title, another regarding insurance assignment and private pay charges, an odd one regarding oxygen safety, and one that said I'd been told and given everything I needed to know and was taking responsibility to pay these people to help Dad die if Medicare didn't. It was all new and foreign to me. And none of it was in my new year's resolution.

Then Anne hit me with the extra credit question.

"Is there a particular funeral home you'd like us to work with? We'll handle all the arrangements with them when the time comes. Visitation, church services, burial. We'll coordinate everything when he passes, if you want us to."

"Uh, no. No idea," I said, botching her quiz but happy to hear they'd take care of all those things I'd never handled before.

My dad had cared for all of my mom's arrangements, we were overseas when my grandmother passed, and managing my brother's remains was a process we muscled through with numerous feats of improv.

Fortunately, Anne was prepared for my failure. "Well, here are a couple that are near your father's home. They're both pretty popular."

She pulled out her cell to show me the search she had done prior to our meeting, obviously anticipating my wrong answer. She was prepared and surprised me, in a weird Houdini-esque kind of way. I was pleased with her prescience.

"Great, thank you. I really haven't thought about this at all."

She had caught me completely off-guard; Dad was still alive, and I hoped he'd stay that way for a while, avoiding the immediate need for an embalmer and hearse. And in many ways, in my sleep-starved, one-cup-of-coffee fogginess, I was still mentally cruising down the veterans' home path—we expected to receive their admittance approval soon—and had not fully down-shifted and detoured to a funeral home. But I understood. Anne was only doing her job, part of which was to dot all the i's and cross the t's in preparation for the end of the road.

"Do I need to pick one now?" I asked.

"No, but when the time comes, we'll need it as soon as possible. It would be good to know in advance."

Our meeting seemed to be ending, when she pulled a brochure out of her folder.

"Also, as part of our service, we offer grief counseling to the family. It's available for his close friends as well. Anyone who needs it." She opened the brochure and appeared keen on explaining it in detail.

I saved her some time. "Okay, thank you."

I took it and quickly slid it into my folder without reading it. The squiggly font was difficult to decipher, and I wanted to tell her I preferred to grieve with my family and not with strangers nor with the help of someone who didn't know my specific sadness. Along with my hourly self-reflection the past fifty years, TV was one of my weaknesses, and I'd seen enough quasi-counseling there to inform me how to acknowledge and address my feelings—and to lean and cry on my family's shoulders. And walking through the five stages of grief with an intense introvert like me was only going to stretch and stress the powder keg, not relieve it.

We'd surely had less misery and suffering in our lives than most families, but we'd had much more than others—and enough to give me practice at avoiding implosion, or at least controlling the blast. And my dad had outlived most of his close friends, so there were few others for the brochure to help with in that regard. I didn't know anything about funeral homes or caskets, but I knew I didn't want to sit in a circle and blubber incoherently about my dad. Call me silly. Or vain. Or ungrateful. Or just call me his son.

"Okay, well, it's available if you need it," she said with a dash of disappointment. "One last thing. Would you like me to ask the hospital chaplain to come by and pray with your father?"

Anne's question was unexpected, another subtle surprise. I tried to put myself in Dad's place to answer her: horizontal and full of tubes, not knowing if I was dreaming on my own or being hijacked by the narcotics diluting my veins, trying to suppress the pain while readying myself for whatever the next phase might be. Yeah, I'd probably want another hand to hold at any point in the coming days or weeks. And as a Catholic altar boy who knew his religion and respected it—though he didn't spend much time indoctrinating us—he'd probably like a few minutes of peace with a professional.

If it were me, I knew I would.

"Yes, please. Thank you."

It felt strange conceding defeat on my dad's behalf. And the vision of him praying or being prayed for made me equally uncomfortable. The finality was upsetting. *REALITY* had arrived.

"You're welcome. He may not be here right away, but likely within an hour or two. Before the end of the day."

I snuck a quick look at the wall clock as Anne packed up her things. The relentless second hand powered past its sluggish comrades stacked in alignment. 2:10 and ticking.

"Great. I think my dad would like that."

On second thought, I *knew* he would.

HOUR 14: The WALLET

I shook Anne's hand and walked her towards the glass doors. Dad remained still and left her escorting to me.

"We'll take good care of him," she assured me as she paused and looked at my dad.

It appeared the pain from that goddamn stent had finally met its match as the morphine dripped in a slow monotonous tempo.

"I'll be back in a little while, after I talk to my director and start the paperwork."

Anne pulled the curtain aside, then stopped.

"Sorry, one more thing. I just need to verify ID. I've got most of your father's info from Marcia, but do you have his social security or Medicare card, or a state ID?"

As quickly as Anne stopped her exit from the room, Katie entered it. They greeted each other with familiar "Hi's" as Katie squeezed past me on her way to my dad.

"ID? Um, I don't know."

I continued to fail Anne's tests. Until then, I hadn't thought at all about my dad's personal belongings or where they might be. Whatever he was wearing when he arrived at the hospital in the back of the inhalator was of no interest to me as he laid wired, tubed, and tormented by pain in the ICU bed. Until then.

I looked at Katie, who was logging into the computer.

"Hi, excuse me. Katie, do you know where my dad's clothes are?"

"No. Let me find someone who might know."

She exited the room past Anne and me as quickly as she'd entered. I'd forgotten she'd started her shift after he arrived.

"I'm sorry, I really hadn't thought about that today."

I apologized to Anne, while also feeling a little queasy not knowing where his wallet and keys were in that big hospital. I never liked that feeling with my own wallet, my kids', my wife's, or anyone's for that matter. Even though most of us had mountains of critical information packed conveniently into our phones and computers, there was still a significant mass of non-digital importance we tucked in our wallets and purses. And for my dad, his wallet—normally stashed in the buffet—was the primary dwelling of his personal data.

Katie hustled past us back into the room with another nurse in tow. The shorter, black woman stopped by Anne and me while Katie zipped over to the computer.

"Hi, I'm Carissa. I'm an aide here. I'll try to find your father's things. Excuse me."

She had a friendly smile and full lashes, and seemed focused on solving the mystery at hand as she ducked behind us toward the cabinets. A colorful headband popped brightly against her wavy, coal-black tresses, marshalling them away from her face in a snug, flowing bunch.

Carissa, Carissa, Carissa I thought to myself, trying to keep track of the staff for assistance later if needed. She was older than Katie, and probably Anne as well, but I still had a good ten years on her, if not more. Determined and agile, she moved quickly about the cupboards by the glass doors.

"I wasn't here, but usually they bag up their things and put them in a closet," Carissa said as she continued probing the cabinets. "Is this it?"

Out of one of the closets, she pulled a large plastic bag branded with the hospital's name and abstract watery logo and handed it to me. I peered in. That was it. I recognized his light blue jacket immediately, then, poking around, his off-white velour sweatshirt and rust-colored slacks. His weary, gray Velcro-laced gym shoes lined the bottom of the bag. Surprisingly, there was no Cubs hat. The pain must have hurried him along.

"Yes it is; thank you so much," I replied. I was truly grateful.

"Is that all?" Carissa asked.

"I think so, for now. Thanks."

"Okay. If there's anything else you need, just let me know."

She grinned and departed, leaving Anne and me literally holding the bag.

I reached in and pulled out the slacks, then set the bag at my feet. His belt jingled as I groped his pockets for the wallet. *Bingo!* I opened the light brown wallet retrieved from his back pocket, expecting it would have everything Anne needed to confirm his identity. It did. It always did. Sometimes I'd help him find what he needed when we visited the doctor, but usually he could self-manage the stack of cards he'd arranged carefully in the slotted compartments.

"Here's his state ID," I said.

Issued in 2010, as his vision disintegrated, it included the thumbnail photo of an alert, wide-eyed, white-haired eighty-five-year-old who no longer had a driver's license but looked capable of the privilege. A privilege I was thankful he gave up on his own without complaint or collision.

Anne pulled out her phone. "Great. I just need a picture of it."

I held the card as she clicked the photo, her other hand still occupied with the hospice documents.

She validated the quality of her snap, then slid the phone back into her jacket pocket.

"This helps, thanks. I'll be back before the end of the day. The chaplain, too."

"Okay. Good. You've got my number, right?" I asked, just in case.

"I do."

We shook hands again, and Anne disappeared through the doors behind the curtain. I was happy to have her on my side. Our side.

I put Dad's ID in his wallet and stuffed it back in his tattered pants. The pocket sported the faded outline recorded by years of sitting on the bi-fold's contents when he was more mobile. I shoved the slacks in the bag and took the wallet to my bedside post as Katie continued at the keyboard across from me.

"She's a nice lady," Katie offered.

I struggled briefly for a name to come to me. "Carissa?"

"Yes. And Anne."

"Yeah, they were great. And you, too. Thanks for all your help."

I took advantage of my second chance to tell her that.

"You're welcome," she said, turning toward me, her modest smile penetrating the loose strands of hair no longer restrained by the ponytail. "It's hard, hospice. It's hard on people. You know, the family. But in some cases, like his, it's definitely better than the alternative. At least that's what I think."

She sounded tired but was still convinced my dad had made the right decision.

I let go of the bag and grabbed Dad's hand to validate his choice. He moaned in approval.

"Hey Dad, how ya feeling?"

He awoke slowly. His glassy stare and weighted eyelids reflected the drip's success.

"Hi Martin. How was your nap?" Katie asked, still perky but dialed back considerably from her earlier energy level.

I realized then she was on the back half of her twelve-hour shift. I wasn't looking forward to it ending.

"Dad, how's the pain?"

He looked at me. He was spent and confused, and didn't have the faculties to deal with multiple questions.

He chose mine.

"My back hurts," he said in a slurred whisper.

It seemed his sad refrain and helpless grimace had become the post-slumber status quo, one which Katie, the doctors, or the drip couldn't fully exterminate. At least they hadn't yet.

"I'll see if the doctor can help with that," Katie said. "I'm sorry you're still having so much pain."

A feeble wince surfaced on his brow as she apologized. His eyes closed again.

"Can I get you anything before I leave?" she asked Dad, thinking he was still aware.

Fortunately, what the morphine lacked in numbing his agony was made up for in his sedation. So I answered for both of us.

"No, thanks. Just more painkiller I guess."

"They might increase the dosage for his next drip, or something. I'll get the doctor to come look at him or just change his meds."

Katie wrapped up her work at the keyboard and turned bedside. With both hands, she held my dad's IV-infused arm at bicep and wrist and talked to him as if he were present.

"Martin, you rest now. I'm going to talk to the doctor. We'll get you feeling better soon," she said, repeating her earlier promise.

Dad groaned softly in agreement, preferring to stay asleep in his pain. His thumb pressed weakly against my knuckle for instant comfort—mine.

I looked up at Katie across the bed. Dad's dying conduit connected us.

"What's it like at the end? When they pass." I had to ask.

She answered softly, as if he were actually listening. He wasn't.

207

"Sometimes it's peaceful. It's quiet. They just go."

She rubbed Dad's shoulder as if she was wishing it so for him. He let her.

"But a lot of times, they gasp. They kind of gasp…wheeze. And like, tense up before they pass."

It was hard for me to listen to her. To picture him. To feel what it would eventually feel like. But I had to ask. I wanted her to tell me. Her calm was soothing, her response disturbing.

"Thanks," I said dryly.

I appreciated her candor but was done with the impromptu clinical. It hurt.

She could tell.

"I'll, uh, I'll go find the doctor. Can I get you anything at all?" Katie asked.

A quick sniffle of emotion escaped her professional armor.

"No, I'm good."

I lied. I looked deeper at my dad as he snored in hushed bursts. I felt powerless. And afraid.

"Okay, I'll be back."

"Thanks again. Really."

"No problem. Just doing my job," she said as she headed out of the room.

I didn't believe her. Or she was an overachiever. Either way, she was making the day less shitty for both Dad and me.

I reached over and grabbed my phone off the counter, unplugging it to call my wife with the hospice status. Oddly, at 56 percent charged, it seemed more lively than before, an obvious figment of my drowsy imagination or just a change in my projected perspective from hungry to satiated. It didn't matter. What mattered was it was fed and ready for action at 2:57 p.m.

"Hi. Are you okay?"

The cottony velvet sound of my wife's voice was like a weighted blanket draping over me. "Did you get something to eat?"

"Hi. Yeah, I'm good. I got something a little while ago."

"Good. How's your dad?"

"He's in and out. Mostly out now. They started him on a morphine drip earlier. He kept waking up in pain."

"Are you able to talk with him at all?"

"Not really. Not much now. He's pretty out of it with the morphine."

"Well, I think I'll head down to see him. I'll log off of work and make you guys a snack or something to bring with me. Probably leave here around four or so."

She was insistent about wanting to visit my dad.

"You know that'll be rush hour, right?" Tired and retired, I forgot it was the holiday week.

Half of me wanted her to drive down to see him and be with me, the other half wanted to save her energy for another time when Katie, Anne, and the ICU crew weren't around to assist.

"Maybe I'll come sooner, or wait a little, but I'm coming down tonight. I'll look up visiting hours and get there to see him for a few minutes at least. I'm coming down."

Anymore arguing would have been useless. She had decided. I was more fine with it than I wasn't. I just didn't want to be a burden.

"Okay. Come later and avoid the traffic. Be careful driving," I said.

"I will. How did the hospice meeting go?"

"The woman was nice. She had a bunch of forms for me to sign and asked me which funeral home to use. I had no idea. It's not urgent, but I've got to find one. She's coming back later to give me a binder full of info. We can go through it at home. Looks like Medicare will cover everything."

I didn't tell her about the part where if not, we would. Dad had virtually no assets left. She knew that. His reverse mortgage was

209

depleted years back, before he told me he had one, so he lived in the bank's house. He'd saved some money from his teacher's pension after I started helping him pay his bills, but nothing significant. His financial acumen, and his luck at the slots, were suspect to say the least.

"That's good. When are they going to release him to go home?"

"She said they may send him home, or they may actually keep him here on a hospice floor. Depends. Based on what I've seen today, I'm almost thinking it would be better for him to stay at the hospital. Especially if Medicare covers it."

"That's interesting. When will they decide?"

"I asked the same question. I'll see when she comes back."

I was hopeful Anne would have a full plan of attack when she returned.

"Okay, good. We can talk about the hospice stuff when I get there. I love you. Get something to drink!"

I felt the blanket lifting as she concluded, exposing me again.

"I will. Love you, too. Be careful driving." I hoped she'd listen and not race Ruby beyond its limits.

"Oh, wait," she said, keeping our connection alive. "The mail came, and there's something from the veterans' home. Should I open it?"

"Sure." *Perfect timing for an approval letter,* I thought to myself.

"He got approved," she said.

Yep, perfect.

"Just hold onto it. I'll call later and let them know he won't be going there."

"I'm sorry."

My wife knew how much effort was needed to submit Dad's application. Not all had been wasted, just not the outcome we'd planned. Even less so for my dad.

"Take your time getting here. I'm sure they'll let us stay with him as long as we want," I said.

"Alright. I'll let you know when I'm leaving. Love you lots."

"See you in a while. Bye."

I let go of the blanket.

As I reached for the cable to continue recharging my phone, I realized it had been a few hours since I updated the kids. I pulled back and got myself re-situated in the armchair to send them a blurb in our family group text. I decided I wouldn't give them the gory details about hospice. I couldn't. I really didn't have any yet. Plus, hospice isn't something that I wanted my twenty-somethings to fret about. Hell, I was probably in my forties before I heard the word for the first time, and it certainly didn't carry a positive connotation. I'd tell them more about it when we talked live, when I knew more about it myself.

And it wasn't the time to take a photo. Or Facetime. It just wasn't. As much as my dad liked mugging for the camera and taking pictures with, and for, the kids, it just wasn't the right time. It wasn't like I was cutting his hair and sending before-and-after shots of his scalp. Or showing the kids how happy he was in one of their college T-shirts. Or capturing him blowing out a single birthday candle, because ninety-plus would have been a hazard.

No, those times had passed. But I wanted them to remember him that way—unfiltered in every dimension, with his crusty smile and ratty mustache, rarely looking directly at the camera, as he was unable to focus his vision but happy to be the focus of attention. They didn't need to remember him in the ICU, nearly comatose and fully outfitted in hospital paraphernalia. They didn't need to see his pain.

So I figured I'd just send them a brief status—one I wanted them to know and not see. A painless one. My right thumb got to work.

Hey there. Still at the hospital
with Papa. He's resting. They've

got him on a lot of painkiller to
keep him comfortable. Mom's
coming down later to visit.
Papa said he loves you lots! Will
keep you posted. Love you all!!
So much.

Their replies came quickly. Almost instantaneously. My wife *hearted* each one as they arrived.

Tell Papa I love him! You too.
Love u and Papa!
Thinking about you both. Love you!

I was lucky to have them at my fingertips. In every way. They were there dozens of times each day, as the photo of the three of them—on the Capitol lawn in DC, when my youngest son finished a cross-country summer bike odyssey with his frat brothers to fundraise for people with special needs—was pixel-painted on my lock screen. The picture was full of smiles, support, accomplishment, and determination. Three kids—as different as they were the same—in one place, nowhere near home, enjoying a common bond of love. Love of the challenge. Love of travel. Love of people. Love of each other—something my brother and I never truly shared or realized, so I was grateful they did.

The times when I stared at that photo, not just passed it to get to an email or a website, I smiled, sometimes choking up as I beamed with pride. I hoped my dad was a tenth as proud of me as I was of them. I looked forward to their visits to see him in the coming days. To see him for the last time.

I closed my phone and plugged it in, no longer concerned with it running out of gas, then looked at my dad as his tank quietly emptied.

He appeared good for the time being as I reached to hold his hand again. I sat up and leaned into him, kicking the bag at my feet and inadvertently reminding myself it was there. As I pushed it to the side, I thought about its contents again and what I hadn't looked for previously: his house key.

I pulled out his pants and twisted them around to find his front pockets. I could feel his wallet flopping around as I searched. His flailing belt followed. I quickly found his front pocket and in it, thankfully, the key. I had my own, but I really didn't want his key wandering around the hospital. The lone, dulled Schlage dangled on an equally worn metal ring held by a small leather tab. *Simple, like my dad.* The trio fit nicely in my palm, which I then fit into my own front pocket for safekeeping. Next to my keys. *That was easy*, I thought. And a minor relief.

As I went to redeposit his slacks in the bag, I thought about his wallet and how that, too, should come with me, even more so than the key. As long as I was tying up loose ends with his belongings, I for sure better tie up that one. I pulled out his wallet and set it next to my phone, as I wadded up his pants and shoved them back in the bag. They were infinitely beyond shabby. He'd need a different pair to leave the hospital, assuming that would happen on a biting January day. If I were thinking, I would have just lightened the load and sent the synthetic, shapeless slacks and their deteriorating belt to the ICU trash right then. I wasn't. And didn't.

I put the bag back on the floor and grabbed his wallet, unsure where it would fit best on me. *With the keys? In my jacket?* It was a nothing decision I turned into something. The real decision was whether or not to open his wallet and go through it first, to verify that what should be there was. And to satisfy that curiosity that comes with having someone's most personal of things so easily within reach, available and not locked.

I'd been in it before, to help him find his insurance or credit cards, or to fill it with a few bucks when he needed to pay the neighbor who cut his grass. But this time seemed more nefarious. More intrusive. More unrestrained. He was two feet away but unable to give me permission, unable to confirm his trust. Trust less earned than required by age and eyesight, but trust nonetheless. He trusted me with his taxes. With his cash. With his signature. With his power of attorney. He made me co-owner of his checking account. I knew the combination of his vacant safe.

After a lifetime of unsure hesitation, I felt like he finally trusted me to take care of him and whatever was his. In his final days, I didn't want to violate that trust.

So I opened it.

HOUR 15: The RIDDLE

W ith the rationale that I needed to know his personal info was secure, I opened it. I told myself it was okay, that if he was awake and conscious, he wouldn't care if I opened it. He'd be okay with my snooping—or my validation, that is. It wasn't like I was sneaking into his closet to gawk at his collection of *Playboys*, like I did in middle school.

Anyway, he was in no shape to manage his data, so just like I had found what Anne needed for hospice intake, he'd be fine with me inventorying his wallet for important and sensitive items. If I found random tidbits of interest beyond the typical cards and bills we all carried, he'd be fine with that, too, and probably want to talk about them. What could a ninety-five-year-old heading to hospice have to hide? My justification made sense. To me.

The bifold was thin relative to my trifold, and especially thin compared to the overstuffed, mini file cabinets I'd seen men unleash from their pockets at Costco, bars, and TSA lines. A scrawny crepe against their hefty, short stacks. Two twenties and a five occupied its cash pouch, leftovers from the money I got him at the bank to give the kids for Christmas. To the extent possible, he was generous with them on their birthdays and special occasions like graduations and holidays, verbally wrapping his gifts with the mantra, "have fun while you're young." They always told him it was "too much," but he'd never take back a cent. He believed in his mantra and wanted it to be theirs.

I left the cash where I found it and moved on to the side of his wallet with the cards. The front compartment contained his priority pieces, at the ready when duty called: his Illinois state ID, his government Medicare card, two generations of his private insurance Medicare card, a Citibank credit card, and an odd, blue card I'd never seen before. I pulled that one out to inspect it further.

Of all things, it was a Medical Device ID card for that goddamn stent! It included Mahanti's name and number, the serial number and model number for what looked to be three components of the stent, and their implant date in August 2012. I flipped it over. The back of the card contained guidelines and restrictions for MRI scanning and spelled out the official name of the little bastard—Survero II Abdominal Stent Graft. Like Dr. Rama, the tiny villain had a business card of its own. And like hers, I probably wouldn't need it again.

With an extra push, I shoved the card back in the wallet and went on to the next compartment of info. It appeared to be a mix of interesting and important—and items he could have easily left in a drawer but chose not to. His social security card—issued days before Christmas in 1940, then crudely but effectively self-laminated sometime later—shared the space with a well-aged, all-events game pass, #247, issued by the Eastern Illinois State Teachers College circa late 1940s, acknowledging his varsity football contribution.

His voting card and another older version of his Medicare card were in there, along with his card-sized certificate of naval service. In a better-laminated twelvish square inches, front and back, the naval card summarized my dad's service with the pertinent military details: name, rate and rank, active duty start and end dates, service number, and the certificate number were still crisp and legible on the card's ocean blue background, well-preserved under plastic for almost seventy-five years. Even his fingerprint had a place of its own on the backside of the card, just above his signature. A Lieutenant Reeves signed the front with his approval of my dad's honorable discharge. I was always grateful he made it out of the war alive and in one piece when so many others, then and since, hadn't. And he never pushed my brother or me to serve, nor held it against us that we didn't. I was sure he'd have been happy if we did though was also glad we didn't have to. He was a patriot but not a war monger. And when I was old enough to understand and appreciate it, I was thankful he drew that line.

I slid the certificate back into place with the rest of the cards and registered them mentally for future reference. On the right side of the wallet was a snapped flap to secure photos. I'd never looked there before and assumed there weren't many based on thickness. I unsnapped it to find out what he'd kept underneath.

"Hello?"

I looked up. Carissa had poked her head through the curtain into the room. I closed the wallet, surprised and embarrassed.

"Umm, hi, there," I said. "Carissa, right?"

I amazed myself with the clumsy but accurate recall.

"Yes. I just wanted to check if everything was okay. Is there anything I can get you?" she asked.

I held the wallet tightly, lowering it out of sight and hoping she hadn't seen me rifling through it, acting as if I didn't have it at all. I was almost sixty years old but still as paranoid as the horny middle-schooler who fumbled around Dad's closet. The nearly half century in between hadn't changed a thing, other than what I held in my hand.

"Thanks. No, I think I'm good. I'm going to walk around later. Maybe I'll get something. But thank you."

"Okay. Well, if either of you needs anything, just let me know."

It was nice of her to offer, and I expected her to duck back into the hall. She didn't.

"Excuse me? Mr. Grojnecki there. He's your father, right?"

She was correct, but I was confused by her sudden interest. I was also surprised she pronounced our last name so effortlessly and with the silent J. That almost never happened on anyone's first attempt.

I perked up and got ready to engage.

"Um, yes. He is."

"Katie told me. I thought I sort of recognized him earlier but wasn't sure."

Carissa had my full attention. The wallet, still in my hand, quickly became old news.

"Mr. G was my freshman math teacher in high school. At Westridge." She smiled wide and held it as she eased further into the room.

"It was a long time ago, but I thought that might be him. He was one of my favorite teachers."

She made it over to his bedside across from me, before I could respond or fully stand to greet her. I turned and put the wallet on my chair as I got up. She reached out to shake my hand, and I hers. Her grip was soft.

"Really?"

I was slightly dumbfounded by her announcement, as she appeared too young to be one of his students—though it was possible she had him for a class just before he retired. She must have been on the cusp of his final days at the blackboard. And his disheveled appearance was not an obvious clue to his identity.

What didn't surprise me at all was that he was recognized so randomly. It happened all the time when I was growing up. At the hardware store. At the gas station. At the bank. At my games. Without fail, someone, or their child, or their grandchild, had my dad as a teacher or a coach during his thirty-plus year career across three local high schools. I got used to it, and it continued to happen as I chaperoned him to his various doctors' appointments and lab visits as he aged. The waiting room was a regular source of "don't I know yous?" or "didn't you teach ats?" For most, he was kind in his comments afterward; for some, not so much. But he generally seemed to remember them all. I doubted, however, the morphine would let that happen with Carissa.

She reached for his hand and held it with both of hers. Neither he nor I minded her taking the initiative.

"Yes. In the eighties. It was general math, but he always took his time with me and helped me out. I think I got a B."

Her speech slowed as she looked closely at his withered face and body, enlaced with tubes and transmitters.

"He was always so nice." She started to cry softly. "So nice. I'm so sorry."

"Thank you."

I didn't know what else to say, so I reached across my dad and put my hand on hers and his.

She continued to stare at him.

"I'm so sorry," she repeated.

Katie must have told her his destiny.

"He's had a good life. He loved teaching. I'm sure he'd remember you," I said.

I felt her squeeze his hand tighter.

"He was such a nice man. I'm, uh, I'm really sorry. God bless him. If there's anything you need, please let me know."

"I will. Thank you."

Affected by the view and sincere in her emotion, Carissa turned quickly and left the room. It seemed as if Dad's pain had become hers.

I picked up the wallet and planted myself back in the chair, thinking of what she said about my dad. I was proud of him. I was proud he had helped her. I was thrilled she remembered and glad she held his hand. Her visit was comforting—but equally difficult to digest; I was cheered to know he was appreciated, though unhappy she left sad.

Her blessing meant a lot.

I took a deep breath to refocus my attention.

I was ready to look at his pictures.

I opened the bifold, and the flap followed. There I was. With him. Just the two of us. Looking dapper and posed in the pearl-gray tuxes we wore on my wedding day. The wide lapels and tails, accessorized with shiny silver vests and ascots, was pure seventies prom motif, my only reference for a tuxedo at the time. For whatever reason, James Bond's suave, black-tie style didn't register as an option.

At the time, my dad was a couple inches shorter than me and only a couple years older than I was in the ICU. It was just before he retired, likely around the time Carissa knew him, and he was heavier and rounder than what was asleep next to me. We both wore smiles in the photo, mine more nervous than his.

He had a jolly look as his bright white hair and bushy beard stood out next to my non-descript self and the faint leafy background. I tried hard to remember the pre-ceremony picture-taking that birthed the shot and the various other pics of him—and my mom, and my brother, and me—but I couldn't.

I remembered climbing the fence and jumping into the Holiday Inn pool with my new wife and our friends after the reception. The soaked dresses, tuxes, and suits included. And the police retrieving my drunken brother from the shoulder of the Eisenhower Expressway. Twice. And the sunny June day at the church when we tied the knot, neither of us expecting all that would follow over the course of six presidents and the same number of Bulls' championships.

But I couldn't remember taking pictures with my family. It made seeing his chosen photo of the two of us even more special.

I slipped our picture out of the plasticized pocket. Underneath it was another. A grainy black-and-white with two young, moon-faced boys standing next to each other toward the rear of an old classic, like a Ford or Studebaker. I'd seen those faces before in similar shots, as my dad and his older brother shared the camera frame frequently, a cost-effective option back when printing and retakes mattered. Dressed in suits, the two young Poles looked solemn as their image was recorded. Their full cheeks and matted, combed hair were consistent with other pictures I'd seen, some in albums my mom maintained, and others that surrounded my grandmother in her small apartment above the tavern. My dad didn't say much about his brother or their time together, nor did my grandmother; but he obviously wanted to keep their memories alive in his pocket.

I removed the vintage photo to see what else my dad carried with him. Next, under the plastic covering, was a small, time-yellowed newspaper clipping the size of a passport photo with the headline, "Grojnecki Wins MVGC Tourney." It was a summary of golf scores from a local tournament, one that my dad won with a score of 67, including his 6-stroke handicap. Like the seventy-year-old college game pass retained with pride in his wallet, he was equally as proud of his accomplishment in that tourney.

I read the brief article, reviewing the other golfers' names and scores, but was unable to find a date of the event in the recap. As I slid my thumb in to remove the clipping and look for a date on the reverse side, a white border appeared as the clipping slipped out. Another photo was behind it. I stopped caring about a tournament date as a wrinkled black-and-white revealed itself.

Faded and creased by time, the studio picture of a young black woman posed with a small boy on her lap was the last item in the pocket. I stared, mesmerized by the two people I'd never seen before, her beauty and his youth still obvious despite the photo's age. Being suffocated in the wallet's bowels likely saved it from further decay.

She smiled broadly, as did he, both looking at an intentional diversion off-center of the camera's lens. Possibly a stuffed animal or noisy toy to hold the child's attention for the shot. Her dark, wavy hair bobbed playfully above her shoulders, its side part evident but mostly hidden by the angle of her gaze. Her smooth skin and youthful look—punctuated by her heavy eyebrows, shaded lips, and gleeful stare—gave the impression of someone in their twenties, maybe mid-twenties. The monochromatic photo failed to do justice to her tight complexion, which was lighter than her hair and other features, but darker than the boy's less ebony skin. His close-cut hair was neatly fashioned, and the arc and width of his eyebrows resembled hers. Their selections of a light-colored blouse and white, buttoned-down shirt with tie accentuated their tones.

I put the other items on the counter and focused myself, amused and curious, on the picture in the wallet. It was a happy picture. I assumed he was her toddler son. And I wondered who they were and why the photo was there.

Could it have been one of those stock pictures that came inserted in the wallet, like the fake credit cards, when Dad first bought it? Maybe, but it didn't seem to be the "stock" type, especially since it wasn't in color.

Could it be someone my mom had known, possibly someone she met in nursing school? That seemed quite possible, as my mom loved her photos and had packed her billfold with dozens of pictures of friends and family alike. But why would Dad carry it in his wallet? So it probably wasn't.

Could it be related to one of the live-in helpers he'd tried a few years back? Unlikely, given it was an old black-and-white shot.

Perplexed, I dug my thumb into the sheath to slide out the photo and examine it further. The years had adhered it to the leather, requiring me to add more pressure to force its escape. After a couple of tender tugs, the wallet released its grip. The photo appeared richer in detail, and its mysterious subjects even happier when not under the plastic;

but it didn't reveal anything else that would help me with its origin.

Until I turned it over.

"To our Martin with love, Doreen and Joey (2)" was written legibly in fading blue ink at the top. It was dated *"Oct. '54"* in the same, smart cursive near the bottom. I read it again. Then a third time. Then a fourth. I read it like I was trying to decode a hidden message or a new language. The words were clear, but nothing else was. My brain cramped and spun at the same time. I gave up and flipped it back over to the two faces, looking for more clues. Looking for answers.

They were still there, smiling and fresh, though slightly less anonymous. Their expressions hadn't changed, only mine. I flipped it over and scanned the backside again, not knowing where to start the deciphering: *"To our Martin"*? *"with love"*? *"Doreen"*? *"and Joey"*? *"Oct. '54"*? I was in no shape for puzzles, and that's what those ten words and two faces had become. A time-stamped riddle whose only solver was lying tranquilized next to me.

"Hi there. How y'all doing?"

Katie plowed into the room, unaware of my discovery and the quiet fuse of angst it lit. She beelined to the computer with an IV bag in hand.

I turned my attention from the photo to her, then to the wall clock—3:28 p.m.—then back to her.

"Hi. I'm fine. Uh, we're fine," I said.

To myself, I sounded short. I didn't mean to project my new set of feelings on her nor reward her friendliness with my customary lack of personality. She didn't deserve it.

"Thanks. Yeah, we're fine. He seems okay," I said, nodding toward my dad.

My icy welcome didn't faze her.

"Well, good news. I got a change in his meds. Hopefully this will take care of the pain." She talked as she logged in and scanned the bag.

"We'll get this hooked up here and get him all better. Does that sound good, Martin?"

Her bubbly pitch fractured the hypnotic tedium of the room's beeping and humming, as Dad woke to her call. His mustache twitched, then eyelids followed—fluttering before opening slowly, as if they'd gotten heavier throughout the day. A day, like him, that was evolving gradually into darkness.

He looked so damn tired, exhausted by the fight. But he was still fighting. With the help of the oxygen, the morphine, he was fighting. He wasn't going to give in to the pain or the constant arterial leak inside him. Dad kept punching, and Katie was still in his corner. I needed them both to stay in the ring.

"Whaa? What?"

Dad was beyond groggy as he tried to respond. He looked her direction, then at me.

"Hi, Dad. You were out for a while. You okay?" I asked, still clutching the photo. I reached for him with my free hand.

"Oh God. My back still hurts."

Katie jumped in.

"We're going to try and help with that. I'm almost done, and hopefully that will get you feeling better right away. Can I get you anything else to help?"

I could tell she was getting as frustrated as we were. She was making the best of things, but the best needed to be better.

"Make it stop. Please," Dad begged.

"You should feel some relief soon. If not, I'll get the doctor back here for you."

The defeated look in her eyes was the result of a long shift, made longer by the ineffective attempts to make him pain-free. I felt bad for her, but was sure it couldn't have been the first time she gave 110 percent in a no-win match. And like my dad, she kept punching.

"I'll come back in a bit and see how you're doing, Martin. Hang in there!"

She looked at me.

"We really are doing what we can to make him comfortable," she assured me. "If he doesn't feel any better after this, I'll have the doctor come back to see what else we can do."

"Thanks. I know you are," I said.

Katie stopped smiling and turned on her nurse face. The sharp, serious one. The concerned one that concerned me.

"His vitals are okay, but I'm worried he's still in pain. Let's see how this next drip goes," she said, exhaling as she turned and left the room.

I watched her go, then refocused my attention next to me.

"What can I get you, Dad?"

"Thirs...thirsty," he groaned.

I grabbed a cup and the straw from the table and helped him the only way I could. He closed his eyes and sipped with purpose, like it was one of those rum-soaked, fruity concoctions from Trader Vic's as opposed to the ice chips' tepid, drab remains. Either way, I saw a hint of relief in each strained gulp.

"You can go. You don't, you don't have, have to stay," he said haltingly.

He was stuck in a loop, unable to craft new thoughts and rehashing old ones—repeating what he'd already said in his bid to stay as present as the morphine would allow.

I put the cup down and grabbed his hand. His thumb rubbed my knuckles again without pause. He really didn't want me to leave.

"It's okay, Dad. I'm going to stay."

His eyelids wobbled up and down, more closed than open. But I needed to ask him about the photo. I needed to know more about the two people. About the heartfelt handwriting on the back. But I didn't want to aggravate him and stir up his vitals. I didn't want the monitor going berserk and Katie flying in to flog me. My exploding

225

curiosity had to be weighed carefully against his collapsing form and frailty, with the balance tilted in his favor. He was in no condition to be interrogated for details, but I had so many questions. Questions whose answers were sure to spawn more. And his rapidly failing health added a new dimension to the puzzle. I realized what I was holding in my hands—him and the photo—was more of a hazy Rubik's Cube than a riddle, and the worn-out corners of that Cube might soon stop turning.

"Dad? Hey. Dad?"

"Mmm?"

He grunted faintly, eyes closed.

I held up the photo so he could see it, or try to, with his disease-ridden, opioid-sopped eyesight.

"Dad? Dad, what's, what's Doreen's last name?"

I figured if he could give me one more clue, one more turn of the Cube, I could keep going to find out more about the two people in the photo and where he fit into the bigger picture.

The response was subtle but immediate. His eyes cracked open in a narrow glare, resisting the glue of his sleep-crumbed lashes. The languid squint appeared to be his maximum effort, and likely would be for the foreseeable future—as would the reddish-yellow membranes around his hazel irises that no longer lustered.

But they didn't close. He didn't blink. He stared at me, not seeing the photo but focused squarely on me. It was as if my question not only hit a nerve, but *the* nerve. The one that cut through the pain, through the morphine, through the exhaustion, through the dreams and hallucinations, and brought him laser-focused on whatever smacked it.

Yeah, he stared at me hard, as if he were angry. As if I should stop talking.

As if he'd been caught.

HOUR 16: The SEARCH

"**B**rewer," he said, in a low, raspy slur.

His eyes closed again. He stopped rubbing my knuckles. I was afraid I'd lost him. Not physically. The monitors confirmed he was still alive. But as a father. That I asked him something I should have just let die with him. I didn't know what it was or if it was anything at all, but it felt as if I'd gone too far. Like I should have stopped but couldn't help myself. I'd felt that way before. And it felt lonely. Again.

#

"Are you a righty or lefty?" my dad asked.

"Righty," I said. I was certain he knew.

"Okay, so when you jab, do it with your left hand," he said. "Now move your feet over here. Get in a solid stance. Here, bend your knees a little, and put your left foot forward."

My dad, always the teacher, took to his knees in the dining room of our ranch to teach me how to box. Inspired by George Foreman's success in the Olympics, and being able to watch it on TV in the company of his sons and a few Old Styles, Dad felt the urge to give me a few gloveless pointers, while my brother sat ringside at the dining room table to watch the action.

"How does that feel? There, you need a good base. You feel comfortable?" Dad asked.

I let him move my feet into position as I paid attention to his instructions. Best case, whatever he told me would lead to a gold medal of my own. Worst case, and most likely, my brother and I would become more lethal to each other when verbal irritation escalated to physical dominance. Thinking the same, my brother watched intently, mentally recording each move to try out on me later—or to dodge accordingly. He never shied away from a confrontation, preferring to run headfirst into a losing battle, which he did a lot.

Dad continued the lesson.

"Okay, there! Now you want to keep both hands up and your elbows close to your body to protect you. Like this."

Wearing his typical tank undershirt and crew cut, Dad looked the part of a pugilist as he raised his hands. His stocky build and thick neck rounded out the profile. His appearance was convincing. It was quite possible he'd gained some real-world experience with the sport while in the Navy, though he never said how he acquired his knowledge. Nonetheless, he was very confident in his guidance.

"Okay, put your hands up. The left one forward, to jab, the right one below your eyes, to protect your face. And to cross."

"Like this?" I asked.

We faced each other like mannequins with hands poised to punch. I stood a few inches taller than his kneeling torso and was definitely more mobile than he was in that position, but his muscular arms could have sent me into orbit with one good punch. So I continued to follow directions with eyes wide open.

"Yeah, that's good," he replied. "Now I'm going to hold my hands up, and you just practice jabbing them, like you're jabbing me in the face."

He opened his palms vertically in front of me, and I took a few weak pokes at them with my left hand.

"Wait, wait. When you jab, when you punch, twist your hand inward like this as you make contact."

He engulfed my hand with his and pulled it toward him, turning it clockwise in my view as it approached his face. He went back and forth, puppeting my hand and arm with the punching-twisting motion four or five times.

"What's that for?" I asked.

"Well, when you make contact, they don't just feel the punch, but it also twists into their face. Like this."

He slowly reached out with his left hand and pushed it into the fleshy skin under my eye, then gave it a slow twist of 90 degrees.

Pretty cool, but pretty evil, I thought to myself. My brother smiled as Dad made his point, likely hoping Dad would come in at top speed and full power for that orbital launch.

"Try it again."

Dad held up his palms in front of me.

I got in my stance and threw a couple of jabs at his open hands, practicing the new motion with a bit more speed. Dad smiled as I repeatedly caught his palm square with the rotating technique. At my brother's expense, my confidence grew.

"That's good. That's good," Dad said happily, rewarded by his student's results. "Okay, now let's try the right hand. Put your hands up and get in position."

I got into position as instructed—left foot forward, knees flexed, left hand forward, right hand back by my face. Dad struck the same pose with his hands. *Oh shit*, I thought, *this is going to hurt!*

"So with your left, you're going to jab a few times at the face, then use the right to come across with a big punch to the body or face. Like this," he warned.

I squinted and went rigid with fear as he cocked his fists, tucking his head and dipping it slightly to his right. Dad was intimidating, even on his knees. His forehead tightened in seriousness, and his eyes zeroed in on their target as I breathed through it and smelled the Old Styles he'd befriended. I expected the worst and braced for Foreman-like impact. The kind I saw on TV. The kind that hurt grown men. The kind that would shatter me.

"Jab, jab, cross. Jab, jab, cross."

He repeated the sequence as he mimed the terror-inducing punches with synchronized emphasis. The blows never landed. Luckily, my fear was more misguided than he was, and I only received the slow-motion, coaching version of a lopsided bout.

My dad was kind. My brother was disappointed.

"You try now," he said, coaxing me with proud anticipation. "Hit my hands. Jab, jab, cross."

Exhaling nervously, I let my shoulders drop with relief as I raised my clenched hands in position and adjusted my stance. I was ready to pop his palms and "sting like a bee," when my mom called out from the living room.

"Are you finished in here? I want to watch something else besides this Olympics crap."

Dad replied quickly as he readied himself for my practice punches.

"No! Leave it on. We'll be back in a minute!"

He did not want to lose programming control in our one-TV house. Not for the quadrennial "thrill of victory and agony of defeat."

"You can turn it back when you come in. I'm just going to look around."

Mom was unconvinced that Dad's minute would be a sixty-second one.

With her reply came his angry response, as he dropped his hands and turned his head to make sure he was heard.

"No! I said leave it on!"

He was no longer focused on me. And for whatever reason, I saw his diverted, unshielded attention as an opportunity. An opportunity more misguided than my earlier fear. Without hesitation, as soon as he dispatched Mom's distraction and returned his gaze towards me, I forgot the jabs and who he was, and connected with a reluctant right-cross to his face as it rotated unprotected into my virgin fist.

The punch surprised him. It surprised me. I wasn't sure why I did it, why I chose to take advantage of the moment. I'd gone too far but couldn't help myself. It didn't feel good, but it didn't feel bad. It felt like a reaction. A thoughtless, empty reaction. One that drew blood, his nose dripping slowly onto his haggard white undershirt.

"Are you okay?" I asked guiltily.

He sensed the blood on his upper lip and wiped it with his finger to verify. He rose to his feet as I shrunk below him in my stance.

"Yeah, I'm fine."

His reply reeked of disappointment as he walked away, pinching his nose. Nothing more was said. My brother followed him to the bathroom. I stood in the dining room, my hand tingling with pain; the rest of me was numb. Mom continued watching, against her will, whatever event was on TV.

#

My dad had let his guard down, and I crossed the line, as I did with his wallet. And like the knuckle rubbing in the ICU, his coaching session stopped. My loneliness in the dining room felt shameful. As it would fifty years later.

The wallet, the photo, the question—they all may have been too much, too quickly, at the wrong time. *And what did it really matter? What if I'd found that brain-jarring photo, his long-delayed counterpunch, a year later? Or never found it? Who was I to question what was in his billfold?*

But Dad's hoarse response through his darkened stare made me think I wasn't wrong to ask. *Brewer, Brewer, Brewer,* I cycled in my head.

As Dad slept, I woke my phone from its charging nap on the table.

It was 3:59 p.m. and time to put it to work looking for Doreen and Joey Brewer.

I summoned Google and filled up the search bar with my dad's name and the Brewers'. It wasn't the most surgical or analytical query, but in my eagerness to discover the truth, it was a start. *If there was an obvious or official connection between my dad and the people posing in the picture, it would—might—pop up in the first few pages of hits*, I thought.

But what I received, and should have rightly expected, in lightning-quick return on my tiny screen was a mishmash of results, including government sites, obituaries, Facebook pages, and the typical "Find This" and "Locate That" sites. Unfortunately, none of the hits rang with the make-it-easy-on-me caption "Your Father Knew Doreen Seventy Years Ago" or "Doreen Gave Your Dad a Picture Because..." That definitely would have been too easy. And my initial scans of the site extracts that showed up confirmed my search would only yield results where their first or last names appeared coincidentally on the same page, but with no relation to my actual subjects of interest. I was thankful for those extracts, saving me gobs of useless clicking and scrolling, but was also a little frustrated that none of them presented any linkage to what I was hoping to uncover. A side trip to the images tab proved fruitless as well, showing nothing that resembled my dad nor the twosome in the photo. It was time to rethink my search. But it was past time for a bathroom run.

I staggered to my feet and slipped the phone in my pocket, readying myself to see the late afternoon occupants of the ICU. Convinced I looked as ghastly as I felt, and keen on getting back to Dad's room to continue my search for Doreen and Joey, I hurried through the curtains and down the hall toward the bathroom. The floor was busy with nurses and doctors, while visitors entered and exited rooms with varying shades of emotion. I was certain I held the record for visiting tenure for the day but wasn't at all happy to hold it. I was less happy to find the bathroom busy in the lounge and again not thrilled to hold it. Luckily, my wait was brief.

On my way back to room 10, no longer cramped and restless, I ran through in my head various search permutations that might get me closer to an answer—without involving my dad's participation. I resigned myself to maximizing the single crumb of info he'd already provided. That was unless he wanted to talk more about it once he moved to hospice, which I couldn't see myself asking for, nor could I see him offering it. The fact that he never offered me more boxing lessons after the bloody-nose incident informed my assumption.

Dad was still dormant as I entered the room and seated myself next to him. Confident that I could somehow find a connection to the photograph, or at least some details on the young woman or the boy, I pulled out my phone to take another crack. *Maybe*, I thought, *if I untangle the three of them from each other and just focus my search on Doreen or Joey, I could limit the hodgepodge of name combinations in the results? Or if I just searched on the two last names together, that would also filter out the errant hits that involved others having their same first names?* Forgetting probably the most important element of the search—that the photo pre-dated the retail internet by a good forty years—I took a shot at finding Doreen anyway.

Starting with only her first and last name, between quotes, I rolled the dice. In response, I was flooded with results that directed me toward hundreds, or thousands, of Doreen Brewers via obituaries, Facebook, LinkedIn, Instagram, and a multitude of other sites in the webiverse. Given the girl in the 1950s photo was likely near my dad's age at the time, or slightly younger, I ruled out the social media hits and focused on the obituary results. I wasn't sure how to search more intelligently, or filter any more elegantly, so I just started reading the extracts and poking at the results that superficially showed some abstract promise.

On those where I dug deeper, I didn't exclude any geographies as funeral homes from across the country appeared, but I gradually smartened up and stopped scanning through obits for Doreens born after 1934. Sites that included photos of the deceased were also helpful in guiding my time and interest. But after a few minutes of failed manual scanning—regardless of how compelling their lives may have been as mothers, daughters, professors, or nurses—I concluded my effort would continue to fail with that clunky methodology. And time-guzzling insanity layered on top of the day's events was not an option, so I gave my search a minor twist by adding "Mennawa" to the string, in hopes of improving the outcome by adding the town's name—in hopes of landing the big catch with no other hooks to help me.

It didn't, Google confirmed. *No Results Found.*

My rejection was coincidentally met with an alarm on Dad's monitor, one of many beeps experienced temporarily throughout the day as a vital fell below or rose above a norm. However, this one served to remind me he was still there, and I needed to back out of the rabbit hole I'd traveled down with my search. I put the phone in my pocket and grabbed his hand again. He didn't wake or respond to my grasp, though a twitch of his mustache followed by a gravelly snore let me know he was relatively fine.

My mind was still transfixed on the photograph from Dad's wallet as I stared past him into the apparatus-filled background, wondering what more I could do to solve the puzzle. I wanted to keep searching but really wasn't sure how to optimize my screen time, while also trying to maximize the alone time with my dad.

Should I keep at it while Dad sleeps and refocus on finding Joey? Or go back to slogging through the Doreen obituaries one by each while I hold Dad's hand and pass the time until my wife arrives? Or just defer my internet investigation to later at home, on a bigger display, with a faster connection, better coffee, and a lot more sleep, and instead spend time with

Dad as he battles that goddamn stent? Deferring and battling made sense for both of us, regardless of how infatuated I was with the idea of cracking *The Case of the Unknown Couple*. Ellery Queen books were my favorites as a kid.

I'm not giving up on the mystery, I rationalized, *just deferring*, as I steered my view back to Dad's sedated physique. He was calm on the outside. I assumed, however, that he was still struggling below the skin, his nerves strangled by the morphine while blades of pain fought to escape and have their way with him. We were both strong in that way; my brother was, too. At least physically.

Over the years, as we were challenged repeatedly as kids by sports injuries, there were few, if any, that kept us from playing. My dad never kept us off the field, always confident we could "play through it" or believing that a pain-pocked performance was better than none at all. He had faith in us and our ability to overcome, and in his skills as our in-home trainer. Our bathroom closet swelled with rolls of elastic bandages and athletic tape, and warehouse-sized supplies of gooey, hot salve. Dad kept it well-stocked, courtesy of his high school's locker room.

As the shadows crossing the river extended themselves in concert with the sun's wintery descent, I settled myself in the chair to wait. For what though, I didn't know. For my dad to wake up? For another doctor or nurse to drop in? For Anne to return with hospice approval? For my wife to arrive with homemade cookies or snacks? I didn't know, but the thought of food made the last option my first choice.

Out of habit, as if as a species we could no longer exist with unstimulated free time, I pulled out my phone again. Not to search for Doreen and Joey, but to cycle through my regular apps. I clicked for email and scrolled through the junk it presented. Then another check of the stock market, which thankfully had closed higher for the day. Then to a few news sites to see what I'd missed outside the walls of the ICU. Nothing spectacular to report. I truly had not missed out on anything during the day, which made me even happier to have spent it with my dad. Hopefully he agreed.

As I went to close my phone, I thought again about the search. Not about the new people in Dad's wallet, but about him. I'd never googled just him before, thinking I knew everything about him—at least the important stuff. But with time on my hands, I figured I'd see what about him was available to the rest of the online world.

So I opened the app, wrapped his name in quotes, and sent it on its way. As was typical for name searches, the usual suspects arrived on my screen: sites to find his address, his phone number, his public documents, his family, his anything-for-a-fee. I scrolled past them. Next on the hit list were a couple of sites from the early 1940s that looked like they were PDF versions of his high school yearbooks, the dusty paper versions of which were still on his basement bookcase. I'd leafed through them in the past as a kid, but never really paid much attention to the details, usually just looking at the old black-and-white photos of individuals or sports teams. The second site took me to his senior year, where he was voted the "hungriest boy" of his class, and he willed his "ability to talk himself out of the doghouse" to an underclassman. Both were somewhat comical, and neither surprised me.

The last result at the bottom of my phone seemed odd, based on the partial title and its limited extract. I opened it. Authored by someone I'd never heard of before, it was a seventies-era thesis, in PDF format, recounting the life of a person who turned out to be my dad's college football coach. I found that fact in the paper's introduction as I scanned it for references to my dad. The document's original typeset was raw and unsteady, bringing back memories of my first typewriter. It was actually our family's first typewriter, a powder-blue K-Mart special that required full effort from each finger and was unforgiving of mistakes. My mom was a proponent of the purchase; my dad, not so much.

After combing the paper, which chronicled the coach's career across many decades, I found near its end a series of team rosters, by year and sport, listing the names of athletes who had played for the man. Google had found my dad's name much more quickly than I did, but I eventually spotted it on a couple of teams in the late forties, which coincided neatly with the game pass #247 I'd found in his wallet. He was one of hundreds of names listed in the paper—a faceless line item in the twenty-three-page inventory of players—but it was interesting to see him identified, nonetheless.

I looked at the names on Dad's 1949 team. About forty were listed in what appeared to be random order, definitely not alphabetical. There were multiple Johns and James, Geralds and Genes, Williams and Dons, a Russell, a Richard, and a Roy. Classic and common male names at the time, though an Otto, Vernon, and Virgil also made the list. Much different than the current NCAA, NFL, NBA, or MLB rosters and those of the last twenty or so years.

I scrolled up the paper to the prior season's 1948 team and saw a number of the same names, including my dad's. It was a smaller team than the following year's squad and had an Emmett, an Earl, and a couple of Franks. It also had a Reggie, who I noticed appeared on the subsequent 1949 roster along with my dad. *Reggie Brewster.*

I did a double take on Reggie's last name, as an awkward reaction fluttered inside me. Having typed and re-typed a similar name, Brewer, into the search bar for the past fifteen to twenty minutes, I looked at both rosters to verify the spelling. My closer examination put the weird feeling to rest. I could go back to scrolling through Dad's search results or clean out more spam email while I waited for whatever it was I was waiting for.

But then I thought: *What if I'd misheard my dad? Or what if his speech, or his recall, was compromised by the morphine? Or both? What if he actually meant Brewster instead of Brewer?* The weird feeling quickly returned.

I reneged on my decision to defer further searching and plugged both Reggie and Doreen Brewster into Google, along with "Eastern Illinois" to help narrow down whatever came back. It was a long shot anything coherent would show up, but I had nothing to lose.

I tapped search. The usual suspects instantly appeared.

But so did an obituary. For Reggie Brewster. With Eastern Illinois in the extracted preview. Along with Doreen Campbell. I tapped the link and held my breath.

Apparently, Reggie Brewster of Earth City, Missouri, had died August 10, 2006, at the age of seventy-nine. His funeral home tribute contained a flattering picture taken later in life: a wide grin under his salt-and-pepper mustache announced his happiness at the time. His dark brown skin was wrinkled but healthy and complemented the suit-and-tie outfit he wore. The photo of the elder Reggie was a good one.

Beyond the statistics of his passing, and that he was born and raised in St. Louis, the obituary noted his survivors. I peered beneath my glasses to read it closely. Reggie had left behind a wife, Janice, two sons, Robert and Charles, and five grandchildren. Reading on, the list of survivors also included a lone sibling, Reggie's sister. Doreen Campbell. Of Delmont, Illinois.

Holy shit, I thought! She'd lived just a few miles north of our ranch in Beaufort, in the same small town where my brother and I suited up as kids to play midget football, as it was shamelessly called back then. The weird feeling raced back and forth in my chest. I wanted to wake my dad and ask him if I was on the right path. I wanted him to share more about the photo and two people in it—why they were there and what they meant to him. I wanted to understand what I had found in his wallet. What I thought I'd found. More than ever, I wanted him just to be there as my dad again. Yeah, I wanted a lot right then.

The coincidence all but evaporated, and the link to my dad was solidified, when I read further in the obit that Reggie was a two-sport athlete at EIU in track and football—a major accomplishment for anyone, let alone someone who was likely one of the few black athletes at the school. I'd found the "right" Reggie, but what about Doreen? Did my dad know her through his college football teammate? It seemed likely. But what about the proximity to our ranch? The Cube spun again.

Confused, anxious, and slightly unsettled, I had more questions and needed their answers. They prodded me along like the caffeine I was lacking. I went back to the search bar in my new quest to find Doreen. I entered what I knew about her—maiden name, married name, brother's name, cities, Joey—and tapped search.

As with Reggie's query, multiple links to internet spam returned, along with an obituary. An obituary for Doreen Campbell. The preview included Delmont. And Joe Campbell. I opened the page, while Dad remained silent next to me.

Doreen's picture appeared. Like Reggie's, it was taken of her later in life, but even on my small screen I could see her resemblance to the photo I'd wrestled from Dad's wallet. I held them side by side. The cheek bones, the eyebrows, the fair skin—in color, it was a beautiful, smooth caramel.

I started reading the text under her picture. She was eighty-four when she passed away June 4, 2013, in Delmont. I paused to do some quick math in my head and flipped the photo over to confirm its date. She would have been twenty-five at the time it was taken; my dad, thirty, and a few years out of college. And if Doreen's shorthand on the back of the photo was Joey's age, he was two as he smiled on her lap. The Cube began to align as I read on.

She died of complications from a long illness. Her husband of fifty-one years, Walter Campbell, preceded her in death, as did her brother, Reggie Brewster, verifying what I'd previously found. She was survived only by her son, Joe, also in Delmont, and his wife and children. And like my dad, Doreen was a teacher. I read it all again. And again.

My head snapped up to look at Dad, thinking *what the hell have I stumbled across!?* There was nothing surreal about my rational, practical life—until then. And then that's all it was, surreal. I stopped slouching in the chair and hunched forward, ready to launch more searches or just analyze the clues and information jumping at me. Likewise, with all its cyber-exercise, my phone had warmed with the workout it was getting. I gave it a well-earned break and let it cool as I stared at the back of the photo in my hand. I read her salutation anxiously, *"To our Martin with love."*

It seemed more genuine and personal than it was casual and friendly. *Am I making that up in my head? Was it really just a sociable keepsake from an acquaintance or close friend? Like when we handed out picture day photos to classmates as kids? Or was Doreen like a sister to my dad, via his friendship with Reggie?* It could very well have been all of that. Innocent and uncommitted. Just a wrinkled, black-and-white FYI.

Or was it why my dad never talked about that period in his life in the fifties, between college and the time my mom came along? And could it be that that photo, one of the few items he kept in his wallet, reminded him of that decade? I put the picture back in the wallet and dropped it in the bag with Dad's clothes. I was on to a new pursuit: I needed to find Joey. Or Joe.

Could he still be in Delmont or somewhere nearby, I wondered? Again, the quick math told me he'd be about sixty-seven, assuming his longevity was on par with his mom's and athletic uncle's. I opened my phone again to find Joey. Or Joe. I entered his details, what I knew of them, and clicked search. The phone, though rested, was still warm. I hoped it was ready for more online gymnastics, as the results painted across my screen.

Unlike me, Joe Campbell of Delmont, Illinois, had a Facebook profile to go with the other for-profit spam links that popped up on the hit list. Doreen's already-viewed obituary showed up as well. As did a link to an article in the local newspaper, the *Mennawa Daily Gazette*, which mentioned football in the extract with Joe. My interest piqued, and I opened it.

It was an article highlighting Joe's volunteer work, helping kids at the Delmont Youth Center. I read through the article, a feel-good community promo, and quickly got a sense of his character. He was a fine, caring man, it appeared. A photo including Joe and a few kids in a rec area popped up midway through the article, which also noted his football prowess as a teenager. At Beaufort Community High School!

The eerie weirdness flip-flopped inside of me again. More math was needed. I calculated Joe's high school years must have been in the 1967–1970 timeframe—the same time we lived on the ranch, across the road from the field he played on!

In a flash, the surreal became more surreal. And Dad was sleeping, or hallucinating, through all of it. I re-did the numbers in my head, then double-checked the simple figures on my phone's calculator, just in case. Just in case I was over-tired and missed a digit. Just in case I was dreaming and making it all up.

Just in case it was true.

Dad's monitor beeped again, startling me in the rabbit hole I had re-entered. I looked up as the heart rate flashed on the screen. It stopped flashing as soon as my eyes were able to focus, having reluctantly dragged themselves away from the fuzzy font of my phone. The beeping stopped as well, as if Dad just wanted to get my attention and remind me of the day's main event. He succeeded.

As I looked at him lying in bed, unable to help me connect the dots, I attempted to attach them on my own, starting with the biggest ones: was Doreen, my dad's teammate's sister, more than just a mutual friend? Why would he carry around a photo of her and her son taken four or five years after he graduated college? A photo with a cryptic message of possession and affection? Was she a crush? A girlfriend? Or was she more? And if she was, what about Joe? Was my dad like a big brother or an uncle to him? Or maybe his godfather?

Or, if that photo was as special as it seemed, to both Doreen and my dad, could Joe possibly be his son?

My half-brother?

The stiff armchair had kept me painfully immobile all day, but the thought of a possible second family in our life paralyzed me even further. The onslaught of emotions had me second-guessing myself and wondering why I'd even gotten to that point—the point where my inability to accept my dad's ultimate demise intersected with the excitement and fear of discovering something that might be everything, or nothing. *Had I chased the rabbit so far into the internet forest I could no longer see the reality of the aging oak and his weak limbs dying helplessly in front of me? Or had I actually found the young saplings of years long past and stumbled into a quicksand that was meant to stay hidden by their fallen leaves forever?*

I couldn't tell if I'd drawn too many conclusions. Or not enough. My mind raced.

Was it really Mom's idea to move to the ranch, from the house Dad had just built? Or had we moved so Dad could be closer to Doreen and Joe? And did my mom even know about the pair? Was that, not a pre-planned plot, what drove my parents to separate on our return from California that fateful summer? Could Mom have found out while we were on that vacation, or did she know of Dad's pre-Mom life before that trip? Likely not, given the acidic prejudice regularly dispensed at her family's gatherings. And if

Dad wanted to be closer to Doreen and Joe, maybe even to watch Joe's games at the end of our lane, did Dad also support them financially? Was that why he taught drivers ed in the summer to pick up extra cash? To fulfill his obligation, his responsibility?

I wanted him back. I wanted Dad back with me, like we were last year. Not in the ICU, both silent and waiting. I wanted him at his kitchen table, or on his front porch, just joking or complaining, or reminiscing, healthy-ish and ready to talk. I had so many questions. So many new questions about old things. Things that weren't Doreen and things that were. I just wanted him back. I needed him back.

"Knock knock. Hello Martin, how are you feeling?"

Katie peeked through the curtains, then quickly walked into Dad's room. Another nurse followed her.

I was startled by Katie's entrance and equally surprised by her associate. I looked up at the clock for some sorely needed perspective. As anticipated, the second hand defied my earlier request and maintained its unwavering pace. It was 4:48, but the day ached as if it were later than that. The thickening darkness beyond the windows didn't help.

Katie lowered her volume as she noticed my dad was still sleeping. "This is Kevin. He'll be taking over for me."

"Hi there," Kevin said, greeting me enthusiastically at full volume, and reaching across Dad to shake my hand.

He looked a little younger than Katie as he leaned closer, though his short brown hair had begun to thin. His patchy but trimmed facial hair matched. Slightly taller than her, he appeared fit in his loose scrubs, and his smile brought a new energy to the room—one that neither Katie nor I, nor my dad, could match.

"My shift ends in a few minutes. I'm going to refill your father's meds and get Kevin up to speed," Katie said softly.

She looked at me as if she were unhappy that she was leaving, but I was sure she wasn't. With confidence, I was sure I was.

243

Poorly timed but well-earned, her departure added another corkscrew to the mind-bending roller coaster I'd been strapped into all day. And what I really didn't need right then was to lose Dad's once-perky cheerleader and my favorite advocate for what was best for him. Without asking, Katie had made everything that was so wrong in that...in that...in that goddamn suicide suite so much better. She got it. She got him. She got me. But Dad's "angel" was leaving, just how she arrived—in the dark.

I understood and responded with a deflated, "Okay, thanks."

As Katie and Kevin reviewed Dad's chart on the computer and changed his IV, he heard their conversation, or just wanted to give Katie some guff one last time, and exited his long sleep. Re-entry was subtle and without fanfare. He opened his eyes, if that's what his bloodshot coin slots could be called, and let out a faint gasp to alert us of his arrival. The three of us turned our attention to him immediately.

Katie welcomed him first.

"Hi, Martin! How are you feeling?"

She rested one hand on his arm and pulled the blanket up to his neck with the other.

"You're still here?" my dad asked her, in a deadpan moan.

We all chuckled with relief. Yeah, he was back.

"For a little while. This is Kevin; he'll be taking care of you."

"Hi, Martin, pleased to meet you!"

Kevin spoke loudly, making sure my dad knew he was there. Making sure we all knew he was there.

"If there's anything you need, you just let me know. Okay?"

"Where's *she* going?" Dad asked.

He obviously had a preference.

Katie smiled, a little embarrassed, a little flattered.

"My shift is over. You'll be in good hands with Kevin!"

Bryant had said the same about her. Hopefully Kevin would follow her lead.

"That's right. Is there something I can get for you, Martin?"

Kevin's extra helping of helpfulness was a little much, or so it seemed. To me.

"The pain. The pain's bad," Dad complained.

His voice was scratchy and already giving out on him after his feeble flirting with Katie. He grimaced while his hips and shoulders contorted under the tubes.

"Well, I've got something that can take care of that," Kevin exclaimed confidently. And loudly.

Really, you do? I thought. *Or were you just pacifying my dad, and me?*

"I'll be right back," he said as he left the room on a mission.

I wasn't sure what to expect from the new guy, but I wasn't expecting the prickly skepticism that hit me when he exited.

"You'll be okay, Martin," Katie said, making things all better again. For both of us.

My dad tried to open his eyes, but they were too much for him.

"Thank you. For everything…"

His voice trailed off as the new batch of morphine snatched him away before he could finish. The hand he'd opened to find hers fell gently to his side as he returned to sleep.

"Yes, thank you, for everything," I said, completing his thought, and tearing up at the prospect of her, and him, leaving.

Katie walked around the foot of the bed toward me, her own tears fighting a smile doing its best to break free. I hugged her hard, and she hugged back. Like my wife in the kitchen on that rotten Sunday many Aprils ago.

"It's okay," she said, allowing a tired, old introvert to mourn on her shoulder. "He'll be in a better place."

With that, I lost it.

I released everything that had balled up inside me and sobbed quietly in her hair.

"I know. I know. Thank you. So much."

The moment felt strange, but for a few minutes she was family. I had no regrets. None.

The emotional purge was quick, but it was total—as if every feeling I'd had that day came with a receipt I filed in my gut, waiting for someone to just give me the okay to shred all I'd collected—all that was odd and painful and busting at the seams—and disgorge it on the spot. Katie was that someone.

"You're welcome. Good luck."

And like that, without leaving a business card, she was gone.

The room quieted. The shredding stopped.

I glanced at the enemy on the wall: 5:03.

As Dad slept, I sat down to pull myself together.

And hunt for Joe Campbell.

HOUR 17: The TRUTH

Whatever Dad's connection was with Doreen, I wondered if Joe even knew about him. Just because I was ignorant of the relationship didn't mean the other parties were. In Joe's case, it may have been even more difficult for Doreen to conceal. The extent of the connection may have made things more or less cumbersome to contain as well. But then again, was there really anything at all to contain? Was there even an *anything*?

I needed to find Joe.

I opened my phone again and pulled up the earlier search results for him. I knew some of the find-a-human spam sites provided a few tidbits of information before they pestered you to pay for more; probing those sites had proved a somewhat useful tactic when needing to verify returned Christmas card addresses or find lost classmates. Their teasers weren't always current or reliable—or at all helpful if you didn't supply your credit card—but if the same info appeared on two or more sites, then you may have gotten lucky.

I gave it a whirl and found Delmont's Joe Campbell on a few sites at 310 W. 2nd Street. In a small town like that, it had to be him. I took a screenshot of the address to save some brain cells. I was making progress.

"Hey there! Let's see if this helps."

Kevin bounded into the room with a smile on his face and a vial in his hand.

Almost on command following the nurse's excited arrival, the monitor tracking Dad's vitals started beeping. The blood pressure and heart rate stats flashed. His EKG line squiggled differently. Kevin put down the vial and stopped smiling. He checked the monitor and inspected the pasta of wires and tubes hooked up to my dad. He stopped and looked at me.

"I'm not sure if this is it. But it could be," he said solemnly, then grabbed Dad's wrist to check his pulse.

The *it* was what I feared, what my dad had requested, in so many words. I wasn't ready for *it* by any means. But the feelings I exorcised and shed on Katie's shoulder left me calmer and less anxious about the moment. About *it*. I squeezed Dad's hand again, hoping he was okay and feeling no pain. His pale, stoic face provided no clue to his level of agony, if any. He didn't squeeze back.

The beeping and flashing continued a few more seconds, longer than it had in previous episodes during the day, then stopped. Quickly, I redirected my stare from Dad to the monitor. The vitals returned to their less frantic state.

"Okay, that's better." Kevin sounded relieved.

"Hang in there, Dad."

I didn't know if he heard me, but I didn't know what else to say. I knew he was doing his best; I just wanted to encourage him to do better. To hang in there long enough to see my wife and our kids again. He deserved to feel their hugs and see their smiles again, and to hear his voice in theirs when they shared their lives and laughed at his corny jokes. I knew the end was coming and sensed it was near, but I didn't want it to be then. Not yet.

"Okay, good. I'm going to give him this additional painkiller to help him out," Kevin said. "Then I'll come back in a few minutes to check on him again."

He swiveled to the computer and logged in, then injected the painkiller into Dad's tubes and logged out. His moves were tight and efficient.

"I'll be back in a bit. Is there anything I can get you?" he asked as he turned to leave.

There wasn't.

"No, I'm fine. Thanks."

But I kind of wanted to know what was in the vial, what supplement could be added to morphine to give it more zest, more potency. *And had a doctor just prescribed it, or was there a standing order to add as needed? Did Kevin know something Katie didn't? Was I wrong about her? Or him?* Regardless, it wasn't an argument worth having with myself right then. My dad had been medicated. I wasn't a doctor. And the staff had been doing their best all day long to make him comfortable. *Find a flaw in that logic,* I thought to myself. There were many, but none mattered at that point.

With Dad stabilized, I thought about Joe again and pulled out my phone. It was down to 22 percent, though I didn't mind, knowing its umbilical was nearby. But instead of going back to the Delmont info in my browser, I tapped on my photos app first.

Over the past few years, I'd tagged photos of our family for my favorites folder to send out for birthday greetings, event recognitions, or just randomly for fun. They were all happy pictures. Many were silly, many were selfies, others caught us by surprise, most showed our love. Many included my dad. It seemed a good time to send some of those out in our group text to remind everyone of the positive memories we shared with him. And after the incident a few minutes prior, I wasn't sure there'd be many more. Or any more.

So I teed up a few to text, maybe ten or twelve. There was the pic of him a couple of years back with a wide grin holding up an Easter basket full of chocolate like a little kid. And a 2016 photo of him mugging for the camera with my daughter on one of his last restaurant outings. There were a few front porch selfies with him and the kids, others of him wearing their college swag in his kitchen, and a number of memorable pics from annual Christmas visits. I added a shot of his ninetieth birthday with balloons and cake and a cameo appearance from my mother-in-law. I was in a giving mood.

As I looked up to see how much of him had changed since that makeshift birthday party, I noticed his face was flushed and no longer pale. His neck strained under the blueish-purple mask, eyes still closed. The vitals flashed and beeped again. *Oh, shit!*

I jumped out of the chair. I hadn't seen him like that before and didn't know what was happening. Was he having a reaction to the painkiller Kevin just gave him? He began to heave and gasp. Then I remembered what Katie had said much earlier about the end. About *it.*

I ran out of the room to find Kevin. He was sitting at a workstation a few feet away and looked up as I approached.

"My dad's having a reaction or seizing or something. Can you come see him? Now."

Kevin got up and followed me back into the room. We stood on each side of the bed as had been the day's protocol. Kevin studied the vitals on the monitor, while I held Dad's hand. He continued to wheeze slowly with his eyes closed, when I realized I still had my phone open in my other hand. And hadn't yet sent the text with his pictures. I scrolled briefly to verify what I'd plucked from my file. They were many moons away from what I was looking at gasping in the bed right then. And there was so much life in the photos. That's how we needed to remember him. I tapped the arrow to send them across the country and shoved the phone in my pocket.

As we bookended my dad, both holding his hands, Kevin looked at me stone-faced.

"I think this is it," he declared softly.

He stared longingly at my dad as if he were his own.

With that, like I did on the mighty palomino sailing full-speed across the dusty field, I held on for dear life as I watched Dad fight for it. At least that's what I assumed he was doing as he tackled his last breaths. As much as he was at peace with the life he'd led, and "wouldn't change anything," I was sure he was fighting for more of it. I was proud he was fighting for more of it. He didn't wriggle or convulse as life left him, but with every gasp he fought for more. Jab, jab, cross.

Until he didn't.

Before long, Dad went silent. His complexion faded as his neck eased down on the pillow. The line on the display went flat. Kevin nodded to confirm the end of the match. The monitor quieted as he turned it off. "I'm so sorry," he said.

The goddamn stent won. Its friend on the wall cheered. The second hand took a victory lap of its own. It was 5:12.

"Can I have a few minutes with him?" I asked, or *told*, Kevin.

It's not like I'd been shorted on time there with Dad, but I just needed a bit more to say goodbye.

"Yeah, sure, of course. I'll come back when you're ready."

As he left, I looked at Dad, peaceful under the beige blanket. Like he was sleeping in his recliner. Like he was glad the fight was over, even though I wasn't. I still had questions, some only he could answer. But the moment wasn't about me. Well, not all about me. It was about me saying goodbye when I still couldn't believe that goddamn stent decided it was time to unwind, to test his age. It had to be tough being ninety-five, I guessed, so wherever he was right then, he must have been somewhat relieved. For that, I was happy for him. But more than that, I missed him.

I leaned over and kissed him on his cool forehead.

"I love you, Dad. We all do."

He was already in a better place.

I pulled out my phone to call my wife, hoping she hadn't yet left to drive down or hadn't gotten very far if she did. I opened it to find a bunch of texts from her and the kids replying to the pictures I'd sent. A lot of hearts and ha-has and witty comments about the memories the photos triggered. I felt the warmth in their responses as I sent an update:

Papa passed peacefully a
few mins ago. Grateful to
be with him today. He
loved you all so much
and knew you loved him.
Love you all!

I immediately dialed my wife.

She'd already seen my text. "I'm so sorry. Are you okay?"

"Yeah. I'm fine. You haven't left yet, have you?"

The connection sounded too clear for her to be in the car.

"No, but I'll come down now if you need me to."

"No, no. Don't. I'm not sure what I need to do here, but don't come down. It's okay. I'll keep you posted, but don't drive down."

"I'm so sorry."

"Yeah, he was in a lot of pain. I was hoping he'd make it a little longer so the kids could see him, but he's in a better place now."

Katie was right.

"I know, me too. I'm sure he is. Do you need anything? Need me to call anybody?"

"No. I've got to figure out what's next. The people here have been great though. I'm fine. I'll let you know when I know more. Thanks. I love you."

"I love you, too. I'll let the kids know you're okay. And my mom.

Call me when you leave there, alright?"

"Yep, will do. Thanks. Bye."

It felt good to talk to her—just enough home-grown grief counseling to propel me past the unsettling scene of watching Dad pass in my hands. I was sad and needed her connection, her two-minute therapy session. But I wasn't crushed into despair or teetering on dysfunction by Dad's death. Likely because of his age and the health hypotheticals we'd previously posited, and also because I'd been so drained by the day, with much of that dam-breaking and discharge having taken place in the last hour or so, there wasn't much left of me to mop up. At least not then. Not on the phone.

And I didn't mention Doreen or Joe to her. It wasn't high on my list at the time, but it was still on my list. At some point soon, it would surely take top spot.

"Hi there. I thought I'd give you these."

Kevin returned to the room as I hung up. My phone was down to 9 percent. I plugged it in before walking over to him by Dad's bed.

He held out four small, glass tubes—the kind used to collect blood for a lab test. The tubes were narrow, about four inches long, with red caps. And a piece of paper sat inside each one.

"It's just a printout of your father's EKG. Some people like to keep them. To remember."

My earlier skepticism of Kevin dissipated as I accepted the tubes from him. I could see the rolled-up strip of graph paper with the heartbeat pattern through the glass. It was an interesting memento. One that looked like a souvenir from the first-floor gift shop. But it was thoughtful, and I appreciated it. We shook hands. And when he leaned in for a comfort hug, I accepted that, too. He seemed to be a genuinely good guy, minus the volume.

Then he asked, "Do you know which funeral home you'll be using?"

He caught me by surprise.

"Um, no."

I hadn't thought of that since Anne asked earlier in the afternoon. It seemed though that this was the signal the moping was over, and it was time to get on with the business of moving my dad out of the ICU and recycling room 10 for the next patient. I understood, but was just surprised by the ask.

"When do you need to know?" I countered.

"Well, the sooner, the better. But I think they'll hold him downstairs for twenty-four hours. Let me go check."

"Okay. I'll try to find one. Let me make some calls."

As Kevin left, I looked up at the damn clock again, wondering if any funeral homes would even be open to talk about my dad. It was 5:23. The second hand rotated fearlessly, eager for the room's next occupant.

I turned to get my phone when I heard, "Hello? Hi there."

It was Anne from hospice. I stopped and let the recharging continue as she entered the room.

"I'm sorry to hear about your father."

"Thank you."

She spoke as she looked at him lying lifeless in the bed.

"I brought you the binder. It has copies of what you signed in it. And you can still take advantage of the grief counseling if you'd like. That information is in there, too."

"Thanks. So, so, you won't be making any of the funeral arrangements for him, right?"

I had to give it a shot, even though I was pretty sure of the answer.

"No. Since he passed away in the ICU and hadn't been released yet to hospice, there's nothing we can do. Sorry."

Her logic made sense. It was the answer I expected. But I had to give it a shot.

"But anyone you call, whoever you work with, will be able to walk you through the process. They'll take care of everything."

My dilemma must have been obvious.

"Okay, thank you. Thanks for everything."

"Good luck," she said sympathetically.

I let her leave without more questions and grabbed my phone to search and make some calls.

I didn't tell her the chaplain never showed.

Fortunately, one of the homes she identified with me earlier rang a bell. I'd attended a wake there for a high school friend's mother a couple of summers back after visiting my dad. It was up the street from the local DQ near my dad's house, the one that had supplied his Dilly Bars. I opened my phone and searched for funeral homes in that area. The one I recalled showed up, as did its phone number, which I allowed to be dialed.

With much surprise, a live person answered—a friendly woman who listened to my story and took my information, committing to having someone get back to me the next day. Her tone and empathy reminded me of my experience with my brother's arrangements, many of which were handled by phone.

I hung up and looked for the next funeral home in the search. I was of the mind that the first to respond—and agree to process my dad—would be the one we used. I knew nothing about the services or costs involved; I just knew I needed to get him out of the hospital soon. And neither Anne nor anyone else was going to do it for me.

As I went to tap on another candidate, my phone rang with an 815 area code in caller ID. I answered.

"Hi, this is Bill Halloran. You just called the funeral home about your father, correct?"

"Yes. I did." I was stunned at the speed of his response, even more so at that time of day.

"Yeah, Jennifer, who you spoke with, just called me. She gave me your father's name, and I just happen to be out to dinner right now with someone who had him for a teacher in high school. I'm really sorry for your loss."

I should have been surprised, but I wasn't. Of course, someone having dinner with the director of the funeral home I randomly called after hours would know my dad. Some things never change.

Our short conversation went better than expected. He agreed to care for my dad's arrangements, and we quickly exchanged the relevant details for the hospital pickup so he could get on with his dinner. A face-to-face meeting at 11:00 the next morning in his office was also arranged—to plot the next steps for my dad. I was relieved. *Anne was right.*

I hustled out to the ICU floor to find Kevin and give him the information. He was at the workstation again, talking on the phone.

"Excuse me," I said, "I've got the funeral home info you're looking for."

He didn't seem to mind the interruption, for good reason.

"Great, I'm talking with the morgue now," he replied.

I expelled all I knew to him and returned to the room to pack up and leave. As Dad laid next to me, I gathered my phone charger, the EKG tubes, and the purple binder from Anne, shoved them in the bag with Dad's clothes and his wallet, and threw on my leather coat. I checked my pockets for my keys, phone, and wallet, then scanned the room for any other belongings before leaving. *Nothing else. Just my dad.*

I stood and looked at him, resting my hand on his shoulder. He was gone, but the two of us were still together. Like we were a month ago, a year ago. We'd become a team, and I got used to it. It was a simple team. No coach, no GM. No overpaid .200 hitters. Just pitcher and catcher. Kicker and holder. Simple but special. I'd gotten attached to the old guy, and he became dependent on me. Sometimes he had a lot to say. Sometimes, like then, not much. It was hard to leave him there for the morgue attendants. It was hard to leave him and go solo. But it was time.

I kissed him on the forehead again and said goodbye. "I love you, Dad. Give 'em hell up there."

I was sure he would. And it was time for me to let him.

Kevin was still on the phone as I left room 10 for good. I waved goodbye as I walked. My departure through the ICU, then the third floor and hospital lobby, was swift. The speed wasn't a reflection of my experience there, just a reflection of my need for normal. For familiar. For food.

The blast of fresh evening air was a welcome slap of cold reality as I pushed open the glass door and made my way outside. Cold, but not too cold. It felt good to inhale and feel the cold in my eyes and on my neck while I walked to the garage. My thinning hairline felt it, too. It felt alive, like the rest of me—and like I was moving on, no longer just waiting. Waiting for someone or something. Or for death. It felt good.

Luckily, I was still warm under my jacket as the chilly car seat did its best to change my mood. I figured I'd stop at my dad's house once I left the garage, check things out there, then get on the highway and head home. Some kind of soup would be waiting for me when I got there. I didn't know it, but I knew it. My wife spent her winters heating up the house and filling it with the aroma of minestrone, chicken noodle, and other savory creations that made all your senses dance and warmed you from the inside out. November through March, I looked forward just to opening the front door to the smells she'd concocted. And if it wasn't soup, it was homemade cookies. I got excited thinking maybe both would be there when I arrived that night. I started the car and turned on the heated seat to keep me in the mood.

As I reached over to get my charging cord from the bag I'd plopped on the passenger seat, I remembered the documents I'd hid when I arrived. I shifted my focus and stretched down to find them, careful not to wrench myself. I grabbed the clamped pile and shoved them in the bag, then pulled out my cord to feed my phone.

It was 5:53 as I plugged it in and noticed a handful of texts waiting to be read. Condolence responses from our kids. I was elated they got to see Dad for Christmas but really wanted them to have another shot. I'd been in their shoes before: I had been overseas when my grandmother died twenty-one years before her son, and I still felt the hole of the goodbye I never got to say to her. And to my mom. And my brother. The day with my dad was a bittersweet end to the trend.

Before getting on my way, I texted a big thanks to my family, then set an alarm reminder to bring Dad's documents to the morning meeting with Bill. I felt myself getting into project mode again, as I threw the car in reverse to retrace my early morning's route and get home.

I exited the garage and the hospital campus, both livelier than I'd found them. Much livelier than me. My lack of energy became obvious in the middle of my turn onto Jury Street, as I realized I'd forgotten to text my wife and let her know I was on my way. I tapped the dash display a couple times, barked out my status, and sent the text. My wife replied quickly to confirm. All was good.

Then, ugh.

In switching my attention between Siri and steering, I drove past the turn onto Roosevelt Drive leading to my dad's house. *A trivial setback.* I thought about taking the next left after Regents. There were plenty of side-road options. I'd been on most of them before. All were easy recoveries from my negligence.

But the weight of the day dragged on my reflexes, and I immediately thought twice about my plan: *Do I really need to turn back to go to his house if I'm going to be down here again tomorrow morning? Or should I just stay the course and jump on the highway in ten minutes?* It was an easy decision. I kept heading east toward the interstate.

The weather was good, and the roads were clear. Lucky for January.

And the drive to the highway wasn't long. But it had plenty of stoplights to remind me of the present as my mind raced around in the future and the past.

How long do I have to deal with Dad's house before the bank takes over?

Do I need to find out about Doreen and Joe before I do that, even though my brother and I are the only beneficiaries in his will?

What was the uber-narcotic Kevin injected?

I'll wait until after the meeting with Bill before giving the kids another status. Or should I just call them when I get home? I hope they remember to "have fun while they're young."

That church over there used to be a clinic that housed our dentist who sang as he scraped our plaque. And where we got vaccinated with a big gun. I'm sure I still have the ringed scar.

There's the fish place where we bought pans of perch that Dad and the kids loved. And the liquor store where we bought beer in high school.

Dad's friend's dry cleaners and the ancient Dairy Queen were just a couple blocks down that street there.

There's a McDonalds straight ahead, just before the highway. I should grab something there to hold me over for the drive.

What kind of casket should we get him? Definitely not fancy, but not too not-fancy. Simple would be fine.

Will my wife come with me tomorrow? I forgot to tell her about the meeting.

What do I tell her about Doreen and Joe?

Wait, when Dad blurted out what sounded like "Dori" in the ICU, was that really "Doreen"? Or my mom? Or both?

Did my mom know the truth?

What was the truth?

As I got closer to the highway, a road sign alerted me that I-57 was straight ahead. As was Delmont. The town was only fifteen to twenty minutes past the on-ramp, straight east on Jury Street's alter ego, Route 12. The same road that used to carry traffic to and from the since-deserted drive-in a couple miles away, then carried us dreaming and drooling back to the ranch at midnight. My thoughts came faster as I approached the interstate.

What if I drive to Delmont and look for Joe Campbell? Just knock on his door and introduce myself? I have his address and could be there by 6:30. And if he's not there, I could get back on 12 to Route 6 towards Chicago. A minor detour and a manageable change of plans.

If Joe is who I think he might be, and knows what I think he might know, he'll also want to know my dad passed, right?

Or do I call him tomorrow after the morning meeting and head to Delmont with my wife?

Or keep searching and make some phone calls from home before I just show up out of the blue?

Or do I need to let my potential half-sibling know face-to-face, as soon as possible, he's also got some new family in his life? Or did he already know?

I missed the McDonalds and hit the red light just before the highway overpass. Cars and trucks zipped back and forth above me, a good sign for my drive north. The on-ramp was just the other side of the bridge. But so was Delmont.

As I waited patiently for the go-ahead green to get on my way, I realized what was unlit and very lifeless to my right. The cemetery my mom was buried in was gated shut for the night. It had been years since I'd been to her grave at St. Stephen's. I'd have to search way back in my memory to find her plot without Dad, but would soon need to find it for him. Yet another reason to bring his documents to the meeting the next morning.

The red light had yet to change as remorse and regret piled into the passenger seat. There was no excuse for not visiting my mom's grave.

I just hadn't. And never offered to take my dad to visit her either. It wasn't intentional; I just hadn't. That rotten realization was magnified when I thought about how our rural clan of four had been whittled to one in the past hour by that goddamn stent.

Or did Joe change all that?

I put his address in the Maps app on my phone. 310 W. 2nd Street. He was sixteen minutes away if I decided to go there. It wasn't far, but I wasn't sure.

The light turned green, and I inched forward, still thinking about which direction to head on the other side of the overpass.

Take the on-ramp to go home? Or keep heading east on 12?

Should I suck it up and just drive to Delmont and find Joe Campbell?

Was it time to change my life even more? To find the truth?

What would my dad do?

What would he want ME to do?

I glanced at the dash. It was 6:13 p.m.

The night was black. So black. So very, very black.

Epilogue

"Here, I can take that. We'll put it in a nice case. You can pick it up at the funeral home when you come by for your photos and things."

"Thanks, Bill." *I'm sure he'll take care of Dad's flag. Amazing how the soldiers folded it perfectly into a tight triangle. It feels legit, too. Definitely the real deal.*

Bill's a good guy. Worth every penny of his five-figure funeral fee. Glad he called me back at the hospital. Yeah, that was a long day. Never made it to Delmont. Hell, barely made it home that night. The drive seemed like forever.

Then it got busy. The kids all flew in, we gathered up pictures for the wake, brought Dad's clothes and his Cubs hat to Bill, met with the cemetery guy, arranged the lunch for when we leave here. *It's been a long week. Maybe I'll make some calls or go to Delmont after the kids leave.*

Glad my wife asked about the military burial. Glad Bill handled it. Nice touch.

Dad loved my wife. His daughter. She's been great today, as always. The kids, too. *They must be hungry. I am. Time to go. It's actually warm in here now. Kind of hate to go back out in the cold. Sleet storm or mausoleum—is there a shittier choice?*

"Thanks for coming. We'll see you at the restaurant, right?" That's my go-to line when folks come up. Trying to avoid any small talk here.

Can do that later when we eat. *Can't believe how many people showed up in this storm. So nice to see them. I hope the Italian place is decent. I've got a taste for gnocchi.*

I'm tired, too. This weather doesn't help.

My eyes hurt as the doors open and close. The flashing of the day's snowscape against the murky innards of the chapel is nauseating. *Can't get a fucking migraine now! Nope, can't. Holding my wife's hand seems to help. Squinting helps more.*

Bill and the priest wait behind with my dad. The soldiers guard them. Everyone else is heading outside ahead of us.

Except two people near the doors standing straight and still. Short and tall. Both wrapped in winter gear, with hats. Church hats. Their faceless silhouettes turn to somber features as I approach them.

I've seen her before. At the hospital. *Damn, what's her name? She was in Dad's math class. Cassie? Chrissy? Dammit! It's been a long week.*

"Hi, Mr. Grojnecki."

The morning was going so well. I feel stupid now. Can't recall her name.

"Umm, hi." *My wheels are spinning but getting no traction with a name. Her right hand is warm. She improves things by smothering mine with her left. I see her tears. I doubt they're caused by my horrible memory.*

"I work at the hospital. Mr. G. was one of my teachers."

Yep. Got that.

She pauses, noticing my dilemma. "I'm Carissa."

That's it! I knew it! Carissa, Carissa, Carissa. I squeeze her hand tighter.

The older man next to her is starting to smile. He's tall and seems to have a few years on me, but looks damn fit for his age. I see his tears, too. They capture whatever light sneaks into the chapel, glistening in pools under his dark eyes. They streak his thick brown skin when he blinks and they fall.

I don't want to let go of her warm grip, but I need to shake his hand.

Her voice is cracking, "We just wanted to come by and…pay our respects to Mr. G."

The man's hand is strong and strangles mine while she talks.

"Mr. Grojnecki, this is my father, Joe. Joe Campbell."

Acknowledgments

I'm Grateful For...

The medical professionals and first responders who treated my dad with kindness and respect. And the funeral, church, and military personnel who treated us the same way.

Donna, Mary, Phil, Rosie, Debbie, Michael, Sandi, and Peter, whose friendship and feedback helped make this happen. I can't thank you enough.

Editor Jocelyn Carbonara for being a coach, cheerleader, and overall motivator to write better. Your positive approach is invaluable and contagious!

Cover designer Philip Studdard, whose creativity and flexibility brought a concept to life.

Above all, I'm grateful for my beautiful and talented wife and children. Without your edits, ideas, and encouragement, none of this is possible. Thank you! You are everything to me!

Discussion Questions

1. What was your impression of the book's title, *To Martin, With Love*, before, during, and after reading the book?

2. People process grief differently. How did the lead character process the reality of his father's impending death?

3. Family relationships can be complex. The book focuses on that of a father and son. Would you consider their relationship to be *healthy*? How did their relationship progress over time? What events seemed to impact it the most?

4. Sibling rivalry was a continuous thread throughout the early years of the lead character's life. How do you think he felt when his brother committed suicide?

5. Was the author effective in using *time* as an antagonist in the story? What are some examples? Were there other antagonists besides time?

6. Sometimes people avoid conversations due to lack of knowledge, respect for privacy, or fear of the response. If you could ask or discuss something right now with your parents, grandparents, or lost loved one, what would it be?

7. There was an age gap of seventeen years between the father and

mother in the book. Do you think that dynamic would be perceived differently today than it was in the 1960s?

8. From your personal experiences with hospitals or health care, did the setting of the book evoke any positive or negative reactions while you were reading? If so, what were those experiences and reactions, and do you think they influenced your feelings about the story?

9. The lead character's cell phone played both a practical and symbolic role in the story. What are your thoughts on how those roles were depicted?

10. What are some of the dominant cultural themes in the story? How is your life affected by those same themes?

11. Prejudice and addiction are referenced in the book. What are your thoughts about how they affect our culture today versus when you were a child?

12. The lead character was faced with the decision to pursue his potential half-brother or drive home. What would you have done and why?

13. What is one thing you would ask the author if you could talk to him? What key messages do you think the author wants you to take away from the book?

14. What aspects of the story do you most relate to, if any?

About the Author

To Martin, With Love is Brad Bujnowski's debut novel and was inspired by a longtime urge to write creatively. His early life in the southern outskirts of Chicago was followed by degrees in electrical engineering and finance, a decades-long career in the telecom industry, and a post-retirement flirt with stand-up comedy. He and his wife now reside near the Windy City after living briefly in Belgium with their three children. Their cat, Harley, puts up with them.

Contact Brad via email at *ToMartinWithLove@outlook.com*

Made in the USA
Monee, IL
15 March 2022